NO MORE SECRETS

BECCA SEYMOUR

RAINBOW TREE PUBLISHING

NO MORE SECRETS

BECCA SEYMOUR

RAINBOW TREE PUBLISHING

ALSO BY BECCA SEYMOUR

Zone Defense

No Take Backs | No More Secrets | No Wrong Moves

Fast Break

Rules, Schmules!

True-Blue

Let Me Show You | I've Got You | Becoming Us | Thinking It Over| Always For You | It's Not You | Our First & Last

Outback Boys

Stumble | Bounce | Wobble

Stand-Alone Contemporary

Not Used To Cute | High Alert | Realigned | Amalgamated

Urban Fantasy Romance

Thicker Than Water

Cover Design: BookSmith Design

Editors: Hot Tree™ Editing

E-book ISBN: 978-1-922679-13-0

Paperback ISBN: 978-1-922679-14-7

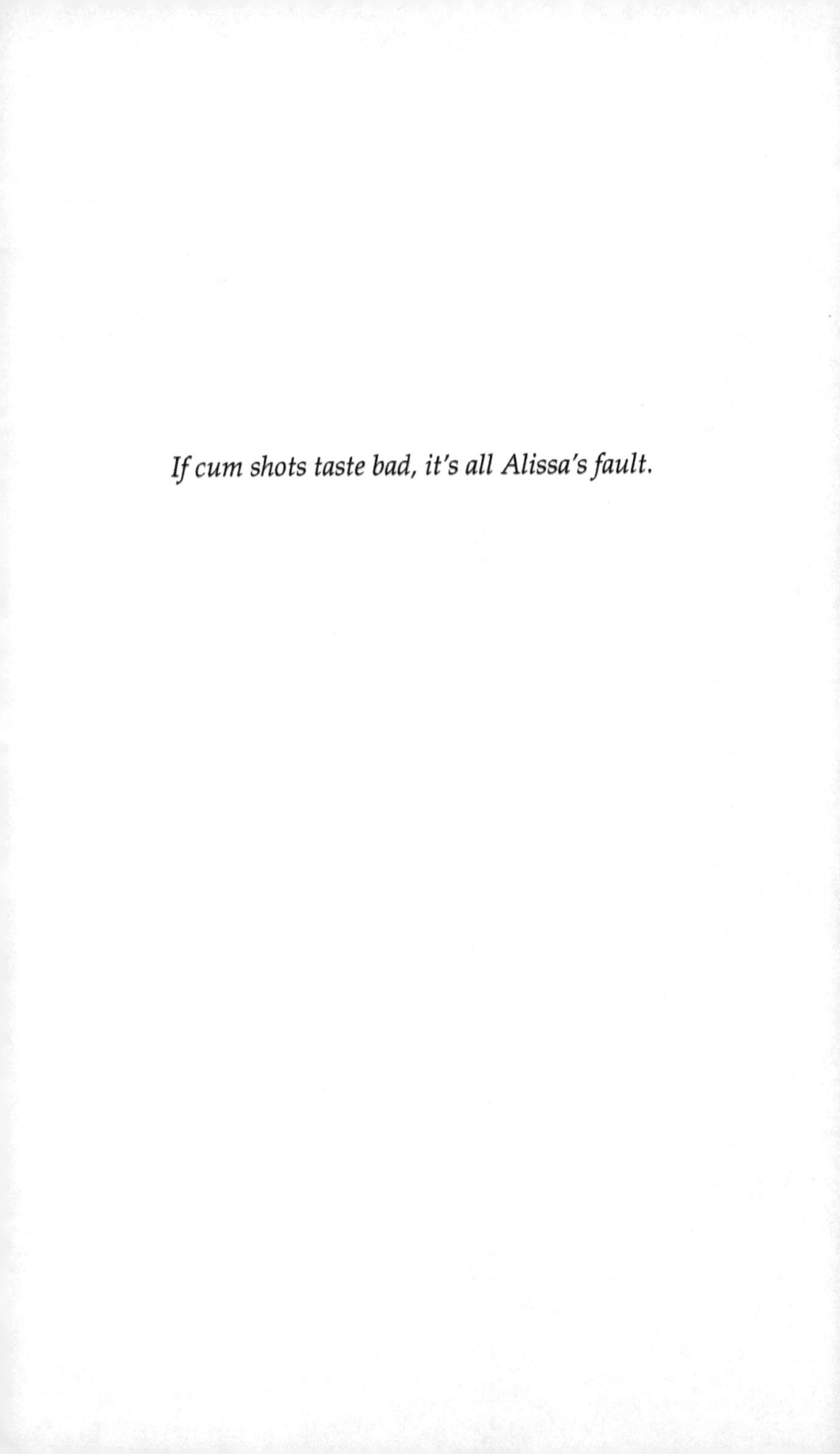

If cum shots taste bad, it's all Alissa's fault.

PROLOGUE
SUTTON

A FEW MONTHS BACK

THE FLASHES OF THE CAMERAS WERE BLINDING. ADD IN the chorus of cheers and some chants, and the atmosphere was electric. I hugged my friend Ryan close, saying, "We've got you, man," then moved on to embrace his boyfriend, Nate. Both were over-whelmed but clearly trying to keep themselves together and their reactions controlled.

With a quick glance at Jayden at my side, whose idea this cheerleading-slash-welcome party was, I had to hand it to the guy. He'd done the right thing. He tended to joke around and play up to the media—both on and off the basketball court—but he'd read this situation right.

Ryan coming out on his terms was a hell of a thing, and Jayden immediately dragging me on a plane from Minnesota to Vegas so that when Ryan returned from his break in Mexico, it would be to a support party was genius.

While Ryan would hate the media attention, there was no getting away from the stories that were already blowing up after he came out on Instagram. This way, Jayden had made sure our friends had support. Heck, Jayden had even got Ryan's new coach and a bunch of his new teammates on board too.

Jayden was lapping this up, and I couldn't fault him for it. He was good at this sort of thing—playing the media, helping to shape narratives. He played a part and put on an act, a cockier version of himself. It was his big personality that had swindled me into being his friend years back when we spent summers at basketball camp together. I'd known then that it was likely I could never be rid of the guy whose smile was contagious and whose hairbrained schemes were questionable.

Our *Ryan loves Nate* tees were probably one of those questionable touches, but the smiles they'd earned us from Nate and Ryan meant they were the right decision.

"You're not expected to do anything. Maybe wave and invite us all in for a beer."

Jayden's words drew my attention to him as he spoke to Ryan. Grinning widely, Jayden looked so pleased with himself. I held back my smile, proud of him for trying his hardest to be the best friend possible. I understood his motivation. It wasn't like I was any different, especially when it came to Jayden and making him happy.

"Really?" Ryan's relief was palpable. "You know I've been on vacation and have no beer or food, right?"

I gave him a chin lift. "All taken care of." It hadn't taken much to sweet-talk my way into Ryan's condo to take in the beer and enough snacks to feed a group of hungry basketball players.

In convoy, we headed off the small stage area that Jayden had arranged. That was the thing about my best friend: he tended to go over-the-top and all-out, especially when it impacted someone he cared about. I kept my expression light as we made our way to the building, Jayden before me. At this side of the media circus, we were closer to a cluster of reporters. I tried hard to keep my face neutral as questions were thrown out, most aiming to get a rise out of Ryan.

"What do you say to the fans who are saying they'll no longer support a team with men that kiss?"

I locked my jaw despite my best intentions at hearing the absurdity of the question. Where did this guy get off asking something so asinine? My tight jaw threatened to pop when "Men kissing are sick" made its way through a small group of bigoted dickheads.

Jayden abruptly pausing almost had me running into him. He angled to look at the small group of idiots, and I winced and reached for him, hoping he didn't do anything rash.

"The stupid fuckers," Jayden sneered just as my hand latched on his forearm. It was his "I'll fucking show them" that had me worried. His gaze snapped to mine, and I searched his expression, wondering what he was playing at.

My "What—" was cut off when Jayden cupped my cheek and leaned in, too fast for me to react beyond staring wide-eyed as his lips pressed against mine. I froze as our mouths touched, and then my brain blanked when he opened his mouth. My body reacted, my lips following his lead as he kissed me.

Heat and shock unfurled in my chest, and when his tongue touched mine, awareness zapped through me. And then he was pulling away, grinning, his smile so wide and satisfied that you'd have thought he'd won the playoffs.

He tossed me a careless wink, laughed, smacked

my arm, and carried on walking, completely unaffected. Nate's "Holy shit" got me following, but beyond putting one foot in front of the other, everything else faded away.

What the fuck had just happened? More to the point, why the hell did I want my friend to kiss me all over again?

It was that thought that plagued me throughout the impromptu party, just like it lived with me for the next few weeks. The whole time Jayden alternated between being proud to have flipped the haters off, helping take the heat off Ryan and Nate, and shrugging the whole thing off with a laugh while ribbing me about how hot a kisser he was.

There was no apology for putting me in the spotlight, regardless that I didn't mind assisting. There was definitely no "sorry" for stepping out of bounds and planting one on me. And there sure as shit wasn't any hint that his kiss had shaken something loose in him as it had me.

All it took was a joking moment for him to unravel our friendship. It took weeks of me shifting from confusion, anger, lust, and something so much more, the four cycling in a loop, for me to finally say enough. I'd slammed the brakes on our friendship, leaving Jayden perplexed. And the reason? Despite me talking a big game about friendship and honesty and how I was a man of integrity, I didn't sit him down and tell him the truth.

What was the point? Sharing my truth would have meant I'd lose him anyway. At least this way, it was on my terms.

CHAPTER 1
JAYDEN

NOW

"But I wanna ride one." I didn't know whether to look at the weird giant rat or marvel at the pulsing vein in Ryan's temple. I'd spotted it a few times over the last week, and now, with the fresh pulse, it was impressive enough to be given a name.

Something sophisticated. Something mature.

George.

Impressed with my name choice, I smiled, eyed George again and then looked at the weird rodent who lay on the grass, chewing.

"Jayden, I swear to God, I'll find the crocs and give you a shove so you can get to know them better if you carry on."

My brows shot up. "What did I do?" I whined. "I

showed you my list before we left the States, and not one thing on my 'awesome shit to do in Australia' list did you veto."

George woke again.

"Fuck me. For a start, they're not even kangaroos. They're wallabies."

Wide-eyed, I glanced at the wallaby. The creature still munched away, ignoring the bag of tasty treats I'd bought to get close.

"I feel cheated. Where are the kangaroos?"

"They all died. They're gone. They no longer have them at Australia Zoo."

Opening my mouth to respond, I was cut off by a loud wail. Both Ryan and I looked down at the small boy standing just to our side. The kid was sobbing, staring up at us. The man next to him quickly picked up the loud kid, shooting us a dirty look while reassuring his nosey kid that the kangaroos weren't dead.

The shake of my shoulders was inevitable. The laughter that followed was loud and abrupt, enough to startle the wallaby and make it jump up and bounce away.

Still laughing, I glanced over at Ryan. He was struggling to contain himself, his lips twitching, the amusement evident on his face.

"Come on." He tugged on my arm. "I think we need to get out of here before we're kicked out."

We left the pen, still grinning. "You know, you've probably scarred that kid for life," I teased.

"Piss off," he mumbled under his breath, side-eyeing the overwhelming number of people with young kids about. "You want to keep looking around or are you ready to go?"

"I'm good to head back." We'd arrived at opening time this morning. It was now past lunchtime, and the weird burger I'd had with beetroot had freaked me out too much to eat it. "I could definitely eat."

Ryan nodded. "Can do. We can stop somewhere on the way back."

Weaving through the crowds was straightforward. Our height advantage made it easy for people to see us coming and step out of our way.

Before long, we exited and headed to his pickup truck that was apparently a ute. I didn't think I'd ever tire of the fun Australian sayings, especially since over the last year or so, I'd heard Ryan sound less American during our catch-ups and calls. A given, I supposed, since he and Nate had got together.

The last year had been hands down the most frustrating of my life, though. And the strangest.

It made sense to add confusing to that list too.

Sometimes it was only my calls to Ryan and Nate, who'd been in Vegas with Ryan playing for the Vegas

Stallions, that kept me grounded. Now, this vacation to Australia was as far away from my life in Minnesota as I could get, finally giving me the space I needed to get my head on straight. Or at least that was my plan. The jury was still out with how successful that was.

We headed to an eatery on the beach. It was worth the drive just to see the waves rolling in and the almost white sands.

"You want to sit outside?"

"Definitely," I answered, loving that not only could we do so without phones and cameras being pointed in our direction, but that it was winter here, yet the heat was just the right side of perfect.

Ryan ordered our food at the bar and returned with drinks. I'd quickly become addicted to the sugary sweetness of lemon, lime, and bitters, and smiled contently when I took a sip. "Thanks."

Ryan nodded in response and took a seat at my side so we could both take in the view of the Coral Sea.

"I finally understand why you were such a wuss in Minnesota during winter."

Ryan snorted a laugh. "Right. This is what I'm used to in winter. Bright blue skies, low seventies, bloody perfect. Sure, you can freeze your ass off at night, but come midmorning on the Sunny Coast, bliss."

Angling to look at him through my sunglasses, I couldn't help the sliver of jealousy that needled at me. He'd had so many incredible seasons playing professional basketball in the League, no significant injuries. While the media were pains in the ass last season when he came out and shared his relationship with Nate with the world, he'd had a killer one.

It was so much more than that, though. Ryan was also in love with a great guy and lived in paradise.

Not to get me wrong. Ryan still hadn't convinced me every creature I saw wasn't going to kill me. But still, the man had it all.

Me? I'd run away for the off-season, as my best friend had… hell, I didn't even know what. Abandoned me? Cut me out? Confused the few smarts I had out of me with the last words we'd spoken to each other that weren't about the game? *"I can't do this anymore. I think we just need some space."* And hadn't that been a kick to the gut.

My best friend had gone and broken up with me.

Ever since I'd planted one on my friend before the beginning of last season, my friendship with Sutton had been screwed. Perhaps not immediately, but after a few weeks of things not being right, we'd finally reached the point of breakdown.

The surprise that I'd misread how he'd react had hit me hard. Without a doubt, I knew gut-deep that was the turning point. There I'd been, all up in his business, kissing him in public, camera flashes all around us, and so sure he'd go with it and laugh it off.

How wrong I'd been remained a struggle to get my head around. It shouldn't have been a surprise, really. Sutton had spent years letting me get away with nonsense, putting up with his dumb-jock friend causing grief.

That kiss had been a step too far.

"You still good to go out tonight?" Ryan's question pulled me away from my thoughts.

Immediately, I fixed an easy grin in place, so used to ensuring it looked natural. "Hell yes. A night out with my boys. Looking forward to it."

Ryan peered over at me with a look of contemplation. Whatever he was thinking, I didn't want to hear any of it. Both Ryan and Nate had attempted to dig for the past week of being here. Each time I'd changed the subject or blown off their concern with a joke. Not a chance I could talk about the muddle of thoughts and emotions that had bombarded me since last season.

I was saved from hearing any of it when our food arrived. Clapping and rubbing my hands together, I winked at the pretty server. "Thanks," I said, laying on my American drawl and enjoying the blush tinting her cheeks.

When she left, Ryan snorted.

"What?" I cast him a quick look while piling on the ketchup.

"I swear, everywhere you go, you can't help yourself and try to see how many women you can make blush."

I picked up a fry and grinned. "I have a scorecard. It's good to keep tabs and know that I've still got it." He rolled his eyes at me and took a bite of his fish. I eyed it speculatively. "What was the name of that again?"

"Barramundi," he answered after swallowing.

I wrinkled my nose, not a fan of fish at the best of times, and fish I'd never heard of would be a hard pass from me. "It stinks."

"It's fish. It's meant to stink."

My nose remained wrinkled, and I shook my head, "Well, shit stinks, and I don't—"

"Mate, fuck off."

I laughed and carried on eating my delicious-smelling burger. It didn't take us long to polish off our food and head to Ryan's pickup to go back to his and Nate's place.

As we pulled out of the parking lot, I focused on

the beach and the ocean. It would be nice to live close to a beach one day. In all honesty, maybe sooner rather than later.

At thirty-three, I was considered a dinosaur in the League and was kinda surprised Minnesota renewed my contract for another season. But maybe after this year, it would be time to stop.

Last year hadn't been the best. While we'd had solid games, my heart hadn't been in it. The joy of playing with my team had all but disappeared. That was partly because of Ryan's transfer to Vegas, but more honestly, it was because of my and Sutton's separation.

I sighed, leaning against the headrest. *Separation.* As much as people joked when comparing mine and Sutton's relationship to that of a married couple, they hadn't been that wrong. We'd done everything together, but last year it seriously felt like a marriage breakdown. The guy pretty much broke my heart with how he'd handled everything. I hadn't known a friendship could have that effect on me. But fuck, it hurt.

"I'm just going to call Nate and let him know we're on our way back," Ryan said.

I bobbed my head, still not looking at him. A moment later, Nate's voice came through the speakers. I tuned out the conversation, not wanting to hear their sweet talk.

As we went around one of the larger round-abouts, I gasped, eyes widening. "Fuck, Ryan, fuck." I held on to the door, the other hand on my seat belt as the car reaching the roundabout entrance we were passing didn't stop. I felt the hit. Felt my head smack against the window. And I sure as shit heard my yell as a second slam followed by an ear-splitting crunch surrounded me.

I didn't even have a chance to check on Ryan before my world turned to darkness.

CHAPTER 2
SUTTON

The bounce of my knee wouldn't stop. As soon as I became aware of it, I attempted to control the movement, but it was pointless. It started right back up. Fear wrapped around me, refusing to let go. Only seventeen hours ago, I'd been chilling with my brother, appreciating the distraction of hanging out with him.

One minute we'd been kicking back, watching my nephews shoot hoops. The next I almost dropped my phone when I listened to Nate on the other end.

Somehow I'd managed to give enough information to my brother, who'd chartered me a flight to LAX to get me there in time for a flight out to Brisbane.

"Would you like another drink before we land, sir?"

The voice cut through my bouncing leg and the thought of Jayden unconscious in a hospital bed. I shook my head and offered a tight smile, not having the energy to speak. There was always the possibility that my voice could crack.

The woman smiled kindly and moved on to the next person. Taking a moment to calm myself, I peered out the window. In the distance I saw an endless ocean, the horizon kissing the sky in a bright hue of blue.

There were no clouds to distract me, no land that I could see, just the never-ending sea, tips of white waves only just becoming visible. The lack of distraction meant that Jayden was on my mind, and all that had happened played on a loop.

I shouldn't have been surprised when Nate told me that Jayden had traveled with him and Ryan to Australia. That didn't stop the twist in my gut when I'd found out either. And this, all this, Jayden being in Queensland, him being in a car crash, was all because I'd pushed him away and couldn't be honest with him.

If I hadn't cut him from my life, no way would he have come to Australia without me, and likely that wouldn't have been until next year.

I slammed my eyes closed, finding no comfort in the vast ocean. The only thing that would ease my terror was knowing Jayden was okay and seeing his dark oak-colored eyes for myself.

Nate had updated me by the time I'd traveled to LA hours earlier. Ryan had a broken wrist and was sporting a new cast, and beyond that was unscathed.

Jayden not so much.

He'd been struggling to stay awake. I reminded myself that he was alert and responsive, for the most part, even as my brain still clung to the thought of him being unconscious. It wasn't true. Thank Christ. Somehow, the only broken bone was a finger in his left hand, which wasn't his dominant one. He had lacerations on his face and apparently a significant cut with multiple stitches spanning from his temple to his cheek.

It was him struggling to stay awake and his brain being knocked around that had held me frozen before I'd boarded my flight to Brisbane. With the flight being so long, I hoped I'd be able to contact his parents with good news when I saw him with my own eyes. They'd been my first call when I'd been able to get my brain functioning.

His mom had cried, his dad taking over the call, and I'd promised them I'd do everything I could to bring their son home. Safe and well.

With Mary, Jayden's mom, wheelchair-bound and not always in the best of health, I hadn't even hesitated to take on the responsibility to fly out. Not that they asked—my brother had been driving me to the airport when I'd called them.

But still, Jayden was my best friend, whether he still believed it or not. And there was no way he wasn't going to be okay.

The man would be playing at my side next season. He wasn't breaking free from me that easily.

It took another hour and forty-five minutes to finally land, pass passport control, and head toward the arrivals gate. I knew someone would be meeting me, Nate had promised as much, and as I finally pulled out my phone to power up, a string of text notifications pinged.

Amber, Nate's sister, would be picking me up.

I exited through the automatic doors, searching for Amber. I'd seen plenty of photographs of her over the past few years.

"Sutton." The sound of my name snapped my attention in the direction of a young woman. Relief settled into me that she was already here.

I greeted her, surprise slamming into me when she wrapped her arms tightly around my waist, giving me a squeeze. Even though she was tiny compared to my towering height, her head reaching no higher than my pecs, the woman knew how to hug.

Emotion clogged my throat, her greeting touching, and then I froze. "Fuck, Jayden—" I couldn't finish that sentence, too terrified to voice my fears.

"Shit, no, he's fine. Well," Amber winced, "he's still struggling a bit to stay awake for long periods but is already doing so much better."

I gasped for breath, adrenalin zipping through me so quickly, I went momentarily light-headed.

"Come on, let's get you to the hospital. I'm under strict instructions to get you straight there." Amber took hold of my hand like we were old friends and led me to her parked SUV.

"Your flight okay?"

It took me a moment for her words to register through the buzzing in my ears. "Yeah, good, thanks." I stared out the window, not quite believing I was in Australia.

Since meeting Ryan Broadwater a few years back, Jayden and I had made half-assed plans to visit Ryan's home country. Often it was linked to us giving our Aussie friend shit, but beneath it all, there'd been an edge of seriousness. But here I was, having traveled in a panic to see the man who should have been at my side.

A wave of frustration threatened to drown me when a series of what-ifs swept over me.

The asshole had run to Australia without me.

And run he did. Why he'd done so was as clear to me as the bright blue sky I stared at out of Amber's car.

It was my fault. I'd shut Jayden out, pushed him away. And all because of that damn kiss last year. Him making a statement. Giving haters and the media the middle finger to support Ryan and Nate may have been ill-thought-out. But fuck if it hadn't been at the expense of my… fuck, I didn't even know what.

Jayden was my friend, without a doubt my best friend. But that kiss had rocked my world in a way I'd never envisioned. Ever. And while I questioned every feeling, gesture, and conversation between us and spent too many hours going over that kiss, Jayden had acted like it was no big deal. I had no doubt he was right to do so, but that hadn't helped me or my confusion.

"It'll take us just over an hour to get there," Amber was saying. "Most traffic is heading into the city, so we shouldn't get too caught up."

I offered a cursory smile. "No worries." My mouth kicked up a little higher at the phrase Jayden and I used, mainly in a low, relaxed twang to mimic Ryan's accent. "I just appreciate you coming to get me."

She cast me a quick glance. "If you need to call anyone back home, you can use my phone," she said.

"I have free international calls on my plan." She cast me another look, and I noticed her cheeks pinken. "Uhm, yeah, I know calls are expensive from an international mobile. No point in that when you can use mine for free."

This time my smile was genuine. This young woman was worried about my cell bill, and I expected she knew that I earned several zeros on my paycheck like her brother once had.

"Thanks. I'll just shoot off a few texts to Jayden's family and mine, letting them know I'm here." I did so, and we carried on the journey, with mainly Amber filling the quiet and not putting me under any pressure to respond in detail. I appreciated she was letting me offer simple grunts and one-syllable responses. I couldn't give any more than that.

I tried to take in a little of the passing highway, hoping it would distract me. But the bright sun, the industrial buildings, the collection of forestry occasionally breaking up the monotony of chain stores, didn't do much to make the journey pass by any faster.

A new tendril of anticipation threaded into my veins when we pulled off the highway. I sat up a little straighter as I focused on the cars of people going on about their day, heedless of the turmoil making my stomach ache.

The landscape changed again, and signs for the hospital caught my attention.

"Is this it?" I asked, just to break the silence, needing the sound to ground me.

"Yeah. Just need to park in the multistory."

Wide-eyed, I nodded, my pulse picking up speed. What the hell was I even doing here? What if Jayden was so annoyed with me, he told me to disappear? What if he was injured worse than I thought, and I lost my shit?

I cleared my throat when Amber cut the engine after parking. "Does he know I'm coming?"

Her warm gaze met mine. "I don't think so. He hasn't been with it enough, I don't think, but I haven't heard anything from Nate for a couple of hours, so that could have changed."

I bobbed my head and exited her car.

"I'm going to get you to his room. Ryan and Nate will be there, then I have to get back to Ivy."

Guilt raised its head. I hadn't even considered she'd left her kid to come and pick me up. We moved toward the elevator, and I shot her an apologetic smile. "I didn't ask how Ivy was doing. Sorry. And sorry you had to come and get me."

Amber waved me off as we stepped into the elevator, and she hit one of the buttons. "I don't mind at all. She's happy with Gran. And the last thing you need to worry about is my girl, not when you're worried about your friend."

My heart squeezed tight. *Friend.* What if Jayden no longer considered me his friend since I'd fucked up?

A huff of air escaped me as we stepped out onto a corridor. I followed Amber's lead as we traveled along the mazelike path toward Jayden's room.

A few minutes later, we were rubbing our hands in antibacterial gel and stepping onto a quiet, pristine ward. The whole place looked clean and weirdly calm. "This is the private hospital," Amber commented, and I realized my brows had shot high when I looked around the place. "Saying that, the main hospital isn't much different, just bigger. The whole hospital isn't that old."

She waved at a middle-aged nurse as we passed by the nurses' station. "They already know who you are."

Between the loud pounding in my ears and my heavy footsteps, I could barely hear her. I managed a weak "Thanks" before hesitating at the door she pushed open.

Curiosity filled her gaze when she looked back at me. The look morphed into understanding when she reached out and squeezed my arm. "You'll be fine and so will he." With that, she stepped away, and I had no choice but to follow her in.

While I was aware of Ryan and Nate, my focus was on the man in the bed—eyes closed and a bandage on his temple. He wasn't attached to a heart monitor, which was something. I held my breath as I watched his chest rise and fall. He was breathing by himself. I gasped for air, having held it in for too long, so focused on watching his rib cage move.

While I'd been told that he was going to be fine, it hadn't stopped my mind from catastrophizing his injuries.

"Hey." Ryan grasped my shoulder and squeezed. "He's doing really well."

Not ready to pull my gaze away from Jayden, I simply nodded. My brain struggled to connect the bruised, unmoving form in the bed with that of my best friend. Jayden was never quiet. Seriously, the guy talked in his sleep all the time. I'd shared a room often enough over the years to know what could shut him up—only a heavy pillow smacked on his head—and what would get him saying the weirdest shit. I'd done the latter when bored or struggling to sleep by asking him random questions while he slept—hearing Jayden's voice always mellowed me out, while his sleep talking offered me endless enter-tainment.

This right here was different.

There were no twitches, no eye flickers, no mumbled nonsense. Instead, there was only the steady rise and fall of his chest.

"You wanna take a seat? Need a coffee?"

I flicked my attention to Nate and returned his smile, quickly accepting his hug. "Yeah, that'd be great, thanks."

Nate bobbed his head. "Cappuccino?"

"Just black would be great."

He and Ryan's sister left the room as I took the seat closest to Jayden's bed. "What have the docs said?"

Ryan took the seat next to me. "He hit his head pretty hard, and his brain got shook up. They're keeping a close eye on his vitals. He's staying awake longer and he's coherent, so they're not as worried."

A whoosh of breath escaped me. "So he's really going to be okay?"

"He is. Concussed, but they've done an MRI and are pleased with what they found."

"They found a brain, huh," I forced out, trying to grasp onto any humor I could to settle my hurting heart. "I vote not to tell Jayden. He'll start using it as proof in his arguments or something, letting us know he has the brain to prove all his crazy theories."

Ryan snorted in amusement. "They won't release

him until they're a hundred percent sure he'll be okay. Probably until he can stay awake for longer than a couple of hours or something. It'll depend on what the doctors advise."

Knowing that sent a fresh tendril of relief through my system. "Okay, thanks, Ryan." I glanced at his wrist. "You going to be okay?"

"Yeah. It was a clean break. It'll heal up in no time." He paused a beat. "How about I leave you alone for a while? See how they're getting on with that coffee?" He squeezed my shoulder, stood, and left the room.

By ourselves, I hesitated before reaching out and taking Jayden's hand. The asshole was pale beneath his bruises, and his stillness freaked me out.

"Thought he'd never leave." Jayden's gruff voice startled me. Reactively, I made to pull my hand away, but Jayden's grip on my fingers prevented me.

My gaze darted to his face as he blinked his eyes open.

"You look like shit," he grunted.

I snorted a laugh. "Looked in a mirror lately?"

His lips twitched, a frown quickly following. "My head feels like it's going to explode."

"You need some painkillers?"

"Nah. I had some not so long ago." His hand

jerked, and I eased up my hold, but once again, he gripped harder.

I closed my eyes and took a breath before refocusing on the man who fucking terrified me.

"You flew out," he said. I bobbed my head. "Does that mean you're not pissed off at me anymore?"

I released his hand and sat back fully in my chair. Emotion flickered in his expression as I moved before it resettled to the more carefree look I was used to seeing last season.

"Or maybe not."

"Jay, it's not that. Fuck, you were in a crash, and I panicked, okay. Of course I came here." He waited me out, staying quiet when I wished he'd do his usual nonstop talking. "I needed to make sure you're all right. Promised your parents I'd look out for you."

He grimaced. "I bet they're climbing the walls."

"They're worried. I'll call them soon. Tell them you're going to have a brain transplant while you're here. That should make them happy."

A smirk formed. The familiar smile directed my way eased some of the tightness in my chest. But in doing so caused my heart to flip over, my pulse picking up. I swallowed hard and took a deep breath. He was okay; it was the only reason my heart pumped faster. Relief that he was all right was the only reason.

It was nothing to do with my memory refusing to let go of the kiss we'd shared. Nor was it how looking at Jayden now nudged me to remember the dreams that refused to disappear. Ones where we reenacted the kiss over and over again.

I could continue to let any of that plague me, which they had done over the past season. I missed the cocky asshole so much, and knowing I could have lost my friend—I couldn't go there.

"You know, you look constipated with all that thinking you're doing."

I rolled my eyes. "That right?"

"You know it." Jayden glanced down at his hand and opened and closed his palm a couple of times. "You can hold my hand again if you want." His eyes twinkled.

I met his stare and raised a single brow at him. "In your dreams, wiseass. In. Your. Dreams."

CHAPTER 3
JAYDEN

I hadn't lied when I said Sutton looked like shit. That didn't stop him from looking so good. Just seeing his face, having him so close, eased a part of my soul that I couldn't explain. Add that he was talking to me in complete sentences, with only a few of his usual grunts, and I was like an overeager puppy, desperate for any attention he'd give me.

But fuck, I was tired.

Between the pounding in my skull and the occasional dizziness where my sight went fuzzy, it was difficult to concentrate. Plus, there was me drifting off midconversation. Every time I came to, Sutton was staring at me intently, fear etched on his features. And every single time I woke, he was holding my hand.

"What time is it?" I asked around a yawn, my jaw cracking and the stitches on my face pulling.

Sutton mimicked my yawn and unfortunately let go of my hand as he tugged his phone out of his pocket. "Almost seven."

"You look beat." Tired eyes stared back at me, a given since his flight from the States brought him straight to me. While I didn't know what time he'd arrived earlier today, I knew it had been morning. He'd barely left my side since. "Why don't you head to Ryan's?"

"No chance. I'm fine here."

His response rolled through me, relief caressing the edges of my mind. Now that he was here, I didn't want him to leave. I was a needy asshole at the best of times, but this side of Sutton, where he cared and looked out for me, I liked best.

"You heard from Ryan?" I asked, trying to control my overeager smile that he didn't want to leave.

He bobbed his head and gave another yawn. "Yeah. He texted about an hour ago and told me to let them know when I was ready to go, and Nate would come and get me. Told him I was fine staying put."

This time there was no holding back my grin. "Missed me that much, huh?"

I expected a grunt, and he didn't disappoint. He looked away, though, avoiding eye contact.

Concussion sucked. A broken finger pissed me off. But Sutton appearing here after a season of blowing hot and cold before settling on Arctic temperatures messed up my head in a way my shitty headache from the crash couldn't process.

Me being… well, me, I grunted loud enough to capture his attention, opened my mouth, and let my inarticulate words tumble free. "If I'd known all it took was a knock to the head and a broken digit to stop you being a dick, I would have made that happen six months ago." I waited for a beat, my stare on him. The dickstain simply looked at me, his expression impassive. "But apparently, the dick hasn't fallen off your head completely."

Aware I was being over-the-top and dramatic, I didn't have it in me to stop or even care. I wanted a reaction. Needed it like my next breath.

His quirked brow was at least a reaction. Still, the fucker said nothing.

"Yeah, it's still there on your head. I'm surprised you can carry the weight," I continued, trying to get a rise from him.

With a bland tone, he said, "My impressive dick size would have most men struggling. Not so much me. I'm used to it."

A bubble of amusement pushed past my snark, and my lips twitched. "You're not *that* big." Okay, he totally was. Having known the man for as long as I had and inevitably been naked so often, I had no issues admitting as much. Usually. Sutton did not need an ego boost, so there was no chance I'd be agreeing with him.

Once again, the ass quirked his brow at me, calling bullshit.

I lost some humor, my aching head letting me know it was almost time for another dose of painkillers. I hoped one of the nurses would be by soon. "What are you doing here?" My sigh was heavy, tired.

Sutton's gaze danced around my face, reading my expression before he spoke. "I may have overreacted and panicked when Nate called telling me you'd been injured, asking if I could let your parents know." His voice was tight, his concern bleeding through his words.

That was the thing about Sutton. He always told the truth, said it how it was. It was why his distance over the past season had hit me so hard. It just wasn't like him. His concern for me inched its way into my awareness more fully. When it settled, my pulse sped up.

"And now that you're here?" I had no idea what his plans or intentions were. Did I even want him to stay? Hell yes. There wasn't a chance I'd beg, though. I missed him, so much so that emptiness had burrowed deep and taken root in my gut. But I'd tried over and over again to figure out what was going on, and I was exhausted.

With his gaze fixed on mine, he took a swig from his can of soda, taking far too long to swallow the liquid. I narrowed my eyes at him, sure he was doing so on purpose.

"Since I'm here, I thought I'd stick around for a while. Make the most of the trip."

I twisted my mouth and ran my tongue over my top teeth, buying myself some thinking time. "You're staying here? With Nate and Ryan?"

He nodded.

"You sure you can handle being in the same space as me? 'Cause honestly, Sutton, I came here to get away from the sullen shit show you've been dishing out all season." I ignored the heat creeping up my cheeks, but the fuck if I'd hold back. Not with him. I watched him carefully, my heart jolting when a flash of remorse appeared on his face.

I wanted nothing more than to go back to how things were. I wasn't dense enough to not know all this distance was because of my actions last off-season. I'd mentioned it a time or fifteen, but Sutton hadn't confirmed or denied anything.

That simply left me more confused.

I'd apologized and laughed it off, teased, and shrugged. None of my reactions had made a difference, though, and in many ways, they'd made Sutton more distant.

Maybe now, if he could pull his head out of his ass long enough, we could finally figure things out.

"I'll make sure I work at removing the dick from my head. How about that?"

I smiled, the gesture wide and warm. "Sounds good. Just don't strain yourself in the process."

He snorted, the sound relaxing my shoulders.

"So apparently I need to hold back for a week or so before anything high octane."

Sutton smiled, the whites of his teeth perfect and almost blinding in the rays filtering in from the setting sun. Fuck, it had been a long time since I'd had that directed my way. "I think only a week is wishful thinking and it may be closer to three, maybe more, but just to be clear, no bungee jumping."

"Or riding kangaroos, apparently."

He grunted out a laugh and looked at the time on his phone.

"You know, I don't think you're allowed to stay."

Intensity shone in his eyes as he stared me down.

I quirked my brow at him in response until he sighed and rubbed a hand over his face. "I'm not leaving until you stop freaking me out by falling asleep midsentence."

Emotion fizzed in my chest, the reality of the past twenty-four hours creeping into my system. I hurt, ached like I'd been body-slammed by a truck, which wasn't too far from the truth. On top of that, my injuries worried me. It wasn't like I was at death's door or anything like that, but concussions were the worst, and I could totally do without a broken bone. While training for the new season was still a couple of months away, I didn't want this to hold me back from a killer season, especially since Sutton was speaking to me again.

When Sutton gripped my uninjured hand once again, my gaze lifted to his. There was no disguising my watery eyes, and Sutton was the only person alive who I'd allow to see such emotion.

"You'll be okay, and I'm not going anywhere, you hear me?"

I swallowed hard and blew out a shaky breath, forcing a light chuckle. "Fucking meds."

He squeezed my hand in response and pulled back when a nurse entered the room. I hadn't seen the dark-haired woman before.

"Hey, Jayden. I'm Maddy. I'm just going to check

your vitals, and it's just about the end of visiting hours too." She cast a glance at Sutton, whose large frame stiffened in the chair.

"Maddy," I said, aiming for an easy grin and thickening up my drawl; so far, the Australians seemed to like it. "This here is Sutton. He's literally flown in all the way from America just to be with me to make sure I wasn't dying, and I had to convince him it was a car and not a snake that got me."

Maddy smiled. "Our snakes do get a bad rep."

"That they do. You think it's going to be a problem if he stays?"

A sympathetic smile spread across her mouth. "Unfortunately, that's not going to be possible. I may be able to give you another hour, but only relatives are allowed to stay the night."

Disappointment knotted in my stomach. "I'd think my man Sutton here flying fourteen hours or so to be with me would be special circumstances, right?" This time I aimed for puppy-dog eyes.

"Your man?" she asked, tilting her head at me, her gaze bouncing between the two of us.

Before I could answer and say he was my best friend, Sutton's "I'm his fiancé" had me slamming my mouth shut and staring at him bug-eyed. I bit down on the inside of my cheeks. Disbelief was etched on his features, and when he looked at me, I could see the absolute panic there.

Amusement burst to life in my chest. His bullshit admission was absolutely the kind of thing I would do.

Like the fucker I was, I held my hand out to him, palm up. "That's right, baby." I eyed him, then my hand, and grinned hard when he sighed, rolled his eyes, and took it. This reaction was much more in line with what I knew from the man.

With his palm secure in mine, I had too much fun rubbing my thumb over his skin. I glanced at Maddy, who wore a small smile. "So what do you say? Can this sexy-ass beast of a man stay with me? I promise I'll make sure he behaves. Sometimes he struggles to keep his hands to himself." I turned to Sutton, who I could tell was grinding his back molars. "You hear that, baby? No funny business." I followed up with a wink and somehow managed not to snort out a laugh when he narrowed his gaze at me.

"I'm sure I can manage that," he gritted with a tight smile. Sutton aimed a very different smile at Maddy. "Cross my heart."

"In that case, I'm sure it should be fine. I'll need to check with the duty nurse, but I don't see a problem. We can have a cot brought in for you. Now, let's get on with these checks and get you some pain meds."

She set about checking my vitals while I managed to keep my mouth shut. Though the truth was, exhaustion once again was setting in. By the time she finished and left, I didn't have the energy to tease Sutton, a little disappointed at the fact.

"You can barely keep your eyes open." Sutton's voice was light and soothing. I peeked at him under my half-closed eyelids and attempted a smile. "Just rest."

"'kay," I mumbled, sighing contently that through it all, Sutton hadn't let go of my hand.

A NURSE WOKE ME EVERY THREE HOURS TO CHECK MY vitals. Each time, Sutton was already awake and sitting on the edge of the cot, his gaze intent on me. By the time I woke up properly for the start of the new dawn and the rounds from the doctor, I'd washed up and was feeling almost human.

"Give us time to organize the discharge papers, and you should be out of here by ten," the doc said, chart in hand. "Remember, concussions are serious business, and while we're happy with the MRI results, it could be as little as a week, but maybe closer to a month before you're feeling fully recovered. Do not push it. I'll organize a script for anti-nausea medications, as well as painkillers and something to help you sleep should the headaches be too much and keep you awake."

I smiled and gave a careful nod, not wanting to shake my brain any more than necessary. I didn't even correct him that falling asleep was not my problem. He'd already spent ten minutes going over the possible side effects and why that was. I didn't want to give him any reason to believe I couldn't be set free.

"Your fiancé"—a thrill of amusement buzzed to life at the word—"I'm sure will fill the script for you. I'd suggest doing it before you leave. The pharmacy opens in about thirty minutes." He glanced at Sutton, who was clearly listening to everything the doctor said.

"I can do that."

The doctor nodded, returning his attention to me. "I know you're here on vacation, and I'm sure this will put a dampener on things, but I can't stress enough how important it is to take it easy."

It majorly sucked, but with the aches in my body and the throb in my head, I didn't expect relaxing would be too much of an issue.

"I'll make sure he doesn't overdo it," Sutton said from my side, sitting opposite to where the doctor stood.

"As for physical activity, including sexual intercourse, play it by ear, and use your headaches to guide you. Certainly nothing too strenuous for at least a week, but listen to your body after that."

I couldn't help it. I grinned and turned to Sutton. The tips of his ears turned pink, and as always, he grunted. "It'll be hard, I know, baby," I said, reaching out and squeezing his arm, cackling on the inside at his rigid shoulders and the stink eye he shot me. Right about now, I was sure he was regretting reacting to being kicked out and wished he'd just got Nate to pick him up. Me? Hell, I loved every moment of his embarrassment. The man didn't embarrass easily, so I had to make the most of it when he did.

"Righto, Jayden. I expect the nurses may want you to sign a few autographs on your way out. There's been increased chatter once everyone realized who you are and that you play for the League. While the League's not too big in these parts, it doesn't take much for our staff to grab on to the most positive excitement they can get. But just give me the nod if you want me to get them to back off. The duty nurse owes me a favor, and she'll make sure no one bothers you." The doctor gave me a small smile.

"I don't mind at all, and I'm sure Sutton here's up for a few photographs too."

"Brilliant. No overdoing it, though, and I'll make

sure Amanda, the duty nurse, takes control so you don't get overwhelmed." With that, he said his good-byes and left the room, leaving me alone with Sutton and eager to be discharged.

"You think it's a good idea bringing attention to you and signing autographs?" Concern had Sutton's voice sounding deeper than usual.

"It'll be fine. You emailed my agent and Coach, right? Got my parents up to speed?" He nodded, and I eased out of bed to go to the bathroom. "Then it'll be fine. They all know my injuries aren't anything too serious, and it won't impact my season. It means they'll be able to shut down any speculation. You gave the hospital the details of where to send the medical records." I shrugged and stood, waiting for the dizziness that thankfully didn't happen.

Smiling, I looked up, brows shooting high seeing Sutton standing before me, hand clearly ready to hold me should I need the support. My heart constricted, so fucking happy he'd come all this way and we were getting back on track.

Before he could say anything, which he clearly intended to do based on his expression, I blurted, "I need to piss."

He nodded and let me pass, and I was sure if I looked over my shoulder, he'd be less than three feet behind me.

After finishing up in the bathroom, I returned to find my fruit and toast. Sutton, ever the gentleman his mom brought him up to be, was waiting for me before he started on his own breakfast.

"What time is it?" I asked after taking a gulp of OJ.

"Not long after eight. I've called Nate, and he's going to head on over to get us." He worried his lip, something he rarely did, and shifted his gaze away from me.

"What is it?" I asked, sitting on the bed.

He lifted his cell, huffed out a heavy breath, then shoved it at me. "Read for yourself."

Sunshine Coast Qld Chronicle @sunshineqld-chronicle #BreakingNews

Basketball superstars @jaydenmooreofficial and @galesuttonofficial are out and engaged. It seems the month for it this #PrideMonth

image of Jayden Moore and Gale Sutton public kiss September last year

89.3K Retweets 14.7 Quote Tweets 512.7K Likes

Wide-eyed, my heart galloped in my chest as I read the tweet, not bothering with the comments, but I took in the number of reactions. "Shit," I said with a laugh, having no idea how else to react. This was crazy, but then that photo of Sutton and me from all those months ago most definitely looked like the real thing.

I supposed it was.

When I'd kissed him, it had been to prove a point. My own big FU to the bigots targeting Ryan and Nate.

For a while, the media had jumped all over the story. It was only when our club's PR advised us to make a statement making it clear we weren't in a romantic relationship, right alongside the two of us being supporters of the LGBTQ community, that the stories fizzled out. Sure, there'd been a whole fandom of "Jayton" love out there with conspiracy theories of the two of us being in the closet and in love, which I'd eaten up and thought was both hilarious and awesome.

That had been the final straw for Sutton, though. He'd distanced himself completely. The memory made me jerk my head in his direction. I ignored the pain of the fast movement, too focused on Sutton and dreading that he'd act all fucking weird again and back away. "Shit, okay. We can fix this, right?"

He sighed. "This one's on me. I'm sorry. I was the one who panicked about being kicked out and said we were together."

When his tone sounded more resolved than angry, I eased back against the puffed-up pillows, relaxing. "So would you say this is worse than me kissing you in front of the cameras? You know, since you said we're engaged and that means one day soon we're going to get married… you think that is going to be harder to take back?"

His gaze snapped to mine, and I couldn't hold back. I grinned, and laughter burst free. The pain of the movement and the loud noise was so fucking worth it for the flickering emotions crossing his face. I didn't think either of us was sure whether he wanted to punch me, abandon ship, or laugh his ass off right alongside me.

"It's okay. You can admit that this is sooooo much worse," I said, super helpfully.

With a sigh, he leaned back in his chair, his shoulders drooping, shaking his head. Seeing the glimmer of a smile on his face was a hell of a thing, though.

"Only you, Jayden." His gaze connected with mine.

"Only me what?"

He tilted his head. "I swear, since the day I met you and you told me I was going to be your friend and there was nothing I could do about it, life's been… chaotic—"

"And fucking epic."

He chuckled. "Yeah, that too. But I only get involved in shit when you're around."

I gasped, somewhat melodramatically. "I am so not the bad influence in this duo—" I cleared my throat, indicating I was building up to some life-changing speech. "—Mr. He's My Fiancé." As far as life-changing declarations went, my pitched voice that sounded nothing at all like Sutton's, was short but sweet. Sutton flipping me the bird told me as much.

He did that a lot. It was one of the many ways he'd shown me over the years that he was devoted to me and our bromance. He also wasn't exaggerating that I'd latched on at basketball camp and told him he was the jelly to my peanut butter and we were destined to be best friends.

I was gifted with my skill with words and metaphors and remained surprised that I'd actually managed to graduate college at all. Though Sutton may have had something to do with that too. Sure, we'd gone to different colleges, but I may have accidentally on purpose fought hard to get into the college closest to his, as there wasn't a chance I could attend Dartmouth like his big-brained self. We'd met up as often as possible over the four years, and he kept me grounded and made sure I worked enough to pass and not bring shame to my momma.

"Okay, we're out of here soon, and I suppose we need to figure out what to say?" I said after he remained quiet. "Perhaps put your phone away too." I indicated toward his cell, which he'd taken back and scrolled through. At the look on his face, my heart thudded loudly. The usual calm expression was nowhere to be seen. "Hey," I said, concerned, reaching out to squeeze his arm. "Let's not sweat this, all right? Let's not say anything for now. We'll get out of here when Nate arrives and go kick back and relax. We'll figure it out, perhaps talk to the team's PR or something. This doesn't have to be a big deal."

Like last time, his reaction left me confused. For a fact I knew Sutton wasn't homophobic. He'd not only been vocal in his support of the community over the years but put his words into action and helped one of his cousins with an LGBTQ+ rally about six years back. Since then, he'd been a strong ally.

Knowing that about him made his reaction to our kiss last year more difficult to understand. I admitted I'd overstepped and had apologized about how sorry I was that I didn't get his consent first. I wasn't a complete asshole. With each apology, he'd acknowledged he understood my intention, but for weeks after, he'd acted differently.

I swallowed hard. Maybe one day he'd tell me the truth about what was really bothering him, but for now, we needed to deal with this. However we did that, I refused to have it destroy our friendship.

"Okay," he finally answered, his gaze steady.

"Good. Let's get my stuff packed up then, and you go fill that script so we can get outta here."

CHAPTER 4
SUTTON

This was insane, and I only had myself to blame.

Every time Jayden had drifted off yesterday, dread had held me frozen, so terrified something was seriously wrong and he wouldn't wake up again. Fear had me spurting out those words, and now a new shit show was unraveling.

To make matters worse, every moment I'd spent with him yesterday had been as ordinary as before our kiss. We'd laughed, joked, shot the shit. The difference was this time when he laughed, my heart sped up. When the light caught his hair in a certain way, bringing out dark blond highlights in his otherwise chestnut strands, my heart had jolted. And by the time he'd drifted off to sleep properly after whispering in the dark room that he was happy I was there, not for the first time I wondered just when it was I'd fallen in love with my best friend.

For thirty-two years I'd been straight. No hesitation, no questioning, and absolutely no doubt. I knew who I was, inside and out. Hell, I had a bioethics degree. While my degree was rooted mainly in healthcare, the initial part of the course was about understanding my own ethos, morals, and values. We'd had a deep dive into our sense of self, and at no point had I been confused.

Not until that kiss.

That one single moment that had unraveled everything I thought I knew was true.

After that, every touch, look, joke, and every single moment we'd spent together had been too much for my heart to take. My brain went to war with the pumping organ. And now, after months of distance, it had all been for naught.

My heart was in control, a hundred percent, effectively telling my brain it could go screw itself.

"You sure this is the best thing to do?" I finally asked, having remained silent long enough as Nate drove us toward the airport.

"You saw yourself what the media were like when you guys left the hospital. It didn't take long to figure out that you were also here to see Ryan. There's been press camped outside our place all morning." Nate glanced in the rearview mirror at me.

"I know the press can be intrusive cocks here in Australia too, but I think it just took both Nate and me by surprise," Ryan added from the passenger seat. "Out front did you spot the ESPN crew?"

I nodded, having wondered myself about that. I didn't care enough about media franchises to know if reporters had flown in last night or they simply had American correspondents here all the time. The reality was it didn't matter. All that did matter was that Jayden needed peace and quiet to recover, and there'd be no chance of that with every man and his dog wanting a photo op and an interview.

"My uncle's place out in Mitchell is the perfect place to disappear to," Nate said. "You'll jump on the flight to Roma, pick up your hire car, and it'll just take about an hour to get out there. It's small but is powered and has fresh water. Stop by the store before you leave Roma, though, and pick up supplies, and you'll be golden."

"Why does it worry me you felt the need to say it had power and water?" Jayden said from my side. He'd been weirdly quiet since Nate and Ryan got us from the hospital with their plan to take us to Brisbane Airport and for us to jump on the one-fifteen flight to Roma.

I saw Nate wince through the mirror. "I visited a few times as a kid, and the dunny used to be outside, and yeah, it has tank water, but it wasn't until about twenty years ago he got the place hooked up to the grid. Before that, it was on a gene."

"A *jen-knee*?" I asked, having already figured out what he meant by a dunny, and was relieved as hell I wouldn't have to go outside to relieve myself.

"Yeah, an old diesel generator," he clarified, putting his blinker on and taking the exit off the highway.

"Just focus on recouping and figuring out what you're going to do," Ryan said pointedly, angling to look over his shoulder at the both of us. Unasked questions formed in his eyes. They'd been there since he came to the hospital. He hadn't asked a single one, though. Hadn't prodded, hadn't demanded answers or called bullshit.

"We will," I answered, side-eyeing a resting Jayden, his eyes now closed. From the mad dash from the hospital to the developments of this past hour, my own head pounded. Christ only knew how he was coping. A quick glance at the time told me it would be another hour until he could take more pain medicine, which I expected meant the ones he'd had were wearing off.

"You all right?" I asked quietly, leaning closer to Jayden.

He opened his eyes, looking so tired that I wanted to reach out and do something, anything, to make his pain and exhaustion go away. "Yeah. Not really looking forward to a flight."

I winced, understanding that completely. "You can have another couple of painkillers before we get on the plane. You'll be fine. A few more hours and you'll finally be in the outback." A smile tugged at my mouth. "You'll finally get to see kangaroos in the wild."

A sleepy grin was my reward, and I filed it away, despite knowing I should do no such thing. "Maybe if I take enough pain meds, I'll be able to finally ride one."

My chuckle was quiet. "Let's make that a hard no."

"You know, you're super controlling for a fiancé." He quirked his brow. "I always thought you'd be sweet and doting, you know… doing all the touchy-feely caring shit that you do."

"Touchy-feely caring shit?" I said back to him, not wanting to latch onto anything else he said.

"Uh-huh. You know you do that care-for-me thing you always do. And you make people talk about their feelings, but I have no idea how since you never come out and ask them to. It's this whole empath thing you've got going on."

"Empath thing?"

"Yeah, you make people open up and like you and care for you because you read them so well."

Bemused, I frowned, wondering what he was talking about while thinking it was probably the nicest and strangest thing he'd ever said to me. Before I could respond, we were slowing for traffic lights. I peered outside, recognizing we were about to drive into the airport zone. I did a couple of slow blinks, hardly believing it was only yesterday I'd arrived, and that was after two flights, making it a long day.

Between the travel and the sporadic minutes of sleep I'd grabbed last night, I was bone tired. Just a few more hours, and I'd be able to stop, though. Once we were at the cabin, the two of us could rest and catch up with some much-needed sleep.

"I was able to sort you extra legroom for obvious reasons," Nate said as he pulled up outside the Qantas terminal. "You're already checked in. You just need to print out your baggage labels, then you're all set." He left the engine running, and we all exited the SUV. He hugged me tightly. "Look after you both, yeah?"

I bobbed my head. "No worries." I pulled away

and winked. I then patted Ryan's back as he embraced me.

When he pulled away, his gaze was searching. "While you're away, figure out what you want and what's good for your heart, okay?" After a beat of seriousness, his lips twitched, and I shook my head at him. The asshole had thrown my words back at me, ones I'd said to him when I suspected something was going on between him and Nate. Despite his amusement, the way he gripped my arm and stared so intently that it was impossible to look away from, I knew he meant every word.

"I hear you."

He squeezed before letting go. "Text when you get there. Nate's sent you the address so you can throw it into the car's satnav. Just be safe and watch for roos."

I rolled my eyes, earning me a laugh.

"He's actually serious," Nate said, moving to his side. "Those buggers are big out there and cross roads without looking both ways all the damn time."

"It's strange they made a Tasmanian devil into a cartoon when they could have had so much more fun with a kangaroo," Jayden said from my side.

I cast him a glance and shook my head at him. There was no way I was touching that and opening up a conversation that could take the whole of the journey.

"Either he's still high, or he needs another dose." Ryan eyed him.

"Another dose," I answered, picking up both Jayden's and my bags. "See you both soon, and thanks for this."

Ryan bobbed his head. "Anytime, mate. You know that. Now get going and perch yourself where you're not the center of attention while you're waiting. Speak to you later." With that, Nate and Ryan left, and I led Jayden into the airport. He followed without question. A quick glance at him, and it was clear his head was hurting. A frown marred his forehead, and even behind his sunglasses, he was squinting.

We waited for the flight in silence, Jayden's painkillers making him drowsy. The hourlong journey was the same, though Jayden used my shoulder as a headrest. Relieved he was resting, I managed to handle the contact with ease, knowing right now he needed his friend back.

After picking up the SUV from the car rental at the tiny airport, I followed the vehicle's GPS into town, did a mad dash around the Woolworths supermarket, then was back in the car to a snoozing Jayden.

Worry bit at my heels as I drove out, passing the brightening red dirt and flat landscape. Seeing the sign welcoming us to the outback, I hesitated, considering waking up Jayden. A glance in his direction changed my mind. He was sleeping peacefully, which meant he was healing. There'd be another time when we could take goofy selfies in front of the sign.

Once we hit the spit of a town of Mitchell, I grinned. It was the sort of place you could blink and miss it, but the area held a certain charm. By the time I turned right onto the dirt road where every few feet I hit a new pothole, inevitably Jayden woke.

"The fuck, man? Hit another one of those craters and we're going to be swallowed whole." Sitting up, he peered out the window. "Holy shit, the dirt's really red."

I laughed. "Yeah, one of the first things I noticed." I winced when I couldn't avoid the next pothole, the whole car jerking and jolting.

"Are you just aiming at the things? Hello, precious cargo with a concussion here."

My mouth twitched. "Precious cargo? More like a sulking toddler."

Jayden shoved at my arm, the gesture working its magic. For the first time since receiving that call from Nate, my muscles fully relaxed, and I managed a full lungful of air. "Satnav says it's another two minutes away."

Angling around to take in the whole surroundings, Jayden tugged off his sunglasses. "This really is the bumfuck of nowhere."

"Seems to be."

"Holy shit. You remember that movie we watched when we were at camp?"

"Don't even go there," I said with a laugh, remembering exactly what movie he was talking about. Jayden always had the worst ideas. When we were seventeen, he downloaded a movie on his laptop, and we watched it on the floor of our twin room late one night. We'd had a whole midnight-feast, horror-movie moment going on. Single mattresses on the floor, a bagful of candy from the vending machine, and *Wolf Creek*.

"You were just as shit scared as me."

I quirked a brow at him and peered over. "That right? I think you remember this story very differently than I do."

"The mattresses were already on the floor, and it was late, so it made no sense to put them back on the beds."

"Uh-huh. Yet you still shared my mattress."

"I was worried about you, and it was cold."

"It was the middle of summer and seventy-five degrees at night."

Another look at the man at my side, and I caught his wide grin. I returned it immediately before peering ahead when the satnav announced we'd arrived.

"Huh."

I pressed down on my lips, taking in the quaint... house? I wasn't sure if I could call it a house, but it seemed super fitting in the backdrop of red soil, the occasional gum tree, and the empty space behind leading to some scrub.

"You want to grab the keys from the mailbox, and I'll get the groceries?"

"Sure." He stepped out of the SUV, putting his sunglasses back on. Understandable, as the skies were blue and endless, and the sun lowering toward the horizon still blasted out some decent heat, despite it being a winter's day.

When Nate had offered us the house, he'd explained the place wasn't used often. It was also an old one-room house that had been expanded over the years, but his uncle had been steadily modernizing the joint. Looking at the wooden main building with small weatherboard extensions, I could see that. The tension in my muscles unraveled even more.

While this wasn't what I'd expected to be doing

when I finally visited Australia, we were here, and considering the only property I'd seen was at the beginning of the road, we had genuine peace and quiet. Absolutely perfect.

Once inside, my brows shot up in surprise. "Okay, so not what I expected."

Next to me, Jayden chuckled. "Right." The front door opened directly into the main living space. While it was cozy, it was still big enough for a two-seater couch, an armchair, coffee table, and TV stand, complete with flatscreen TV. The other side of an ornate archway was a modern, country-style kitchen, just big enough for a small table and chairs.

"This place looks so much better than I expected from the outside." Jayden peered around the kitchen and turned on the faucet. The water ran immediately, and a few seconds later, a loud groan erupted in the room. "What the fuck is that?" Wide-eyed, he swivelled his head, eyeing the door as though something ferocious was going to come blazing in.

I laughed loudly. "You not heard of the dropbears in Australia?" I chuckled when his eyes widened even further. Yeah, I may have researched the whole dropbear legend a while back when Ryan had mentioned them a time or two.

"The hell are dropbears?"

"You not remember Ryan mentioning them a few years back?"

"No?"

I fought hard to straighten my face and suck back my laugh. "It's the water pump, dufus."

His features morphed immediately, and he flipped me off. "Asshole."

I bounced my brows. "That I am." I dumped the grocery bags next to the stove and collected our bags, still chuckling at Jayden's reaction. When I returned, Jayden leaned against the wall next to one of the doorways. Amusement flickered in his gaze, and I sighed. "What is it?"

"I found the second bedroom."

"Okay," I said slowly, waiting for him to continue.

"Check it out for yourself."

Opening the door, I failed to control my expression, if Jayden's laughter was any indication. A bunch of furniture, none of which appeared to be a bed, was piled together in the second bedroom. A ladder leaned against the wall, and a couple of paint cans were next to it.

I closed my eyes, wondering if I counted to ten before reopening them, then I'd see a bed, complete with mattress and ready for me to pass out on. That was not the case.

"The good thing is," Jayden said, "the bed in the

main room is bigger than a double, a queen maybe, *and* I know this will make you extra happy; there's no big footboard so no having to bend our knees to fit. We can stretch out all we like."

Jayden. Stretching out. In bed. With me.

What the hell had I done in a former life to be punished in such a way?

"Come on, man. Don't look so damn miserable. It's not the first time we've shared a bed. Plus we're in the desert, so it's going to be even colder here tonight than it was at Ryan's." He shuddered for effect, which I wanted to ignore or maybe smack him around the head, but since he cut off his fake shudder superfast, I expected it had hurt to do so.

Finally, I looked at him. The humor and teasing from a moment ago was gone. "You look tired."

With a sigh, he offered a pitiful shrug. "I slept the whole journey. How is that even possible?"

"Concussions suck."

"Yeah."

"Come on. I'm dead on my feet."

Concern lit Jayden's gaze as he studied me. "Did you get any sleep last night?"

"A little." Though it absolutely wasn't enough. My body was crashing, my eyes tired, my sight a little blurry as exhaustion urged me to get my ass to bed. "Let me put this food in the refrigerator, then I'll get us both a bottle of water, and we'll sleep."

Uncertainty washed over Jayden's expression, something I rarely saw.

"What is it?"

"You really okay to share?"

I had to play this right and be the friend I wanted and needed to be. "It's not the first time, and since I'm your fiancé, I suppose I better get used to it," I said dryly, fully aware we still hadn't figured out that nightmare. Since leaving the hospital, I'd deliberately set my phone to not receive calls. The gossip making its rounds wouldn't be going away, so as far as I was concerned, it could all wait.

Sleep and Jayden's health were more important.

With a smile and bouncing brows, Jayden made his way to the small hallway, which I assumed led to the bathroom and master bedroom. "I'm taking the right side," he called out. I grinned as I got to work putting the groceries away. That was more than okay with me. The left side was my favorite spot.

CHAPTER 5
JAYDEN

"You snuggle like a koala bear."

The simple grunt Sutton sent my way wasn't quite what I'd hoped for. Undeterred, I turned and faced the man who'd actually kept on his side of the bed. Or at least I assumed he had. From the moment my head touched the pillow, I'd been comatose, and when I woke a couple of minutes earlier, my friend was on his side, his back to me.

I prodded him in the back, earning me a huff this time. He groaned, stretched, a couple of bones cracking, and sat up, back against the bedhead.

"And your snores are as loud as a freight train." He peered down at me, his gaze sleepy as he took me in. "I'm going to have to go and invest in earplugs at this rate."

I shoved at him and angled up, leaning on my

elbow. "Whatever, man. Just keep going, and I'll fashion you some out of the window putty I saw in the unfinished bedroom." The moving shadows through the window caught my attention. Dusk was heading our way soon, and I was hungry.

A loud rumble escaped my stomach as if it agreed with me. I grinned. "Food sounds good right about now."

"I could eat." A yawn followed, and he covered his mouth.

"You feel any better after getting a couple of hours?" I asked, looking at the time for confirmation and standing up, waiting for the movement to set my head pounding. When it didn't, my shoulders eased.

"A little. I could do with a shower and an early night."

The rolling of my eyes was immediate. "Concussions suck," I grumbled, repeating Sutton's words from earlier and wondering when my thirty-three years felt so old. Sure, I abused my body with the training and with just how hard I pushed to be in peak condition, more so than the average Joe my age, but still, it was a hell of a thing realizing I couldn't just bounce back after an injury. Reminded of my broken digit, I peered at it, bringing it out before me and wishing I could bend it.

"Your hand hurting?"

"Nah. Just annoying me."

The sound of Sutton opening his bag caught my attention. I glanced in his direction, and my gaze landed on his bare chest. A clean T-shirt was in his hands, ready to pull on. I paused, watching his muscles move and ripple, his focus intent on the blue cotton. Struggling to pull away from his movements and the expanse of dark skin, I remained rooted to the spot. For the life of me, I couldn't move, couldn't speak, and couldn't pull my damn attention away.

"You okay?"

Like a bucket of cold water, Sutton's words smashed into me. I jolted into action, nodding, barely making eye contact, before mumbling about needing the restroom and hightailing it out of there.

Once there were two doors between us, the bathroom door safely locked, I stood at the sink with the faucet running. I splashed my face and risked a glance in the mirror. Maybe my reflection could make heads or tails of what that little moment was about. 'Cause fuck if I knew. Sure, I was looking at Sutton. That was something I could acknowledge. What confused me was my difficulty in pulling my attention away. Considering I'd seen his body, seen the man shower and change more times than I could poke a stick at, I just didn't get what I'd been so fixated on.

Was I admiring his chest? Admittedly he was built, fit, but not weight-training buff. Had I appreciated the expanse of brown skin on display? Was it kind of weird that I had? In those few moments that had passed, I didn't think much of anything, truth be told, but now?

I splashed more water on my face and washed my hands as best as I could with the finger strapping. Whatever that moment was, it was over, and I needed to stop being weird. Between my anti-nausea meds, painkillers, and the pills that helped me sleep, I was almost rattling. It meant I couldn't trust anything I said, thought, or did.

Plus, Sutton had flown all this way to be here with me after our, what… estrangement? It was a lot to get my head around.

Then there was the whole fiancé thing that the two of us were doggedly avoiding. But the huge-ass elephant in the room needed to be dealt with. I patted my face dry, not sure I had the energy for dealing with the club's PR or the press in general. Fuck, then there were my parents.

Knowing my mom, she'd have made Dad go to the store to buy a Pride flag by now. Mom didn't give a shit who I loved. To paraphrase, if I met anyone who could put up with my bullshit, keep me in check, and love me like Westley did Buttercup, then she'd be happy. She'd told me that at least once a year since I was sixteen.

No doubt when she read the gossip columns, or tweets, or whatever her source was, and read Sutton was not only the one to love me, but we were engaged, she'd throw a party. It was no secret she adored him. Both my parents did.

Since there was nothing I was willing to do about any of it at the moment, I left the bathroom and focused on the relief of my head not pounding. I could hear Sutton in the kitchen. I smiled as I entered, taking in the scene of a man on a mission.

My eyebrows lifted at the collection of food on the countertops. "You weren't that long in the grocery store. I'm impressed, man." Immediately I moved to his side, picked up the knife he'd laid out, and started cutting the veggies. "Stir fry?"

"You know it," he said lightly.

Preparing a meal with Sutton was effortless. We'd spent enough time over the almost twenty years of knowing each other cooking together; we could do this blindfolded. The thought made me chuckle. "You remember that time in Cali, and we did the blind-folded charity event?"

Amusement lightened his words when he said, "How could I forget? You knocked me on my ass after headbutting my junk while trying to limbo."

Sutton's laughter was warm and soothing. "Left me cross-eyed for an hour. I swear your head is harder than concrete."

"Ha. Well, I thought so too until this damn concussion."

At my side, Sutton grimaced. "Yeah, could have done with that extra protection for sure."

The last thing I wanted was to bring the mood down, but there was still the massive elephant in the room we'd yet to tackle since escaping the hospital. "So, you turned your phone on yet?"

"Nope." He handed me a slice of carrot to munch on before popping a slice in his mouth.

"You know, I let Mark Lonsdale kiss me in college." I grinned as I spoke, waiting for a reaction. Sutton whipping his head in my direction was worth me sitting on this nugget for all this time. "As kisses went, it was decent. A bit too much tongue."

Wide-eyed, he placed down the knife and turned to me. I mimicked his action, not wiping the grin from my face. "You're messing with me."

"Nuh-uh." It was a memory I was pretty fond of, truth be told. While it didn't do much for me and I hadn't wanted a repeat, it was all right as kisses went. "Sophomore year. Mark told me he thought he was gay and was freaking out. I offered my services." My shrug was deliberately nonchalant. I loved getting a rise from Sutton whenever I could. It was one of my favorite pastimes.

Rendered speechless, he simply stared at me, the whites of his eyes more visible than usual.

"Turns out he was gay, and he dated a guy from the swim team about six months later." I stretched, puffing out my chest and adding a wink at my friend for good measure. "Thought about running a community service program of sorts, you know, doing a good deed."

Narrowed eyes formed and peered back at me. "That really happen?"

"Scout's honor. And yes, you know damn well I was a Scout."

"I don't think three weeks of being a member carries much weight," he deadpanned.

"Well, it happened."

His mouth twisted, the cogs in his head turning from the look of things. Meanwhile, I filled the electric kettle and turned it on. By the time I returned to his side, I settled in for his questions.

"You know, I think it's highly unusual for straight guys to allow other men to kiss them."

"Just the one guy." When his brows shot high, I smirked. "Okay, two," I said, referring to the kiss we'd shared last year. And we'd definitely shared it. While there'd been a beat there of Sutton freezing when I'd planted my lips against his, I'd encouraged him to open and kiss me properly.

I'd been determined to do it right.

"You're my friend, so does it really count?"

"Count as what?" he asked, his voice sounding a little edgier than earlier. This was the first time we'd revisited this conversation for months. At this point, I was just grateful we could talk this shit out once and for all and move past it.

"No idea, honestly." I shrugged. "I just mean it was with you. We do everything together." I refused to use the past tense, determined last season was a blip and one I'd sooner forget. "We shared a kiss. It was nice. Kinda hot." My words were as nonchalant as they were true.

Sutton's mouth dropped open, and his eyes bugged. "Hot?" His gravelly voice made me grin, him still being nonplussed by the whole thing apparent. At least this time he wasn't grumbling at me and raising his voice.

"Well, you know. It wasn't the worst kiss in the world." Hearing the kettle click off, I grabbed a pan from the cupboard and put the noodles on to boil. I picked up another carrot slice and passed one over to Sutton. The guy was staring at me like I had two heads. I rolled my eyes at him, the movement hurting my brain a little.

"You had any meds since being awake?"

I swore he read me better than, well, anyone. There were times I was convinced he knew me better than I knew myself. "Not yet."

"Go grab some, then sit down. I'll finish up here."

I hesitated, my gaze roaming his. "Okay, thanks, but we need to talk about our engagement, okay? We can't ignore it." Surprise lit up his features, and I snorted. "Yeah, yeah, Jayden Moore being all responsible and shit."

His smile was small but good to see.

"You're usually the first person to remind me and anyone that LGBTQ+ rights deserve respect and shouldn't be used... nefariously."

"Nefariously?" His lips twitched. "You going for a nineteen-point word, huh?"

I flipped him off as I left the kitchen, searching for my meds.

"They're in the bathroom," he called out, "and you're right. The last thing I want to do is cause shit in the LGBTQ+ community."

As I headed to grab my painkillers, I took a few deep breaths and allowed the relief of our exchange to settle over me. I talked a lot and joked around even more, but it had only been the past thirty-six hours or so that my usual BS didn't feel forced.

That was the thing when you had a role to play

while nursing a broken heart. No chance would I have let anyone see just how hurt I'd been the past few months. It meant I'd played the game and worn my smile like the armor it was. I'd lost my best friend once and refused to do so again.

We had to put the reports straight. I snorted at the word before sobering. A kiss had screwed us up last time, so what the hell would a fake relationship do?

Ice slithered through my veins. I wasn't willing to find out. Not at the expense of my friendship.

CHAPTER 6
SUTTON

After eating, we sat in the cozy sitting room, Jayden on the sofa and me in the armchair. This small house really was a nice place, completely unexpected, and I appreciated Nate organizing the refuge for us.

"So," I started, "what do you think we should be?"

Jayden's sleepy gaze was on me. Between a belly full of food and his painkillers kicking in, he looked close to passing out again. "Not willing to let anything come between us again."

My pulse kicked up at the honesty of his words. It didn't matter that his tone was groggy and that he was even more forthcoming when high on meds. He always, as in *always*, gave me his truth. Sometimes he had a weird or backward way of expressing himself, but from day one, he rarely held anything back. I snorted internally. Well, beyond me not being his first kiss with a guy.

And hadn't that news been a punch to the nuts.

Jealousy was never a pretty emotion, but fuck if a shroud of green hadn't blanketed my vision for far too many moments when he'd told me about Mark dickwad Lonsdale. Okay, I'd met the guy a couple of times when hanging out with Jayden in college, and he wasn't a dick, but still, Jayden had been the first man I kissed, and there wouldn't be another.

And that there was the crux of my jumbled emotions.

Aware he was waiting for a response, I nodded. "Me neither."

"So we what, apologize for the misunderstanding? Explain we're not in a romantic relationship"—nausea twisted in my stomach and tightened my chest at his words—"and that we're a hundred percent behind the LGBTQ community…?"

I swallowed hard and took a deep breath to center myself. He was right. We had to do this. Clear up the mess I created.

It didn't matter that our kiss had rocked my world.

It didn't matter that his mouth on mine had

opened me up to a next-level, mind-blowing collection of emotions for Jayden.

It didn't matter that my love for my best friend had morphed into so much more than I'd ever envisioned.

"Yeah. We need to touch base with our agents and probably the club PR. Not only will they want to navigate us through this, I imagine they want an update on your health."

"That first, then our parents?"

I sighed. "Yeah."

A slow smirk formed on his mouth, the action dragging my eyes to his lips. "You know my mom's going to lose her shit at me and be all levels of pissed that we're not getting married, right?"

I dug deep and pulled forth a light chuckle. "You know it, and you know my mom will be the same."

"Damn straight. I'm a catch."

I raised my brows, my shoulders relaxing into the banter, enjoying the familiar ground with Jayden. "That right? I would have thought I'd be the catch in this relationship."

A part of me wanted to smack myself and beg my mouth to shut the fuck up. Each word tasted bitter, which conflicted with the peace bantering with Jayden gave me.

"Well, you know, Momma always told me to

marry up. Go for someone smarter than me." He winked. "Heck, she really is going to be so pissed off."

Sadness attempted to settle over me. Another version of us, maybe this could have happened, but I'd take Jayden anyway I could. No way would I put our friendship in jeopardy again.

"They'll all cope," I offered.

His mouth twisted, not seeming convinced. "Okay, cells on."

We switched on our cells, our phone services connecting to the Australian towers. It took a few beats, and then the notifications started. And they didn't stop for at least ninety seconds. Jayden's brows shot progressively higher as the alerts sounded, his gaze meeting mine.

"Fuck. This is crazy."

I winced. "We need to deal with this together. Perhaps check a few messages, then whoever we talk to, do it on loudspeaker so we don't have to repeat ourselves too much. Fuck, maybe we should just do a conference call or something."

Jayden's groan caught my attention.

"You okay?"

"Yeah." He sighed. "Just exhausted already."

Guilt flared to life in my chest. He was meant to be healing. Part of that was making sure he was relaxed, yet here I was, causing a mountain of work for him.

"Sorry, man. You know, I can deal with all this. This was my doing."

With a shake of his head, two lines appeared between his eyebrows. "No chance. We do this together, Gale." Once again my heart flipped. This time at the soft use of my first name. "Last season I did almost everything by myself, and I don't know about you, but it was a stinking pile of dung. I'm so used to you being at my side, with me every step of the way, usually dealing with the aftermath of one of my grand schemes." He quirked a smile at me, and the pain that had blossomed at his words eased some. "We do this together, okay?"

Allowing my heart to settle in my chest, I edged back in the armchair, my cell still in hand. "Codependency isn't something I'd usually support people bragging about."

The smile he gave was so smug he looked all levels of hot. "You know better than most I'm all about crossing lines." He waggled his brows, and I huffed out a laugh. Of course I knew that. It was one of the things that endeared him to me while driving me insane.

"Okay, whose voice messages shall we listen to

first?" He glanced down at his cell and clicked a few buttons. "It says I have fifteen."

I didn't bother to check mine since he already had his open. "Go ahead." I gestured toward his phone.

"Here goes."

"*Give me a call when you can. We've received your medical details. I've spoken to Coach Brentworth and have calmed things down there. We have time before training, so no one's worried at the moment. Rest up.*"

I recognized Greg's voice easily. He'd been Jayden's agent for years now.

"*Jayden. A heads-up would have been good, man. Call me ASAP.*"

There were three more messages like that from Greg, and Monty, our team's PR guy.

"*Jayden, it's your momma. You need to get your hiney on the phone or get Gale to call me if you're busy sleeping and recovering, but baby—*" A distinctive sniff followed, and Jayden's mom's voice filled with emotion. "*I don't know why you didn't tell me, but I'm so proud of you, baby. Your dad and I love you. We're so happy for you both. I've already spoken to your aunt Sammi, and we think a spring wedding would be perfect. Don't you worry about a thing.*"

"Fuck." Jayden's gaze slammed into mine, and we both winced. "I expected it, but shit, when she knows the truth, she's going to chase me around the damn house in that chair of hers with a broom and tan my hide."

"Seriously, man, one of you needs to call me. It's about your endorsement with Axle. They've pulled out of your renewal contract you were meant to sign off next week. I've already scoured the contract, and there's fuck all we can do about it. We both can guess why that is, which they'd never admit, of course. Call me."

Surprise at hearing the voicemail from Greg zipped through me. That surprise was quickly replaced with anger, especially at seeing the wide-eyed shock on Jayden's face.

"The motherfuckers," he spat. I clenched my jaw, my back molars grinding. "I should have pulled out myself or never signed up with the bastards in the first place." We made eye contact. "And don't start with an I told you so."

I raised my hands. "Hey, there's no point in any of that. You signed because the brand made sense so you could support Bounce Your Balls charity." At the time, Jayden had hemmed and hawed about the sponsorship. The company's ads tended to be on the cusp of cringeworthy but not quite pushing over the edge. The final decision was their over-the-top masculine ads targeting men while also encouraging them to check their balls. Axle had agreed to 5 percent of sales going toward a testicular cancer charity as part of the sponsorship deal. Jayden donated every single cent of his payment to the same charity. "Fuck, this is all my fault. I'm so sorry, Jay."

"Don't." He shook his head, eyes blazing. "This is all on them, and apparently being gay or bi or whatever isn't masculine enough for their bullshit brand."

"Of which you're neither," I said, trying to be reasonable despite the growing frustration in my gut.

"That's beside the point. If I was bi, so fucking what. I know the brand is about being a babe magnet. Being bi wouldn't change that."

I kept my mouth shut, not sure anything I could say would help this conversation at all. The whole body deodorizer range targeted uber masculine men who played the field… and with their balls. Jayden had supported that brand because of the charity deal he'd struck.

"I know they were a bit on the cusp of sexist," he admitted. There was no argument from me, but his heart had absolutely been in the right place. It always was. "But who do the assholes think they are?" He shook his head. "And fuck, the charity money."

The contract was worth five million, so it wasn't exactly pocket change, especially to the charity.

"Just talk it out with Greg. See what he has to say."

"I'll fucking sue the bastards for prejudice." Pink-cheeked and eyes still blazing, he looked so fucking sexy like this. Full of passion and indignation.

"But our being engaged isn't true, and you're not bi or gay." The obvious needed to be said, but Jayden wasn't always the most rational when he got like this, full of indignation.

"I don't give a shit. They don't know that. And that's not the point."

While I wholeheartedly agreed, I wasn't sure that there'd be anything to pursue based on the short message Greg had left.

"You want to listen to the rest of the messages?" I asked, my tone calm, trying to cut through some tension. Anger wouldn't be doing his head any good. He was meant to be relaxing.

"I suppose." The tone of his voice had changed. He sounded almost forlorn, which didn't sit right.

"How about we listen to one more and take a break?" A glance at the time told me it was not long past six in the evening. After the days we'd had, we deserved a break, and all of this could easily wait till our morning. It was still early in the States, so we wouldn't be making any calls until we woke anyway.

Once again, he hit play on the next message. When I heard Pearce's voice, one of the younger players on our Eagles team, I angled my head, curious about what he'd say.

"Jayden, shit, man. I owe you a drink, and you can make it the expensive one. For two seasons I've had my bet going, each year topping up, and fuck yeah, I won. Totally called that you and Sutton were an item. 'Bout fucking time you guys shouted it loud and proud. I'm happy for you, man. Like seriously." Pearce cleared his throat, the sound of shuffling coming down the line. *"So yeah… between you guys and Ryan…. Fuck, man, this is hard, but if you guys can do it, and playing on the same damn team…"*

My eyes widened and my gaze connected with Jayden's.

"Oh fuck," he mouthed, and I couldn't help but agree as a ball formed in the pit of my stomach.

"…so yeah, I'm gay." Slightly unhinged laughter followed. *"Holy shit, I said it. I'm gay, hell, that felt good to say. So, yeah, I wanna come out, but maybe when you guys come back to Minnesota, if that's all right… I just, yeah, think I could do with the support. Uhm, so I'll talk soon. Oh, and feel better, Jayden. I heard about the accident. Sucks, man. Make sure he's making sure you don't overdo it. Uhm… bye."*

The message cut off, and I was left shellshocked and feeling like a turd. I closed my eyes, guilt eating away at me, wondering what the hell I'd done, all because I was so needy and desperate to be near Jayden. "Fuck," I gritted, opening my eyes.

Frowning, Jayden shook his head, his skin paler than usual, the same guilt reflecting in his eyes as I imagined he could see in mine. "We can't take this back, not now," he said. "Not after Pearce. Fuck, we can't do that to him."

Rubbing a hand over my face, I expelled a weary breath. "I know, you're right. That there took so much fucking guts. Hell, the guy came out to us, thinking we were all brave and shit." It wasn't lost on me how much of a fucking coward I was. I felt an inch tall. Without a doubt, heart and soul-deep, I loved Jayden. Like *loved him* loved him. I'd loved him for years as my best friend, but my love now was all about hearts, rainbows, cocks, ass, and kisses.

Unable to come to terms with why him and why now, since my dick nor my emotions had ever stirred for another man before, I'd bailed. Epically so.

My heart pounded loudly in my ears. Was it time? Should I just tell him? Admit why I freaked? Admit that I loved him and wanted him to be mine? Admit that even before I realized the extent of my feelings, every time he'd hooked up, I'd been weirdly jealous, which I'd only recently understood the reason why?

"Gale, you look like you're going to hurl."

The sound of his voice had my attention snapping to his. Absolute trust shone back at me. I couldn't lay my emotions on him. Not like this. Not now. It would be unfair and way too much considering everything else going on.

"I'm okay. Just thinking and feeling like a prize dick."

He nodded. "So, what's the plan? You're the brains of this duo."

I huffed out a humorless laugh, feeling anything but intelligent considering the current situation. I thought through the options, having heard what he'd said. "We're engaged. We see this through. Just before media week, we… split"—those words hurt my heart far more than they should have done—"saying we're still great friends, and move on."

Remaining quiet, Jayden stared at me. When I finished speaking, he started nodding. "Okay, so we're a couple. Both bi or gay, or any other number of terms I don't fully understand yet?" He shrugged.

My gaze softened, knowing he would be researching up a storm all of those other terms and getting his head around them. "I'm comfortable with saying I'm bi." My brain mocked me, calling absolute bullshit. *Comfortable? Ha.*

"Okay, me too." He huffed out a breath, his shoulders visibly relaxing. "Apparently, it shouldn't be a hard sell, considering the whole team was betting on us. Fuckers." Oblivious to my forced smile, Jayden's features smoothed out, appearing less rigid. "Right, we've got this."

I nodded, despite the uncertainty itching at my skin. "We don't tell anyone the truth."

His wince was immediate. "I know you're right, and I agree. You know both our parents are going to have something to say about everything, right?"

"I know it, and I feel shitty enough as it is, but we do this."

"Definitely." He quirked a brow at me. "So, do we kiss on it or what?"

I picked up a throw cushion and threw it at him, deliberately aiming for his chest rather than his head. I was a swell guy like that. "Keep your lips to yourself, wiseass." I grinned, despite my heart flipping over. I could handle a flirty Jayden, since a "flirty" Jayden was how he'd always been. While now, each innuendo or look he cast my way ignited a needy reaction, it also helped to calm my nerves.

Jayden being himself wrecked me, but there wasn't a single thing I wanted him to do differently.

CHAPTER 7
JAYDEN

WE'D ALREADY ESTABLISHED HAVING A CONCUSSION sucked. There was a flip side to the headaches, flashes of nausea, and dizziness, though. One of the biggest being Sutton fielded the calls for the past three days.

Some he'd had no choice but to pull me into the conversation, where I grunted in understanding when told to do so by Sutton. But beyond those few times, I luxuriated in not dealing with disgruntled complaints about keeping our relationship a secret. Nor the whole planning sessions about the club's PR handling our coming out—we still hadn't agreed to anything concrete—in addition to HR needing additional paperwork signed since we were a couple working for the same company.

Being the patient genius he was, Sutton took it all

in his stride. I was sure he got off on the level of paperwork we had to deal with. It was kinda sweet, really, weirdly so when Sutton actually got excited about pulling apart our contracts. When he got really into something that pushed him and made his brain work overtime, he got this extra sparkle in his eyes. He'd sit a little straighter, his eyes widening a little, and if he had a pen in hand, he'd gnaw it.

I liked those quieter times of him studying or explaining what something meant in complete layman's terms. The man was the epitome of patience, and after the third time I'd slowly removed the pen from his mouth, just 'cause I could, he pinned me with his dark gaze rather than smacking me upside the head.

Another win for the concussed right there.

"Why?"

I grinned at the flat tone of his voice as he eyed the chewed pen I was flicking between my fingers. "Huh?"

The quirked brow he shot my way was impressive. Complete with the look of "what the fuck am I going to do with you?" I knew I finally had his attention. "I'm bored. Let's go to the pub."

"What is it about booze and meds you think go together?"

"I didn't say I'd have a beer." Maybe my attempt

at sounding innocent was what gave me away, as I could totally do with a cold beer. For three days, we'd done nothing more than take a few strolls—yes, *strolls*, not even fast-paced walks—down the gravel road and once along the gently running creek. We hadn't seen another human being. Not to say that was a bad thing necessarily, but I could only sleep, watch Netflix, play cards, and talk nonsense at Sutton for so long.

"If anything, it's for your own good," I explained. "Just think, a bit more normality, and I'll stop stealing your pens. I'll even stop hiding the Post-it Notes."

"I fucking knew I hadn't thrown them away. Asshole."

"You see… for your own good."

He eyed me, and I could see him building up to his ground rules. I eased back on the sofa in anticipation. Sutton was always about planning and laying down the law of the land. To be fair, he was used to talking me out of schemes in the nick of time— usually stopping me from making a dick of myself. So with that in mind, I always heard him out. It was just, in the heat of the excitement, I tended to forget all about his well-laid-out plans.

"I'm all ears."

Despite his sigh, the hint of a smile was obvious on his mouth. "You can have one light beer since your last painkiller was almost four hours ago. No dancing, no doing that weird line dance Ryan taught us last year, no pissing the locals off so they run us out of town, and no admitting who we are. We keep a low profile."

Hell to the yes. Wide-eyed, I nodded and grinned, which immediately earned me a groaned "Oh fuck, why did I say that?"

"Ha." I rubbed my hands together, excited at the challenge Sutton had unintentionally thrown down. And hell if it didn't feel good—eager to have fun and hang out with my friend, the man who knew precisely what each expression I made meant. I stopped myself from telling him how much I missed him. I'd already had a couple of moments. That was my quota of the feels for at least a month.

It didn't matter that I was a touchy-feely guy, and I usually said what was on my mind. When it came to sharing feelings with actual words… I wrinkled my nose at the thought. No, thanks. A hug, sure. Words just tended to get me into trouble and dig a proverbial hole.

"What's with the weird face? What are you think-ing? You need to shit before we go out? Because, man, I read about long drops, and knowing you, you'd end up wedged in the damn thing. To be clear, that happens, you'll be finding a new friend."

"Fiancé," I corrected helpfully. "And you can tell me what a long drop is over my beer."

"That's a hard pass from me."

I waved his words away, refocusing on what mattered. "Okay, my name's Bellamy, and I'm a sheep farmer from… where do they have a heap of sheep?"

Rather than answer me, Sutton angled his face to the ceiling. I could imagine what he was praying for. That happiness in my chest doubled at his reaction.

"Okay, so no sheep. Let's go for we're brothers, searching for our father, and along this journey, strange things keep happening. Obviously, we're badasses, so we figure out the weird shit… ooh, and we have a cool car." Before Sutton could interrupt, I clicked my fingers. "No, the brothers thing is weird since I've had my tongue in your mouth." His brows shot high at that. "Okay, so you've left your girl-friend, and we're here on vacation. You've been down in the dumps, depressed, so I'm here as your wingman. We're looking for big open country roads, but we're also on the run. In that last town we stopped at, something happened. So now we've got a whole team of cops after us." I angled to look out the window. "Do you think there's a cliff or anything nearby? And we'll definitely need to find a convert-ible to rent rather than the SUV."

I turned my gaze back to Sutton. His head was in his hands, and I was pretty sure he was going to drop me off at the pub and leave me there. If not that, he would crush some of my sleeping pills and be done with me for good.

WITHOUT A DOUBT, THE LOCALS AT THIS TINY RUN-down pub in the literal middle of nowhere were a hoot. Old boy Bazza was eighty-two, still lived on the same farm his dad had bought, could drink me under the table given a chance, and spoke with such a thick twang I could barely understand him.

He and the other group of locals in the pub in the early afternoon had me all but rolling on the floor in laughter. Bill, a truck driver, recounted a tale of a kangaroo smashing through the window at his sister's home. "Struth, mate, the bloody thing was eight-foot tall, with guns as big as Schwarzenegger's. It wrecked the whole bloody house as it bounced around the place." He laughed loudly and shook his head. "My sister was there with a bloody broom, trying to shove the thing out, but it was too busy smashing the place, bouncing wall to wall to be worried about her…"

Sutton's soft laughter reached me, and I angled to

look at him. He looked relaxed and ate up the story, amusement evident in his gaze. As always, his laughter was gentle, light, which constantly took me by surprise and seemed at odds with his tall frame and muscular physique.

He made eye contact with me and shot me a wink. The gesture made my belly flip and pulled a fresh smile out, just for him. I turned back to Bill, though I shifted to stand next to Sutton. Leaning against the bar next to him, I edged close enough for our arms to touch and relaxed even further.

This, the contact, the crazy stories, Sutton's happiness, I lapped it all up, drawing it in from touch. Rather than shifting away or even looking at me, Sutton turned a little, making our connection more definite. It was something he'd always done.

No word of a lie, I was a needy fucker and a touchy-feely barnacle. I craved physical contact, and Sutton had always given it to me so freely, knowing without any conversation what I needed. His touch grounded me, settling me in a way no one else ever could.

I'd never questioned it or analyzed it and probably only thought about it now as I'd gone a whole season without it. The thought made my hands sweat and skin itch.

And then his palm was on the back of my neck, squeezing lightly.

Immediately, my muscles relaxed, and I refocused on Bill.

"…like a bloody hurricane as it bolted through a different window to escape." Bill picked up his beer and took a hearty gulp, his cheeks flushed and eyes bright. His gaze took us in, and he bobbed his head before asking, "If you blokes like to fish, there's a good spot along the Maranoa River, just a few kilometers out at Fisherman's Rest. You can get bait over at FoodWorks. You say you're staying at Stuie's place?"

"Yeah, just off Homebush," Sutton answered.

Bazza pitched in, "Look in his shed. There'll be everything you need there. Rods, chairs, the lot."

Sutton squeezed my neck once before dropping his hand. But rather than moving it completely, it settled on the bar, right at my back, offering me the slightest of touches. "What do you think?" He angled to look at me. This close, his eyes seemed lighter, with tiny flecks of varying shades of brown in their depths.

"Sounds good," I agreed, still not sure how long we actually intended to stay in Australia, let alone Mitchell, before we headed back.

Bazza explained to Sutton where we could find

the fishing spot, but I zoned out. I'd had one beer and a soda, all while having a good time, especially escaping the four walls of the house. But two hours of straining to work out the words hidden beneath a thick accent and my head ached, and once again, tiredness beat at me.

The concern in Sutton's tone caught my attention when he said my name.

"Huh?"

When my gaze connected with his, it took barely a second before he stopped leaning against the bar, saying, "Good to meet you all, but it's time we get going back." He reached out and shook the men's hands, and I followed suit.

It didn't take long before we could extract ourselves and make our way back to the house. Almost immediately, Sutton glanced at his phone as we entered. "Time for your meds."

I didn't hold back my smile when he headed to collect them. It had been a long time since Sutton cared for me like this. It was something he'd always done—this season not withstanding. The man looked out for me, cared for me. He was a natural caretaker, something I'd never challenged, just happily accepted, especially considering my own level of neediness.

I'd missed this, *him,* a lot. Heck, that didn't come close to just how much I'd missed the man.

He returned with a bottle of water and the pain meds that'd target my headache and the pain in my chest from the seat belt, which I'd sort of ignored until yesterday since my attention was so focused on my head.

"You need me to break them in half for you?"

"Screw you, wiseass." I grinned and accepted the drink and pills. After swallowing and washing them down with the cold water, I settled on the sofa. "Thanks."

A chin lift was sent my way, and my stomach flipped over at such a normal, casual gesture. That, as well as the warmth in his gaze, hadn't been directed at me in such a long time. I focused on him being here and just how long I could keep him. The thought of us finally getting back to how we were was a huge driving factor.

"So another two weeks of hanging out, and then you can keep me company on the flight back. I like this plan." Apparently, I'd decided this between… okay, just this second.

Sutton quirked a brow at me. "When did we decide that?"

"When you couldn't bear to be apart from me any longer, so headed all this way to see me. I thought we'd make the most of my recovery in the quiet before we're hit with the mayhem."

"That's totally the reason I jumped on a plane," he deadpanned. "Nothing at all to do with Nate pleading with me to come. He must have heard what a pussy you are when you're ill or have an injury."

Lightness settled in my chest. "Uh-huh, keep telling yourself that." This time I grinned. Fuck, I'd missed him, missed this. "Tomorrow I think we can make a break for it, go and explore. Visit that fishing spot, maybe cause a bit of chaos along the way. What do you think?"

He eyed me, a slight frown settling between his brows. That look I knew. He wasn't convinced I would be okay exploring.

True, my head hurt something fierce—it felt like a jackhammer went off in intervals. But at least with the pain meds I was sleeping, and they mostly kept my pain away.

"If you can jump up and down ten times tomorrow, maybe exploring is an option. If not, sitting in a couple of camping chairs fishing is maybe more your speed."

"The fuck!" Just the thought of that movement had my stomach clenching. "My version of mayhem doesn't involve bouncing up and down."

He quirked his brow. "So no kangaroo riding tomorrow?"

The pain meds had kicked in enough that I was finally able to roll my eyes at him. "Not tomorrow. And I know I can be a douche, but the thought of any sort of activity like that is enough to make me hurt." Sutton was one of the few people I'd ever admit that to.

Concern etched his features, and a slight movement of his hand had me glancing down. He fisted his hand and placed it on his knee. Curiosity had me wondering exactly why that was. Why had he held back, especially since in the pub he'd touched me so openly? After a beat, my attention returned to his face. His expression was weirdly neutral. I swallowed down my sigh, hating he still had moments of holding himself back.

"How about we do the fishing thing, then you can buy for lunch?" he suggested.

"I suppose I can do that. It's not every day my BFF admits he can't cope with not being on the same continent as me." That earned me a twitch of his lips.

"The pining for you was too much." His voice was impassive. "My life is finally complete now that we're breathing the same air."

At his words, a flash of memory... of feeling sparked inside me, reminding me of the time we had legit shared the same air when I'd launched myself at him and kissed the hell out of my friend.

Surprised by the spike in my pulse, I forced a laugh, knowing there was nothing natural or easygoing about the sound. "You see, that wasn't so hard, was it?" I sassed, working on my tone, and totally ignored how my mind kept catching on the innuendo of my words. "Fuck, I think these meds are screwing with me," I said aloud, sure that was what was going on.

"Let's get you to bed."

I caught the strangled noise that attempted to break free from my throat. What the fuck was happening? "Yeah, that's probably best."

Sutton hovered over me like a clucking hen as I went to our room and lay down. He closed the blinds and placed my water bottle on the bedside table.

"Sleep, and I'll check in on you in a couple of hours." There was a softness in his voice that sent my heart hammering. Sutton was absolutely the more thoughtful out of the two of us, but just how attentive and gentle he was being made my head spin.

I latched onto that notion as he left me in the dark room. That's all this was—me reaching for meaning when there was none there. That and being confused by Sutton in my space after so long without him being all in my business.

As for those memories, it was only natural they'd flicked through my mind. Our kiss had changed everything. So what if the more I thought about it, the more I wondered what it would be like to kiss Sutton for a second time?

Maybe even a third or fourth if it was as nice as my memory made it out to be.

With a sigh, I turned on my side and closed my eyes.

THE FOLLOWING DAY THE TWO OF US HEADED OUT fishing. We left midmorning after I'd given some time for my pain meds to kick in, and probably far too late for the fish. That was a thing, right? Fish biting early in the day rather than later.

I had no idea, but I was bored after an hour of not catching anything, and thankfully, Sutton wasn't feeling it either.

After packing everything up, we strolled down a small track alongside the creek, the gentle flow of the water calm and soothing. Admittedly, this was kinda nice, the two of us hanging out, actually relaxing together.

There were no awkward silences, no forced conversation. Exactly the way it had always been between us. It wasn't a secret that he was the one I felt truly comfortable with. The only person I could simply be myself with. While we dug at and ribbed each other, every word always held affection, right alongside the certainty we trusted each other.

"Apparently crocs don't travel this far south."

Sutton offered a small "Huh," which translated to he was paying attention.

I smiled. "Too cold for it or something, I think. Can you believe it's winter?"

"It's a little like California's climate." He glanced over. "Except for last night. Did you feel how cold it got?" I laughed at how bemused he seemed. "I thought Nate was screwing around when he told me about there being a log burner."

"Right. Only for it to jump up forty degrees during the day. This place is weird." Out of the corner of my eye, I saw his focus had moved to my hand with the bandaged finger, and I lifted it up for inspection. "You think Coach is going to freak out when he sees me?"

"Nah. He'll already have been pouring over the X-rays, or at least the team's doc will have."

I nodded. "True. Everything looked good. Clean break. It should heal fine and in enough time for next season. Until then, I can train with my right."

"When I learned you were injured, I was sure it

was a crocodile or a snake or something that had finally got you."

I snorted at his words. "You sound disappointed. We can go hunting for something wilder if you want, gain new experiences."

"Let's make that a hard pass. And I'm not disappointed. The news just took me by surprise."

"And freaked you out."

"And freaked me out," he repeated.

My lips twitched. "And made you so worried you jumped on the first available flight to come and take care of me." Sutton made it so easy to wind him up.

"Think of it more along the lines of making sure you were not dead and bitten by something venomous."

"That right?"

"Yeah, and there wasn't a commercial flight to get to LAX in time for the next trip out to Brisbane, so I had to charter one."

I stopped short, my eyebrows shooting high. "No shit?"

"No shit."

While words to keep up the banter were at the tip of my tongue, knowing he'd done that for me blew me away. I locked on to his deep brown eyes, my stomach doing a weird-ass flutter. "I don't know what to say."

"Holy shit, alert the press. Jayden Moore has been rendered speechless." His tone was dry, humor flickering in the depth of his gaze.

Lightness settled in my chest, chasing away the flips in my gut that I was keen to ignore, that earlier reaction too confusing. "And it's passed." I quirked my brow, and we continued strolling along the track, the warmth of the sun pressing against us. "You know, while the circumstances I could do without, it makes a nice change doing nothing, being forced to relax."

Sutton hummed at my side.

"I can't remember the last time we did anything like this. Just chill."

"We've never done anything like this," he said. "Every off-season, if we're not catching up with family, you're dragging me to some dodgy-ass place, doing shit Coach would have palpitations about."

My grin was immediate. "Come on. You wouldn't have it any other way." I side-eyed him, curious about his reaction, considering that none of that had happened in the past six months or so.

With a tilt of his head in my direction, he caught my gaze. "I know what you're doing."

"What am I doing?" I looked more fully at him, my expression a picture of innocence, which, truth be told, I was terrible at. In the past, Sutton had told me more than once that my "innocent" face resembled a constipated marshmallow. Since I had no clue what that even looked like, I'd accepted it with good grace and spent a week buying bags of pink and white marshmallows and emptying their contents in the most random of places.

Of course, those random places were items he owned or used, like his bedside table, locker, and glove box. I even filled up several pairs of sneakers. How could I have known that it would be an unseasonably hot day when I did? Marshmallows melted grossly. He may have had to ditch a favorite pair of his Nikes.

"You're fishing," he finally answered.

I totally was. The past six months had been all levels of shit with the distance he'd put between us. Miserable didn't come close to my general state of being. At times, I'd been annoyed that not having him by my side, in my life, all up in my business, had hit me so hard. It was all kinds of pathetic. None of that had meant I'd missed him any less.

"You saying it's possible to reel you in?" I bounced my brows up and down before snapping my attention away. Why the fuck did that sound like I was flirting? I frowned and tried to loosen my muscles, my head deciding to remind me at that moment to stop making sudden movements.

I hadn't realized I'd stopped until I opened my eyes a fraction to find Sutton before me; his brows dipped with concern.

"Your head?"

The thought of nodding or moving my head made me feel sick. "Yeah," I said quietly. Even at that volume, a fresh wave of pain slammed into me.

"You've overdone it."

My usual sarcasm was swallowed, knowing he was right and not having the energy to banter.

"Let's get you back."

His hand gripped mine and held on tight, the feel of his palm a steady comfort that perhaps should have surprised me. But that was the thing. Sutton and I were tactile as fuck, so his touch was grounding and precisely what I needed.

We made slow progress back to the rental, my head alternating between a groggy spin and a steady pound. Once I leaned against the warm metal, I closed my eyes. "I don't have any pain meds with me."

"It's a good job I do."

I managed a smile, because of course he did, and lifted my eyelids a little as he opened the door and ferreted around in the glove box.

"The water's not cold." He passed over the bottle, along with a couple of pain pills.

"Thanks." I swallowed the pills, flushing them down with tepid water. "What would I do without you?" As I spoke, my gaze caught on his, a clear thread of seriousness behind my words.

Sutton twisted his lips before offering me a smile. "It's a good thing you won't have to find out."

A fizz in my gut took me by surprise, quickly picking up speed and zipping to my chest as it bounced unceremoniously around there. "Fuck, are we having a moment?"

His eyes sprang wide, and he took a step back, moving out of my space completely. Regret at the distance I'd created by letting my mouth run hit me square in the chest. And as he released a forced snort while ushering me into the passenger seat, confusion rose to the surface.

My reactions were freaking me out. On the one hand, this was Sutton, who I'd not so secretly missed a fuckton. It had legit hurt when he'd kept his distance. Surely my reaction to him being here now was a result of my relief.

But if that was the case, why, as he leaned into my space and tugged my seat belt across me since I was sitting there staring at him like an idiot, did I close my eyes and fucking sniff him?

"You okay?"

"Huh?" I asked, following his movement as he put on his own seat belt.

"You spaced out and held your breath there." Concern dipped his voice lower than usual, and his gaze darted around my face.

"Just tired." My half-truth only had him hesitating a moment before he started the engine, pressed a few buttons on the satnav, and pulled onto the road.

A hand on my shoulder jerked me awake, my eyes fluttering before reclosing.

"Hey, we're back. Let's get you inside, and I'll make you lunch, then you can go to bed."

I smiled at Sutton and dragged my eyes open fully. "Satnav worked then?" My sleepy voice filled the cab. "Not in the middle of the desert or anything?"

"*Once*," he said, lips twitching. "That happened the one time, and you're the one who programmed in the address." With a roll of his eyes, he climbed out of the SUV.

Unclipping my seat belt, I stretched, smirking when Sutton opened my door. "You wait till I tell your mom about what a gentleman you're being. You sure your family aren't Southern?"

"How about you ask my mom *that* and see if she's still willing to have you over for goulash nights."

"Hell no." Once out of the car, I stretched again, following up with a giant yawn. "Goulash nights are the best. You will not take them from me ever again."

A flash of emotion crossed over Sutton's features. "Never again," he offered softly, and there went my heart. He cleared his throat and indicated toward the small house. "Come on. Get your ass moving."

The late-morning sun brushed against my skin as we took the few steps to Nate's uncle's place. "It's nice, isn't it?"

"What's that?"

"Not being in the spotlight, being able to walk along the creek, be here. Relaxing."

At my side, Sutton nodded. "Yeah. I know it's part of the price for playing pro, and we have to deal with it, but I could get used to not having the attention."

I angled my head to look at him. "You could, as in, be out of the spotlight?"

He shrugged. "One day, sure."

I exhaled, realizing I was relieved he wasn't saying now. I wasn't sure how I felt about what he said. "So you're not ready to do a Ryan, fall in love with a guy, retire, and escape to normality?" While I smiled, a niggling ball of something I struggled to put a name to rolled around in my stomach.

The slightest of movements in his shoulder had

my eyes springing open. Why was he tensing? Fuck, was he thinking of retiring? Was "one day" closer to today?

Reaching the screen door, he pulled it open and unlocked the front door. "Why don't you go wash up, and I'll get started on lunch?"

Not sure if I was disappointed or relieved he hadn't answered me, I paused in the main room as he headed to the kitchen. I sighed and went to the bathroom. While my head was no longer pounding like a jackhammer—the painkillers and ten-minute nap having done their jobs—it felt muddled.

As I washed the sleep from my face, I thought back to my half-joking question about having a moment and considered his reaction. Patting my face dry, I wondered what "a moment" would actually look like between us. I paused and glanced at my reflection, focusing on my mouth. The last person I'd kissed was Sutton, so many months ago. While I'd had ample opportunities, and when drinking I'd been tempted, I hadn't been feeling it. Maybe that should have made me feel a little pathetic.

"Yo, stop preening like a peacock. Your sandwich is ready."

My gaze latched on to his through the reflection. He stood in the open bathroom doorway. The longer

I looked, the deeper the lines between his brows formed.

"You're freakin' me out, man. What's going on?"

I turned, leaning back against the basin. "You know, you're the last person I kissed." His brows shot high, eyes widening. "Do you think that's weird that I haven't been partying much and getting laid?"

Straightening out his features, Sutton cleared his throat. "Season's been busy. I don't think many of the guys have been partying."

I nodded. "True, but they've been complaining about not having the time. Me? I haven't wanted to."

"Okay?" He dragged out the word.

"So you don't think it's weird I haven't been interested?"

Sutton's gaze was as uncertain as it was unwavering. "Look, Jay, our season has been shit, and I know I'm pretty much responsible for that." He didn't need to clarify. "We haven't talked about it, and honestly, with your accident and how we're just sort of moving on, I wasn't sure if we needed to."

I opened my mouth to speak but stopped at the shake of his head.

"Listen, I'm sorry, okay. I got lost in my mind this season, got caught up with shit, and that's on me, not you. I kinda surprised myself at my reaction, truth be told." He stopped speaking and leaned against the doorframe. While he gathered his thoughts, I couldn't help but agree with the last thing he said.

Sutton was a certifiable genius. But more than that, he was confident, and while he wasn't cocky and talkative, he spoke his mind and wouldn't dream of holding back when it came to defending the injustices of the world. So him shutting down had apparently surprised us equally.

Before I could censor myself, which I knew I really should, I did the usual and asked the random shit on my mind. "What about you?"

"What about me?"

"Have you been hooking up this season?" I held my breath and couldn't even pretend that I didn't know why. If Sutton said yes, there was no doubt jealousy would rear its ugly head.

That shouldn't be so surprising, as I coveted our friendship and was a needy fucker. Seriously, I'd threatened to take out more than one player if they tried to hang out with my friend without me. Sutton was my best fucking friend, and everyone knew it. There was so much wrong with my behavior. I wasn't a complete narcissist that I didn't recognize that, but still, there was no denying the green-eyed monster would be a cockhead if Sutton answered yes.

As clear as day, I could tell he was considering

not answering. The swell guy I was, I quirked my brow at him in challenge. He narrowed his eyes at me, replying, "No."

My shit-eating grin was as immediate as it was bordering on psycho levels on par with the Joker.

"Just shut the fuck up and come and eat." He turned and left me following, a legit bounce in my step and curiosity thrumming through my veins. Did I want to kiss Sutton again? More to the point, why did that question fill me with a thrill of anticipation rather than dread?

CHAPTER 8
SUTTON

WE FISHED AGAIN, COOKED MARSHMALLOWS OVER OPEN flames, went for short walks, and even went to Bill's house for a barbecue. We'd also visited the small medical practice and had Jayden's stitches on his face removed. They'd left a scar, which apparently made him look like a badass—his words.

The past week in Mitchell had been the escape we needed, but after one of Ryan's calls letting us know the press were no longer camping outside his home or milling around the area, it was time to head back.

We just had one more night before we'd be dealing with the fallout of my declaration. And that would mean lying to two of our closest friends.

"Why can't we at least tell Ryan and Nate?" Jayden asked for the hundredth time.

Our conversation was playing out like a game of

tag. Frustrated, I tugged the pillow from under my head, pressed it against my face, and groaned. A moment later, Jayden's fingers wedged into my side, my squeak drawing a laugh from him. Returning the pillow to under my head, I angled to glance at him.

"What?" His lips twitched.

In the low lighting from the bedside lamp on Jayden's side of the bed, it was hard to look at the man sharing a bed with me without my breath catching. Every time I thought I'd got a hold of my emotions and controlled my reaction to him, there he went, looking so peaceful and sexy. Add in the lines between his eyebrows as he shared my own frustration about our deception, and there was something most definitely endearing about the way my friend focused on me.

After taking a deep breath, I spoke. "We've discussed this to death, and just when I'm not sure, you remind me why we should stick to our original plan, and then we go back around in circles."

Still on his side facing me, Jayden grunted and huffed out a breath. Warmth settled over me, along with the scent of mint toothpaste. "It sucks, and I feel like an even bigger dickhead."

My fingers itched to stroke away his frown, but being in bed together would make that action far too intimate. Instead, I nodded. "We both feel crap about it, but we agreed to go all in."

Nothing about our plan made sense, and we both knew it, just like we knew we kept backing ourselves into a corner.

Many times over the past week we'd had the chance to come clean. With our agents, with Monty, with our family and friends. The final deciding factor for holding on tight to our lie was answering a call from Pearce.

Jayden and I had ended the call shaken, privileged, and with a whole mess of emotions.

Then there were our friends who we'd be seeing tomorrow.

If we told Nate and Ryan the truth and explained everything to them along with our whys, they'd understand. I was sure of it.

But I knew all too well how once someone knew the truth, that information often found a way to escape. The truth coming out would be a hundred times worse in this situation.

The deception made me feel ill.

"All in," Jayden agreed, his focus intent. I eyed him curiously, wondering at his intensity, and then he floored me when he said, "So we date for real."

I froze. The loud pounding in my ears made it difficult to think. He couldn't have possibly—

"What?" I finally asked, sitting bolt upright in bed, the sheets pooling around my waist. "For *real*? I don't under—"

Jayden sat up, his voice earnest when he spoke. "Well, if we're together and engaged, we're not going to be dating anyone else. Not that either of us was." A smile lifted his lips as he continued. "So yeah, before the moment that shouldn't be named, which if it's not clear is the time I put my tongue in your mouth, *and* just for clarification, you totally kissed me back"—he didn't give me time to react, or even attempt to deny it, which I wasn't prepared to do as there were already enough lies and secrets between us—"we were pretty much dating anyway, right?" My mind boggled, but he powered on through, saying, "You're the only person I ever spent time with, went out or stayed in for dinner with, hung out with. Hell, we even went with each other when visiting our families. That's like… the most committed relationship I've ever been in."

By the end of his mini speech, he was wide-eyed and looking deadly serious.

Me? Amusement bubbled in my gut, but right alongside that was a feeling that was so fucking dangerous I didn't know how to handle it.

Hope.

It was a hell of a thing.

"You've been rendered speechless as you know I'm right." Humor filled his tone, but the intensity in his gaze didn't waver.

I cleared my throat and got my brain to work. "A romantic relationship usually implies being physically close." Somehow I kept the wobble out of my voice.

"You wouldn't even be able to count on two hands how many times we've hugged or held hands. Plus, there's that thing you do sometimes…"

My brows shot up, and nerves awoke inside me. "What thing?"

"You don't even realize you're doing it." Triumph flashed across his features.

"I have no idea what you're talking about."

"You see, it's so instinctive. You crave me. It's okay to admit it. Everyone knows I'm handsy."

It was true. Jayden absolutely was, but as he continued, I couldn't help but wonder what he was about to share about me. There wasn't a chance I'd touch the "crave" observation either. No fucking way.

"You always touch me when I need comfort"—pink lit up his cheeks, his grin not quite as cocky—"hold my neck, press against my shoulder, squeeze my knee or let me know in some other way that I'm okay. I don't even have to say anything for you to be able to read me."

With no idea how to respond, I pressed my lips together.

"You don't do it with anyone else, and you've always done it, silently supported me, understood what I needed." When he stopped speaking, his gaze roamed my face, searching for my reaction. His lips parted, and the tip of his tongue flicked out so briefly I would have missed it if I wasn't so attuned to taking my fill of him.

Once again, my pulse increased. Jayden Moore should come with a health warning. One of these days, he was going to give me a heart attack.

Needing to say something, anything, I ended up asking, "But dating for real, how would that even work? This is all pretend." The words sliced through me, but they needed to be said.

"Thirty-three years old, and you don't know how dating works, Gale. Seriously?" He quirked his brow. While his cheeks remained flushed, his tone was easy, and a new sparkle appeared in his eyes. The man got off on challenging me.

And hell if I didn't love him the more for it.

"You know what I mean, asshole. I know how dating works, but… why? I just don't get it."

Frown lines appeared on his forehead, and his

exhale was frustrated. "Are you deliberately being facetious?"

"Fourteen points," I said automatically.

While his lips twitched, he didn't follow through with a smile. "We have, what, just over four months till media week? What better way to make our relationship look real than by it being real?"

I prided myself on being an intelligent guy, but I had to wonder if I'd lost a brain cell or fifty, as he couldn't possibly mean a real relationship. How would that even work? It didn't matter that my heart was dancing to the "Macarena," not when what he was suggesting would end up destroying me in four months.

"Spell this out for me." I sighed in defeat.

"We date and do all things people dating usually do."

My eyes shot high at that.

"Well, uhm…" A flicker of unease appeared on his face. "I mean like middle-school dating."

And there it was, the truth of it all and what I had to remind myself of every single day over the next four months if we were doing this.

"And with super strict parents, so no second base." The pink in his cheeks deepened to red. "Listen, based on what Pearce said, this wasn't a surprise to anyone. But we need to find a way of living the lie.

That means technically, there'd be no more secrets, making us feel less like assholes."

I didn't correct him. Pretty sure that being in love with him was a significant secret I was keeping.

"So we date, which pretty much means we behave exactly like before, uhm, last season."

I struggled to maintain eye contact at his reference.

"Just no dating anyone else. Maybe a bit more PDA." The shrug he followed up with was light.

"Apparently all I do is show you PDA," I deadpanned.

He grinned. "You see, so it's easy and super simple. We just need to get in the mindset and convince ourselves it's real by making it real."

Hurt splintered through me. It wasn't like I could even blame Jayden for the agony each word he said created. The whole thing was ludicrous, but I had to admit that while the thought of us "calling things off" hurt and was a slap of reality, having him as all mine for the next few months was something I couldn't pass up.

The thought was selfish and creepy as fuck. No doubt I should have said no. The fine line between what was fake and pretend and how we could make that "real" blurred in my mind.

My energy spent, I bobbed my head. "Fine. Let's

get some sleep, and we'll figure it out as we go." I lay back down and reached for the lamp.

Once settled, I risked a glance at Jayden, who was still sitting up, watching me carefully.

"What is it?"

Remaining silent, he shook his head, an expression I didn't recognize on his face. I frowned, wondering what he was thinking. And then he moved.

The action was slow, deliberate as he leaned down toward me. My breath caught, not quite believing and too terrified to believe he was doing what I desperately hoped he was. A couple of inches from my face, he paused, his breath washing over my skin.

Goose bumps broke out on my arms, and I swallowed hard, trying to control my breaths. His gaze searched mine, and then his lips were on me. Closed-lipped, the pressure was light and lasted but a couple of seconds. He pulled away, eyes opening with the movement. A slight tilt of his head followed before he whispered, "Night, Gale."

As he switched off his lamp and settled under the covers, I finally expelled a breath. The sound was shuddery and loud in the quiet room, with nothing but the sound of the wind drifting through the cracked-open window.

In the freedom of the darkness, I gingerly lifted my hand to my mouth and pressed my fingers to my lips. They tingled at the memory of the all-too-brief connection of Jayden's mouth to mine. I sighed and turned away from Jayden. It would be all too easy to snuggle up to the man. My morning wood, let alone the semi I now sported, was not in the realms of what would be acceptable for middle-school dating.

CHAPTER 9
JAYDEN

There were times I marveled at the ideas that popped into my head. I also wondered how I managed to get away with the things I actually shared. Last night was a moment just like that.

As my brain had worked overtime, all I'd known was that spending time with Sutton was my favorite thing to do. Definitely on par with playing professional basketball. And the thought of sharing a few kisses with the guy was something I was okay with. More than okay with, the more I considered it.

But this was Sutton, so I refused to get spooked or freaked. What was the point? He was the only person in the world with whom I'd happily share everything and anything.

I took a fast swig of my cold water when the possibility of sharing things with the man started to lead me down the path beyond the first-base touches I'd mentioned yesterday.

"You okay?" Sutton's voice was low as he leaned close.

Placing the lid back on the bottle, I nodded. "Just stopping my ears from popping," I bullshitted and looked past him at the tarmac we were fast approaching.

"When I spoke to Ryan a couple of days ago, he mentioned an Everglades tour that I thought we could check out. It'll be something low-key we can do."

"Yeah?" I liked the idea of heading out and doing some touristy stuff. "Please tell me there'll be crocodiles."

Sutton's warm chuckle wrapped around me. "That'll be a no. We're too far south, remember."

"I'm still waiting to see a deadly creature in the wild."

"We saw that mob of kangaroos when we were fishing."

"True." The giant rats were huge too, but kinda fun to watch. "Would you class a kangaroo as a deadly creature, though?"

"Did you not hear Bill's story?"

I snorted at the memory. "They sound like crazy fuckers."

"Uh-huh, it makes sense why you're so fascinated by them."

I rolled my eyes at him, the wheels touching down jolting me and making me latch on to his arm. "These propeller planes are bumpy as hell," I grumbled, loosening my grip on his arm. Before I could release fully, Sutton took my hand and held on. Surprise rippled through me, and I held back a smile.

When taking off, he'd held my hand too. I couldn't help but remember how compelled I felt last night to press my mouth to his. While the kiss was innocent in the grand scheme of things, the connection had sent a lazy trail of heat through my veins. Who would have thought I'd like kissing Sutton?

Realizing I was staring at his lips, I dragged my gaze away, focusing on the movement around me as the seat belt sign was turned off. Sutton stood, releasing my hand. But that was okay. I figured I could hold his hand whenever I wanted. Knowing that was as heady as it was weirdly normal. Something about my palm in his felt right, natural.

"You got everything?" Sutton's gaze was on me.

"Yeah." I stood.

"Come on then. Let's get our bags and meet up with the guys. Don't forget your cap."

Even though it was clear he was trying to hide it, his nerves were easy to read. Whether we were doing the right thing or not, I had to remember our hearts were in the right place. *Think of Pearce*, I reminded myself. Plus, there were thousands of Tweets from fans, so many that I didn't have a hope of reading them all.

Many made my blood boil, but the ones offering support and the ones sharing their own stories were a hell of a thing. There was no way we could let any of them down.

This wasn't just about saving face. We knew the significance of coming out as a couple—something we hadn't officially made a statement about yet. Maybe that knowledge was a little delayed, but it didn't prevent it from being true.

We headed down the staircase. As soon as Sutton's feet touched the tarmac, he paused at the side, waiting for me, and I readjusted my cap. Together, we strolled toward the terminal building and followed the signs to baggage collection. Once there, we immediately saw both Nate and Ryan.

They greeted us with pats on the back.

"You're looking better," Ryan said, raking his eyes over me. His gaze hovered over the scar on my face. "Badass look you've got going on there."

I laughed and Sutton groaned. "Right." I nudged Sutton and raised my brows at him.

"Don't encourage him, Broadwater. He doesn't need any help in growing his ego."

"Hey." I shot my hand out, going for a two-finger dig in his waist. The asshole was too fast for me and caught my fingers before I made contact. Rather than releasing my hand, he turned over my palm and latched on, his gaze never wavering from mine.

Heat flushed through me, and before I made a dick out of myself, I refocused on our friends. Ryan was wide-eyed, while Nate's smile was soft. "How have you guys been?" I asked, trying to distract them.

"Good. Same old. Busy at work. Nothing much else, really. Ryan looked after Ivy yesterday, and he was in bed by six last night." Amusement spilled into his words.

"Toddlers are demons. I swear. She's so angelic when she's sleepy and wanting cuddles, then in a blink, it's like she's possessed and getting into every-thing," he grumbled. We all knew he loved taking care of his niece, though, something he'd been doing a lot of since returning to Australia so his sister could concentrate on studying.

Hearing the warning from the conveyor belt, I glanced over. A light squeeze of my hand brought my attention to Sutton.

"I'll grab the bags." He released my hand and

went to find a spot. As always, it was easy to do. His height and bulk struck an intimidating figure. The small crowd seemed to part for him. A clearing of a throat pulled me short, and I snapped my attention to Ryan and Nate's direction.

Ryan's brows almost hit his hairline. "So it's real?"

"Ryan, I told you not to do this." Nate glanced at me, his stare apologetic.

"Come on, how could I not ask? I'm just, I don't know, blown away, I think." Ryan shook his head. "And engaged? When did that even happen?"

Aiming for casual, I flicked them a smile. "All you need to know is it happened." Already we'd decided to be loose with the details rather than digging further into lies. We'd stick as close to the truth as possible.

"We're happy for you guys," Nate said, his tone warm. "It makes sense he flew all this way so quickly considering," he continued. "I bet he was worried sick."

Aware that Ryan stared at me hard, I cast him a quick glance. "What? Just say what's on your mind."

"Maybe wait till later," Nate suggested, peering around us at the milling passengers.

"Fine. I can wait." Ryan bobbed his head, and I rolled my eyes at him.

As our friend, of course he'd have questions. Me coming to Australia in the first place without Sutton being an almighty one, I expected.

The sound of wheels drew my attention. Sutton headed our way, rolling both our bags, his full attention on me. The way he stared at me with such intensity shot a spike of adrenaline into me. Had Sutton always looked at me this way? I blinked and shook my head, not quite sure what I was reading in the way he focused on me.

All I did know was every time he did, warmth bloomed in my chest and my heart went out of whack. I wasn't sure if that was a good thing or not.

Concern colored Sutton's words when he reached my side. "Is your head hurting?"

I made eye contact. "No, it's still okay." I smiled, genuinely relieved that I hadn't been plagued by a migraine over the last couple of days. I'd almost forgotten what it was like to not have a fluff-filled head.

Relief bled into his gaze. "That's good."

"Uhm, right, shall we get going?" Nate asked.

Sutton handed off one of the bags to Nate, surprising me with a nod. When I realized it was to free up his hand to hold mine, my heart did that wild beat again.

Something was most definitely going on. There

was little doubt in my mind that dating Sutton wouldn't be a hardship at all. What I did have to worry about was figuring out how to make my screwed-up declaration of "really" dating not drag my heart into the mix.

Our broken friendship had hurt my heart once. If real feelings got involved, which made me want to hold Sutton's hand and share kisses with him, I didn't think it could survive the fallout a second time.

But with a squeeze of my hand and the reassuring warmth of his skin against mine, I wouldn't back out. No chance of that.

———

SUTTON HAD GONE WITH NATE TO COLLECT TAKEOUT, leaving me alone with Ryan for the first time. Certainly the first time it felt safe enough to ask the questions I'd somehow managed to keep bottled in.

I'd had a whole day without painkillers. My reward was the light beer I was cradling, complete with a fun stubby holder a term I found both weird and hilarious with the words: "I'm the Rainbow Sheep of the Family."

As soon as he sat his ass down on the chair oppo-site me, I let loose. "When did you know you were gay? Did you just know? Or was it like… a big buildup, like a revelation or something? Have you only ever been gay with Nate, or were there others? Did—"

"Whoa." He lifted a hand out before him, eyes wide. Rather than amusement, concern burned brightly in his gaze. "Let's just take a breath." Both his brows shot high, and he indicated for me to take a deep breath. I rolled my eyes at him but did the whole overexaggerated breathing thing to get him talking.

Patience was not a virtue of mine. I opened my mouth to speak when he continued to stare at me. Before I could get the first word out, he shook his head. "Listen, I'll answer all the questions you have, okay, just tell me something."

Pursing my lips, I waited for him, hoping it wouldn't be a question I had to lie about.

"Are you okay?"

My face scrunched in confusion. "Course I am."

I assumed the shake of his head meant he wasn't convinced. "I mean, the last couple of weeks have been intense. Like, crazy intense. When we left the States, it was clearly without Sutton, and don't even bullshit me by saying nothing weird was going on between you."

I lifted a brow at his choice of words.

He snorted. "Not *that* thing between you. I mean, whenever I spoke to you or Sutton, you were never together."

Trying to control my expression, I held back my wince. "You know, codependency is unhealthy." Somehow I contained my smile as I channeled Sutton's words. "Not spending all your time with someone can be a sign of a healthy relationship."

When his mouth gaped, I couldn't hold back my grin. His stink eye simply made me chuckle.

"You're an asshole. You're telling me everything was fine between you and Sutton?"

I reminded myself to stay as close to the truth as possible. "Secrets are hard. You know that," I said pointedly. He acknowledged my words with a slight nod. "Working together, being in each other's space while having secrets, is not easy. But you know Sutton is the one person in the world who gets me." The truth of those last words rang loud and clear. "I'm not saying last season wasn't difficult and that things were always okay between Gale and me, because they weren't. But it's different now." A genuine smile lifted my lips.

Everything was so very different.

While I wouldn't forget the reason for the decision Sutton and I had made, I couldn't regret it. I had my friend back, and what was more, I liked our version of dating. A lot. Like, a hell of a lot.

Every night before I turned the lamp off, because of course we were sharing a bed since being back, I couldn't resist dotting that same brief kiss on his lips. It was a moment, an exchange I'd come to crave. The touch sent a flurry of butterflies to wake and take flight in my stomach every time I did so.

How on earth could I regret something that felt so right?

"You really love him, don't you?"

"Yes," I said immediately. Maybe it wasn't the full-on romantic love he was referring to, but without a doubt, I loved Sutton. "So, my questions?" I pushed.

For a beat, Ryan stared at me, wonder still evident in his expression before he told me his story.

I listened, my heart feeling lighter the more he explained. That he hadn't figured out his sexuality until he was at college had made my heart flip over. A strange relief formed in my chest knowing there wasn't a single rule that meant if you didn't realize at puberty or simply forever or something, it meant there was something funky going on.

It's stuff I always thought I'd known, just from watching movies and TV, but it had never been a conversation I'd had.

"So falling for a guy later on, even though I've never been attracted to another man before, that's, I don't know, okay?" I asked honestly.

Ryan's smile was gentle when he said, "I'm not the font of all knowledge to everything gay-related. Struth, I've been publicly out for what, a year? Sexuality doesn't come with a rule book. That much I know. You know the term love is love?" He didn't wait for an answer, saying, "You ever think about what that means? How love simply *is* love. It comes in so many shapes and forms, and no one size fits all. You falling in love with your best friend?" A huge grin lit his face. "You know I'm all about best-friend love."

I grinned and put aside the empty beer bottle.

"You think about it. How many straight single guys have straight single female friends and it simply stays that way?" He shrugged. "Sure, I know there's plenty of exceptions, but I think falling for your friend is natural. Here's this person you care for, share all your time with, and it's normal for romantic feelings to get involved. I don't know, maybe millions of people with platonic friendships would call bullshit. Maybe we're the anomaly. I just know that loving Nate is as natural and easy for me as breathing."

Latching on to his words, I absorbed them and

considered them carefully. He stood and indicated if I wanted another beer. "Yeah. Thanks." Alone with my thoughts, I thought about everything I knew and felt.

I loved Sutton.

I wasn't sure about romantic love yet, but the idea was far from horrifying. And that sounded really shitty, but that I *wasn't* as freaked by the possibility warped my mind.

I supposed the question was, did I want to be open for more with Sutton, really explore something with him? Make our "real" relationship *really* real?

Hearing footsteps returning to the outside patio area, I called out, "So tell me more about anal sex. Is it really as good as the porn I've watched?" I was mildly aware that an engaged bi man wouldn't ask these questions. But hell, I needed inside information. I could totally argue the case that Sutton and I were saving ourselves till our wedding night.

When my dick perked up, I looked down at my lap in surprise. I huffed out a laugh. "Huh, you like the idea of some anal penetration, right, big guy?"

A strangled sound came from behind me. I turned quickly to peer over my shoulder. In the doorway stood Sutton, a bag of takeout in his hand and a heat in his eyes that had me freezing.

And as easy as that, my cock hardened, thick and

fast, and totally on board with whatever was happening right now.

Ignoring the tremble in my hands, I gave him a chin lift, an easy smile on my face. "Smells good," I said, completely ignoring the tension. I was 99.9 percent sure he'd overheard at least part of what I said.

Movement behind him drew my attention. Nate appeared. "We good to eat out here? I can put the patio heater on."

Sutton jerked at the sound of Nate's voice and stepped forward, clearing the doorway. His gaze shifted away from me as he reached the outside table and placed the bag down. "I'm just going to wash up." And then he moved quickly back inside. My focus remained on him until he was out of sight.

Doubt sprang to life. Heat had been in his eyes when he'd looked at me. I was sure of it. But with how hastily he'd hightailed it out of here, maybe whatever it was I was feeling—my growing interest—was one-sided.

I hoped not.

"Everything okay?" Nate asked as he turned on the patio heater, taking our lack of responses about where to eat as a yes. While the temperature was dropping, the view of the pitch-black sky and the abundance of stars was spectacular. I was more than happy to stay outdoors for longer.

"Yeah." I shook off the sliver of anxiety and smiled. "All good. Food smells great."

He side-eyed me for a second but gave me a reprieve by switching topics. Launching into a story about something that had happened at work, he didn't seem to notice I only half-listened, my attention drifting to Sutton.

He seemed on form by the time he returned, alongside Ryan with the plates and cutlery, offering his usual smiles, grunts, and nuggets of conversation. More relaxed, it was easy to enjoy the good food and even better company. When Sutton's gaze caught on mine, some silent question in his stare, I'd offer him a wink or a smirk. Each time, his lips twitched and he glanced away, refocusing on the conversation at hand.

The moments were small but somehow significant. With each brief eye contact, awareness flickered to life. The growth warm and comforting and surrounded by curiosity.

When the plates were cleared away and a dodgy action movie played, I could barely concentrate. The need to do something, reach out and touch Sutton, was a steady thrum in my veins.

Every time he moved slightly, my hair stood on

end. With each huff of laughter at something ridiculous on the screen, my stomach tightened. My body, mind, and emotions were on high alert, attuned to him in every possible way.

When he shifted his leg at my side, his thigh brushing mine before casually moving away, I couldn't stand it anymore. Ignoring the spike in my pulse, I leaned into him, pressing myself to his side.

Every muscle in his body seemed to contract at my touch. I ignored it, instead reaching out for his arm and maneuvering it to over my shoulder. When I positioned his hand where I wanted it, I snuggled in deeper, my palm landing on his stomach.

His abs flexed once, twice, and it wasn't until I squeezed lightly and rested my head against part of his shoulder and his chest that the tension seeped out of his body. Relief spread through me, and when his arm pulled me in tighter to him, his hand clasping my arm to keep me in place, I smiled.

This was perfect. My comfort fix was engaged, but more than that, in Sutton's arms, I'd never felt so at peace. Not needing to question it, I exhaled slowly, a wisp of happiness in my breath.

We stayed like that for about fifteen minutes before I repositioned my head on his lap so I could stretch out on the sofa. By the time the movie ended, my eyes were bleary, and I knew getting up would be an effort.

"Work for me tomorrow, so I need to hit the hay." Nate stood, clasping Ryan's hand and tugging him up with him. "You guys staying up?"

Yawning, I shook my head against Sutton's lap, earning me a grunt. "I'm beat." I turned to peer up at Sutton. His gaze was already on me, his irises looking black in the soft lighting of the room. "You ready for bed?"

He simply nodded.

I sighed. "I suppose I best get up then." His stare didn't shift. I became aware of two things. The first was my head was positioned right over his groin, which was firm under my head. The second was the shuddery breaths escaping him.

I gulped before the sound of shuffling reminded me we weren't alone. Reluctantly I sat up and dragged my focus away from Sutton. "Night," I offered to Nate and Ryan, who held hands and were glancing over at us, both with soft smiles.

Aware this was the first time we'd shown couple-y affection in front of them, my skin heated under their scrutiny.

"Sleep well. We'll lock up," Nate said.

At my side, Sutton stood. I angled to watch his

movements, surprise making my heart stutter when he reached for my hand, much like Nate had done to Ryan. I clasped it, and we headed silently to our bedroom.

With each step we took, my thoughts ran rampant.

I need to brush my teeth. Will his cock feel the same as mine? How will he react if tonight's kiss lingers and I go for it? Do I want to? My brain nodded frantically, my heart agreeing 100 percent.

I excused myself as soon as we hit the room so I could wash up. Before I closed the door, Sutton spoke, "Let me grab my wash kit, and I'll use the other bathroom."

With a nod, I held my breath as he walked past me, his arm brushing across my chest. Pulling my gaze away was impossible as I tracked his movements. When he finally left, I closed the door and gulped in air.

The man staring at me in the reflection was wide-eyed and pink-cheeked. Fuck, I looked on edge. My dick throbbed in my jeans, having been not so slowly growing hard over the past few moments. Holding on to myself, I squeezed lightly and shuddered.

"Get control of yourself," I said to my cock. "If not, you're going to embarrass the fuck out of yourself."

My cock didn't listen as I washed up, brushed my

teeth, and stripped down to my tight-fitting boxers. The fit left very little to the imagination, the outline of my erection proudly on display. Unless I wanted to hide out in the bathroom and jack off, there wasn't a thing I could do about it.

All of that shit about thinking gross thoughts or whatever never did the job for me. Hearing Sutton enter the room, I took a shaky breath. It was now or never.

CHAPTER 10
SUTTON

WATCHING THE MOVIE HAD BEEN THE MOST DELICIOUS torture I'd ever experienced. Between overhearing Jayden talking to his dick—this was Jayden so I had no doubts that's what he'd been chatting to—and him cuddling up to me, ending up rubbing against my cock, and I was a walking, grunting ball of need.

I wanted him so badly my nerve endings were alive and pulsing with desire.

Every touch, look, and word we shared buzzed with awareness all night. It had been developing for a few days, something I was viscerally conscious of.

Tonight a change had happened. While I didn't understand fully why that was, if Jayden indicated he wanted more from me, I wouldn't hold back. Couldn't if my life depended on it.

But it had to be him.

Being in love with the guy meant I had no choice but to hold back. This had to be his decision. Only then could I truly be all in.

His words from when we were in the outback taunted me. He'd said the same things. "All in" then was bullshit. We'd both known it. There was only one version of "all in" that existed.

Heart, body, mind, and soul.

I wanted to give him it all. So ready that my body vibrated.

Already in bed, I tried to relax and not act as if this could be it. The moment he asked me for more. Despite my efforts, my muscles were tight.

More than aware he could exit the bathroom, give me his usual sweet kiss—one of my favorite parts of the day—and turn his back to me, I closed my eyes and counted to ten.

Then to twenty.

Moving on to thirty, I heard the soft click of the door opening. I had no choice but to look.

I soaked him in, drank in the light splattering of hair on his chest, the way his muscles dipped and curved. Reaching his stomach, I didn't dare go any further, my gaze snapping to his.

Moving toward the bed, he seemed in control, unperturbed by the invisible current zapping between us. Before he got into bed, he faltered. The first tell his nerves were close to the surface.

"Jay." I stopped there, not sure what else to say.

But he knew. He had to.

The man at my side, now under the covers, his head on the pillow, his whole body facing me, knew me. And I was tired, oh so tired of the wall I'd erected, the barrier I'd felt like I had no choice but to build to protect my heart from my friend.

Jayden would never hurt me deliberately. The certainty of that was as clear as the open expression on his face.

With parted lips, his eyes wide, Jayden's stare remained unwavering.

I lowered beside him, head on my pillow, aware of every inch of space between us. Warmth spread between us, and the slow movement of his hand caught my attention. I held my breath. Waiting, need-ing, wanting. And then his palm touched my cheek, fingers dancing over my skin. The gentlest touch I'd ever experienced.

It surprised me, the tenderness of the exploration. Jayden often dived in headfirst, usually without a first and never with a second look. But here he was, his gaze and fingers wandering, as if discovering the man beyond the friendship for the first time.

I expected him to speak, assumed he would say something cocky to cut through the tension.

I was wrong.

He leaned in, his stare on mine, his breathing uneven. Watching, waiting, perhaps assuming I'd stop him.

He should have known better.

Unable to wait, I closed the gap, my lips pressing against his, and then our mouths joined, moving, exploring, tongues probing. One of us groaned, maybe both of us, and Jayden wasted no time in plastering himself against my body.

When his thigh brushed against my cock, my gasp was guttural and needy. Then he was there, his cock against mine. Two thin barriers between us.

I clamped down on him, wrapping my arms around him as our kiss continued, desire and rightness demanding attention, demanding more from me.

He gasped, disconnecting from the kiss. My eyes jolted open, a tremble of anxiety brushing across my skin. Only heat and wonder reflected in the depth of his oaky eyes. A lazy smile followed, the reaction everything I needed for the trembles to stop.

He wasn't backing away.

He wanted this.

Wanted me.

"I know we said first base only." His quiet words

pressed against me. My cock twitched, earning me a quirked brow. "How set on that rule are we?"

Darting my gaze around his face, looking for anything hinting at uncertainty, I exhaled lightly, not seeing any. "You want to do more?"

He pushed his hips against mine, his pupils dilating. My groin tightened at the contact, and I bit my bottom lip. The movement pulled his attention to my mouth. When he leaned in and pressed a light kiss and a slight lick against my bottom lip, I released it.

"I *really* want to do more."

I didn't need to ask if he was sure. I had to believe that what was happening—or at least his awareness of me—had been building for a while. That this wasn't one of the times Jayden simply reacted. And even if it was, the Jayden I knew never had regrets. Ever. Period.

He screwed up? He owned it.

"Me too," I answered breathily.

There was nothing tentative about his touch. His fingers traced my skin, my chest, swept over my nipples. I shuddered at the contact. He smirked, but rather than teasing, his mouth connected once more with mine.

By the time he reached the material of my boxers, the cotton tight to my skin, I fought hard to not writhe on the bed. I bit back the plea on my lips, begging him to put his hands beneath the elastic waistband.

It turned out I didn't need to worry. Jayden went for it, his hand dipping in, fingers immediately touching the hot skin of my cock.

He caught my gasp with his mouth, but I angled away, needing the space to concentrate on getting my hand in his boxers.

A light chuckle escaped him at my urgency. The sound relaxed me, offering me that perfect reminder of who exactly this man pressed against me was.

His laughter broke off when I grasped him, feeling the full effect of the weight of his erection and the heat of his flesh. Once in hand, I returned my gaze to his, pumping, focusing on the sensations rippling through me, committing to memory his soft gasps, the light groans, and his shot pupils.

The grip on my cock was steady, just the right side of firm, and when he swept his thumb over the end, spreading the satin smoothness of my precum, I groaned. I chased his kisses, my hand picking up speed, his own mirroring mine.

This was too much. Not enough. Everything, and so much more than I'd dared hope for.

"Fuck," he grunted out against my mouth when my fingers dipped and caressed his balls. "Do that again."

Through my lust, I managed to smile, lips barely connected. Jayden smiled back and shivered when I made good on his request. His hand faltered on my cock, and I fucking prayed that meant he was close. The stars appearing in my peripheral vision were closing in. My balls drew tight.

"I'm gonna…," I said against his mouth.

His nod was the only indication he'd heard me.

And then I was flying, soaring in the blinding tingles sweeping through me. My body jerked, my hand squeezing, and thank fuck when I felt him coat my hand.

We both came down, panting. My mouth found its way to his neck. I pressed my lips against his sweaty skin, once, twice, before angling away. I released him, not caring my hand was sticky, not minding one bit about the mess we made.

A loud huff of breath, along with a chuckle I knew so well, escaped from Jayden as he angled back. Our eyes connected. I didn't even have to wait for a beat before I was smiling back, and when he leaned in for a quick press of lips against mine, my muscles became like jelly.

Contentment rolled down my spine, reaching every finger and toe.

"We need a shower." He raised one brow.

"We need clean sheets."

"It's a good job I know where they are then," he responded, squeezing my ass before throwing the sheets back.

I remained where I was, sticky, my sweat drying, and my gaze glued to his movements. When he peered over his shoulder, both his brows shot up. "You coming? The shower is plenty big enough."

He didn't have to ask me twice. With a swiftness that had Jayden snorting out a laugh, I made it to the bathroom ahead of him, turning on the tap and checking the heat. And then I hesitated, hands on my boxers.

"You going shy on me even though I've still got your cum on my hand, Sutton?"

A glance revealed Jayden in the doorway. Once he'd captured my gaze, he tugged down his boxers. Not wanting to miss a thing, I followed the movement, staying on his half-hard cock.

My eyes flared, cock twitched, and the tip of my tongue dipped out, wetting my bottom lip. Jayden held on to his junk and squeezed. My brows shot high, opposite to my attention that quickly lowered.

"You know that just gives me ideas, right?"

"That right?" I asked, my voice gruff.

"Oh yeah. That water good?"

I reached out blindly to check it. "Yeah."

As he stepped toward me, I got into the shower,

happily watching the show. Once he was before me, he moved into my space. We were almost at eye level, me having just an inch on him. It felt right, being here like this with him.

With so much having happened, he was going to hate me for asking, but I needed to know. "Why aren't you freaking out?"

He tilted his head, gaze searching mine. "Why aren't you freaking out?" he shot back.

I rolled my eyes and leaned into the spray. It gave me a few seconds to get my thoughts together. A mighty feat considering the orgasm he'd torn from me had left me shaken and weak.

"Seriously, man, why?"

He sighed, nudging me so he could get some of the spray. "You making me talk about feelings and shit, Sutton?"

"Maybe… are you saying there are feelings to discuss?" My chest tightened, certain he could read the edge of desperation in my tone.

"I don't usually make out with guys and kiss their faces off while we jack each other off to the point my eyes roll back inside my head."

My mouth twitched at the visual. There may have been a little bit of cockiness morphing, too, knowing I'd done that to him. Alongside that was a reality of the man I knew who went through stages of sleeping around with League groupies. Not that I'd been that different, in the early days especially.

"What?" The concern in his tone was clear.

"Just thinking about groupies…" I trailed off, expecting the direction of my thoughts were clear, though already wishing I could take the words back. When the hell did I become this person? This fucking *man*? Butt naked in the shower, and here I was asking my best friend if what we'd just done meant something to him. If it was more than a quick jack-off session. I straightened my back, tension rippling through me, feeling like a dickhead. "Forget I said anything."

Reaching out for the shower gel, I turned my back on him, focusing on washing down and getting out of there as quickly as possible. If not, there was a chance I could humiliate myself even more.

I barely even recognized myself anymore. *This*, whoever this version of me was, was no one I recognized. If this was what it was like being in love and being on the verge of possibility, having hope so close to my grasp I could taste it, I wasn't sure I was cut out for it.

"Sutton."

I scrubbed my face under the water.

"Gale."

Goose bumps appeared at the sound of my name

and the tone of his voice. I could tell with just one word that whatever he planned to say was serious.

"Just look at me, man."

I turned to face him, humiliation heating my skin. Not sure what to expect when I saw him, my breath was all but knocked from my lungs when he immediately reached out and cupped both sides of my face.

"To be absolutely crystal fucking clear, League groupies were great for a quick fuck"—my eye twitched, but he didn't stop—"and a good time. No way I would risk doing anything with you, stepping over any boundary, not like this unless I meant it and wanted more. Which I do. With you. Don't even begin to ask me how or why or even knowing that just the thought of sucking on your dick makes me hard, because it just does." He brushed his thumb against my cheek, the movement so tender, a lump formed in my throat. "And while I will always try my fucking hardest to be honest with you, actually talking about my feelings and that damn muscle in my chest that keeps going crazy when I see you is not my favorite thing to do in the world."

I grinned, unable to hold back the rush of feelings for this man. "That muscle in your chest been getting a workout recently or something?"

He snorted. "Or something." He dropped his

hands and placed them around my waist. "Do you have any idea what we're doing?"

I shook my head. "Not really."

He laughed. "Gale Sutton clueless and without a plan. Has hell frozen over?"

Feeling bold and remembering precisely who this man was to me, I reached around and clamped my hands on his ass. His grin stretched even wider. "You know, you always say you're useless at talking and dealing with feelings. I think it's about time I told you that's absolutely bullshit. You let all your emotions pour out."

Narrowing his eyes at me, he scowled. "Take that back."

"Now why would I want to do a thing like that?"

"Because it's all lies. I don't do feelings."

"Uh-huh. The man doth protest too much, methinks."

"Don't you get quoting *Hamlet* to me."

When my brows shot high, his palm landed on my ass with a loud smack.

"Ow," I said with laughter. "What the fuck, Moore?"

"I know shit. Totally watched that Mel Gibson movie rather than reading the play at high school."

"Of course you did."

"You've known for a while I'm crazy cultured."

"Perhaps drop one of those adjectives," I fired back.

"Stop with all of the grammar shit." He pushed his hips against me. "You see, you've made me go soft. Grammar's not sexy."

"Take that back," I said.

"Or what?"

"I won't be able to show you the hundreds of verbs out there relating to jacking off." I licked a column up his throat, more than happy to put further discussion on the back burner. "Or maybe even sucking," I whispered, pressing kisses along his collarbone. Distracting him from my overreaction was my best idea ever.

"Yeah?" He sagged against me, angling to give me better access. My mouth returned to his neck. "What else?"

"At some point, I'm sure we'll reach the stage of fucking." I swallowed down his groan with a kiss, feeling empowered by his reaction, bolder than I had ever felt before.

As I devoured his mouth, I wrapped my hand around his no longer flagging cock. If he was up for it, working up to sucking and fucking was totally going on my plan. And with the way Jayden moaned my name and cussed up a storm, I imagined it wouldn't take too long at all.

CHAPTER 11
JAYDEN

OUR DAYS FLEW BY TOO QUICKLY. THE NIGHTS EVEN faster.

While I still hadn't had his cock in my mouth or mine in his, jacking each other was my new favorite thing to do. And frotting?! Holy shit balls. I'd been seventeen the last time I had my dick between someone's legs getting off, and fuck, that memory didn't do justice to rubbing all up Sutton.

I expected lube had a lot to do with it.

There was something crazy hot when my dick slid effortlessly between his firm thighs. It took no imagination at all to wonder what it would be like when I got access to his ass, or him mine for that matter.

I wanted to try it all, do it all, experiment with everything.

But absolutely no way in Nate and Ryan's home.

It made saying goodbye easier when we'd boarded our flight yesterday. There was no denying I was sad to be leaving our friends, just like Sutton was. With no idea when we'd see each other again, it was a bittersweet farewell.

The thought of having real alone time with Sutton when we returned to Minnesota was one hell of a distraction, though, to saying goodbye. But that fantasy was shot to shit when we'd gone our separate ways because of the maniacal welcome at the airport. I hadn't liked it one bit.

It turned out "all in" for me meant I didn't like being without him. Maybe in another life, that knowledge would have worried me, but I lived with my eyes wide open in this one. Also, being practically ambushed when we flew into Minnesota after our two long flights meant we'd had no choice but to split.

I hadn't even been able to kiss him goodbye before my agent was shuffling me into the car, Sutton's doing the same to him. It took me a beat to calm down and stop grumbling and shouting at Greg for the weird ambush they'd organized.

Truth was, I was still pissed off, but I was also tired as fuck and over being treated like a rookie.

"Greg, I swear, man, you need to wind your neck

in and drop the subject already." It was barely midday, and I already had a beer in my hand. Greg had driven me to booze. Not only was my head aching, but if I didn't get some proper sleep soon in a real bed, I was likely going to say something I couldn't take back. Though I was quietly impressed that I'd managed to finally use "wind your neck in," on my favorite new Aussie sayings.

"I just need you to be sure, Jayden. While you were out of the country, we were able to spin a few things to stop the vultures from circling. The press got wind of Axle not signing with you."

"And I've already told you I want you to contact my lawyer and see what we can do about that." While I didn't want anything to do with any brand or company who were homophobic assholes, the end of my contract would mean they would no longer have to provide a percentage of sales to the charity. "We stayed away from the media, even managed not to get photographed when we were in Australia. I did what you wanted, what Monty recommended, but now we're back, and this is happening. I'll find another gig to help give my own yearly donation, but them getting out of it this way is not okay."

"I just want you to consider all options. It'll be more press if they decide to push it. You could just drop it, and we'll focus on a better deal with a matching percentage, with a brand that you're proud of."

"Drop it?" I stood, exhausted, even knowing that maybe he had a good point. I'd been unprepared to be dealing with this. Sutton and I had been in our Aussie bubble. That protective layer had well and truly been destroyed since arriving in Minnesota… since my agent dove straight in and started talking business to me.

I knew it was what I paid him for, but couldn't it have waited for a day or two at least?

My cell rang, giving me the distraction I needed. Seeing Sutton's name, I exhaled, relieved. "Can we just be done here? I need to take this call. I'm not going to change my mind."

After a huff of breath and a nod from Greg, I left the main sitting room in my apartment and headed to my bedroom, answering the phone en route. "Hey." At the sound of the door closing, signaling Greg had left, I exhaled.

"You okay?" Warmth threaded his words, helping me calm my mind.

"I am now you've called, and Greg's listened to reason."

"What did he say?" Ice hardened his voice.

I sat in my bed and leaned against the bedhead.

"Tried to talk me into backtracking on trying to file a lawsuit against Axle."

"Really? He say why?"

"With a world of negative exposure about the two of us, and our refusal to make an official statement about our relationship, he doesn't think I need the extra focus. Thinks it might damage another sponsorship deal."

"I suppose he has a point."

My brows shot up in surprise. "Seriously?"

"He's just looking out for you."

"So you don't think this is something I should pursue?"

"I absolutely do think you should pursue it, if there's a case." I grinned at the heat in his words. "Those assholes not renewing like that, especially as you'd just arranged a new deal and were due to sign a new contract, is not okay. Prejudiced fuckers."

I laughed, feeling better after Sutton's rant. "What did Max have to say?"

"Not much, really," Sutton said about his own agent. "Asked me a few things about our relationship. Encouraged us to go public and make an official statement. More than the Eagles' standard 'all our players are supportive of the LGBTQ+ community, and Moore and Sutton wish for privacy while working through rehabilitation post-accident.'"

I winced. "What did you say?"

"That we weren't willing to go on record yet about our relationship, nor would we be confirming or denying anything. And we'd do so without the pressure from the media."

I sighed. "Yeah, I said something similar to Greg." It was something Sutton and I had agreed to a few weeks back. While I didn't expect we could get away with it forever, for the time being, my health gave us a small "get out of jail free" card. I was still annoyed we'd been railroaded at the airport, though. If anything, I was pissed off at myself that I'd allowed it to happen. We could have easily had a conversation together. Codependency be damned.

Once we'd arrived at Minneapolis-St. Paul, the press had been three deep. It had been ridiculous. Greg and Max had been a welcome sight, considering the media and the gathered crowd. Sure, I'd been disgruntled when Sutton and I had been shuffled into different cars, but between the cameras, the shouts, and my exhaustion, I'd just gone with it.

"What else did Greg say? Anything else about us?" he said when I remained quiet, caught up in my thoughts.

"Not really. He actually seemed relieved."

"Yeah?"

"Something about maybe you can stop me doing

stupid shit." Sutton started laughing as I carried on. "I reminded him that in almost twenty years, you hadn't been able to do that, so why would it happen now."

He snorted. "Maybe we'll need to come up with a reward system, you know, for avoiding doing stupid shit."

"Screw you. I'm a fucking catch. It's a wonder you could resist me. The stupid shit I do is just one of the millions of reasons why you finally succumbed to my charms."

This time the laughter I pulled from him trickled over my skin. God, I loved his laugh.

"I'm a lucky man," he said gruffly, and my brows shot high at the genuine tone in his words.

"Brave, more like it. We both know I'm dating up here, right?"

"Can I come over?"

"I wish you were already here," I admitted and rolled my eyes at myself for good measure. When had I turned into this gushy guy? I couldn't even be that disappointed in myself, especially when I was sure Sutton would have smiled at my words.

"I'm leaving now. Be there in ten."

I grinned, already jumping off the bed and heading into the bathroom to take a quick shower. "Bring your key," I reminded him.

"You know it lives on my key ring. Just put some coffee on."

The phone cut off, and I made my way to the kitchen to organize a pot of coffee before returning to the bathroom.

Once under the warm spray, I relaxed even further. While my disappointment in Greg continued to simmer and I needed to vent some more and talk this shit out, I wanted to do it face-to-face with Sutton. Even more preferable would be doing so wrapped up in his arms.

After an orgasm.

Not for the first time, I imagined what it would be like to suck him off. I'd received enough head over the years to know exactly what I liked. Since I was a fast study, I thought I'd do a kick-ass job.

But then there was the swallowing of his spunk. Could I do that? Was I cut out for swallowing jizz? I'd tried my own a couple of times, curiosity driving me to lick a little off my fingers. It hadn't been bad, but it wasn't like I wanted to lick my hand clean. But since it was my cum, that would have been all levels of gross.

Sutton's I could at least try. Make the effort.

And if I gagged or needed to spit, then so the fuck what? If I was going to humiliate myself in front of anyone, Sutton was the guy to do it with.

Over the years, he'd seen me at my worst and my best.

With just the thought of him, a flurry of excitement hit my gut.

It didn't matter if my mouth was on his, his gaze was on mine, or our laughter mixed together. Every moment since my eyes had been wide open to Sutton and the possibility of more, my heart was no longer my own.

And wasn't that a fuck of a thing.

I'd never been in love. I wasn't even sure I'd be able to recognize the emotion. But I did love Sutton. Everything we'd shared so far, I was keen for more, which was a total understatement.

I switched off the shower and dried off. As I wrapped my towel around my waist, I heard the front door closing. My grin was instant, and my feet moved. My whole body knew what it wanted, what it needed.

And right now, it was to lay my eyes on Sutton, get my lips on his, and then finally see how long it would take for me to master a blow job.

In the bright space of my open-plan apartment, Sutton looked especially delicious. I'd likely seen him in my condo thousands of times before, but kisses and shared orgasms changed everything. Despite seeing the man with renewed appreciation, him being here was as natural as the view of the lake and the brightness of the summer sky visible beyond the windows.

"Hey," he greeted, placing his keys on the small table near the door that was the nominated dumping ground. A brief caress of his gaze over my naked torso sent a flush of heat snaking over my skin. Appreciation flickered over his expression, his smile turning lazy despite the alertness in his eyes.

I grinned, eating up the distance between us. "Hey, you made good time."

"If I'd known you were showering, I would have got here faster."

Stopping in front of him, I laughed and reached out for him. He mirrored my action and we pressed against each other, our kiss sweet and slow.

When he pulled away, his gaze turned assessing. "You okay?"

I sighed. Just the thought of Axle threatened to destroy my good mood and my plan to suck Sutton off. "Yeah, other than wanting to throw down and call the company out."

Feeling myself getting more worked up, I exhaled. My cock was soft, my head remained fuzzy, and I wanted to bury my head in the sand about as much as I wanted to fight Axle with everything I had.

A light touch drew my attention. "Couch or bed?"

This man knew me inside out. "Bed would be good."

"Your painkillers still in your bag?"

"Yeah."

"I'll get water, you get those, and I'll meet you in your room." A soft kiss followed his words before he made his way to the cupboard to collect a glass.

I stood there for a beat, watching him.

In my home, Sutton was utterly comfortable. Not for the first time, I wondered how I could have missed how attractive he was. Well, that wasn't completely accurate. The man was good-looking, and I'd always known that. It was more why I hadn't been attracted to him, or at least open to the possibility.

I huffed out a laugh, knowing full well that before the car accident, I'd never seriously considered my sexuality as being anything other than straight. That kiss in college had been my version of a favor for a friend. I had been curious, though. But when I hadn't popped a boner, I'd put a cross in the box next to straight and had accepted that as gospel.

Oh how wrong I had been.

Realizing I was still staring at Sutton, I grinned when he glanced my way. Me standing there earned me a quirked brow from the man I ogled. I shook my head at his unasked question and turned to get my meds from my bag I'd dumped in my closet.

Once my tablets were swallowed with ice-cold water, I lay on my mattress and exhaled. "Man, I missed my bed." I'd planned to sit up so we could talk, but the comfort called to me.

On top of the covers, my head on the pillow, I smiled, and when Sutton lay next to me, I sighed, content. He moved onto his side, his arm circling my waist, and I turned into him.

"You need to off-load?"

My smirk was immediate, and I jerked my hips against his. "Hell yeah."

He laughed. "That too, but I meant talk about your sponsorship."

Annoyance quickly flared to life in my chest. "Greg mentioned something about me being in breach of contract. Not quite a morals clause, since I'm sure that would break all kinds of discrimination laws, but more to do with the story of us being engaged. You know, the whole focus on being single and a babe magnet."

Sutton's wince was minute, but I still caught it.

"And don't even apologize. You did point out before I signed the contract how ridiculous the clause was. And yeah, you said fiancé, but we both went with it and decided on this fake relationship."

Muscles stiffened under my hands, and I wanted to nut punch myself.

"Not that this is fake now...." My gaze roamed his face, darting between his eyes, and unexpected nerves rippled inside me. Tongue-tied, something that had never happened to me before, I tried a couple of times to get my words out without sounding like a dickhead. "I... I know we said... I mean..."

Sutton took pity on me.

Pressing his lips against mine for nowhere near long enough, he tasted my mouth before angling away. "We said all in, right?"

Kiss drunk, I nodded, despite the contact being brief. This was what he did to me, though. One second my emotions were in knots, spiraling out of control and whipping me into a frenzy, and in the next, his comfort provided a calm I'd never experienced before.

"I wonder if that was the shortest fake relationship in history?"

Amused, I responded, "Probably. But there's the whole thing about being engaged." A shiver danced over my skin as he drew circles on my waist, just above the towel still wrapped around me.

"Maybe one day there'll be no more lies."

I nodded. "No more secrets."

Again, there was a slight twitch of his eye. Before I could press him, Sutton's cell rang. Gaze still on mine, he reached over and hooked it off the bedside table. "It's my mom."

"Go ahead." I indicated for him to answer, wondering if now was the perfect time to start my exploration of his cock. Sure, he'd pretend to be pissed, but I figured my mouth on his junk would counter any frustration.

Was I an asshole for my plan, considering who he was on the phone with?

Definitely.

Would that stop me?

Heck no. I needed the distraction, and wanting him to feel good was right up there with it.

It wasn't like he hadn't spoken to his mom all the time we were away. There'd been a few calls, a couple with me involved. His mom approved of me and didn't let on once that she was confused by the revelation of our relationship.

Pushing aside thoughts of his mom and blocking out the conversation he was having about the flight, I eyed the way he turned to take the call. Now on his back, he was in the perfect position for me to do my thing.

As soon as I shifted, his gaze snapped to mine.

Whatever he saw on my face had him narrowing his eyes at me.

Wide-eyed, I attempted an innocent smile. When his expression didn't change, I grinned and went for it.

Shimmying down the bed, my hand went immediately to his jeans. I unbuttoned, unzipped, sat up, and yanked them down to his thighs, earning me a low grunt.

These muscles of mine weren't only handy for the court.

I glanced at him in triumph, so fucking proud of myself. His lips twitched, his gaze molten as he assessed me. My eye contact didn't waver as I eased back down, this time bunching up his T-shirt. I managed as far as his pecs. Since that exposed his nipples, I was good with it.

The whole time, he listened to whatever his mom was saying, occasionally responding with a grunt or an "Uh-huh," but I remained at the center of his focus. Just where I loved to be.

But it was no good.

I needed to get my fill and take in his body.

Forcing my attention away from his face, I zeroed in on his dark nipples. They were tight. Whether from the coolness of the air-conditioned room or from desire, I hadn't a clue. But I was sure I could make them harder.

Trailing my fingers over his hard muscles covered by soft skin, I smiled at the goose bumps my touch left behind. I skimmed over a nipple before I lightly pinched and plucked, mesmerized by the small disc tightening further.

Sutton shifted, his hips lifting slightly, drawing my attention back to his face.

If a simple look was capable of making me come, this would have been it.

Need.

Heat.

Absolute trust.

And all directed at me.

I swallowed hard, licked each nipple once, and chuckled when I realized he was trying to tell his mom he needed to go, but she wasn't having any of it.

That he was at my mercy like this had my dick thickening. I wanted him gasping in desire. I wanted him to unravel and to suck his brains out.

With renewed determination, I trailed kisses down his stomach, wishing I had more time to play with the divots and angles there. Tasting him was imperative. And fuck if I didn't want to do it while he should be concentrating on something else.

I was such an asshole.

I finally reached his cock. The brown skin was smooth, the end sticky and ripe for the tasting.

Not wanting to miss his reaction, I flicked my gaze up.

Wild desperation reflected in the depths of his deep brown eyes. His bottom lip was wedged between his teeth, and his chest was practically still. I was sure he was holding his breath.

And then I licked.

"Mom, I've gotta go. Love you." He threw the phone onto the mattress, where it bounced, landing on the floor with a thud. I hoped like God he'd managed to end the call. If not, that would be a whole hilarious "what the fuck" therapy session right there. "Fuck, Jay. Do it again."

I did, this time focusing on the taste. Committing the smooth tang to memory, I lapped at his skin, at the spongy head, and then down the side.

While I wasn't waiting for a freak-out, I was viscerally aware this was the closest I'd ever been to a cock, my own included. I couldn't help the light chuckle that escaped me as I traced along the vein on the underside.

"What?" Curiosity colored Sutton's words. There was no discomfort, no doubt or uncertainty from him, considering what I was doing.

That was the thing. Sutton had nothing to feel anxious about, even when I laughed as I licked his erection. He was built. Every kissable inch of his skin was perfection. Heck, he could have a marble statue created in his image. Jocks on or off.

"By the end of this, I'm going to know your dick better than I know my own."

He sat a little, shoved another pillow behind his head, then settled to watch me. "I'm okay with that." He grinned.

"I just bet you are." I eyed the extra pillow. "Got a good view now?"

Heat flashed in his gaze. "The best."

At his praise, warmth caressed me from inside out. "Let's see if I can make it even better."

For the first time, I opened my mouth and lowered over him. Engulfing his cock, I eased down halfway, remembering just in time to grip the root.

Not a chance I'd ever be able to deep throat him. There were a couple of intimidating inches too many for that circus act, but what I could manage, I'd make it work and have him screaming my name.

CHAPTER 12
SUTTON

"Intimate" had never been in my vocabulary when describing a blow job. But with the soft licks, the gentle stroke of my balls, and the way Jayden would search for my gaze as he sucked me off, I knew this mattered.

BJs were all about getting off, having fun, and finding that sweet release.

This was all those things, but so much more.

I was the first man he'd tasted this way, the first cock he'd licked like a lollipop, and he was the first person I was going to let own my soul.

What he was doing with his tongue, the firmness of his long, strong sucks… any second now he'd be drawing out my soul and wrenching it free from my body.

He was welcome to it.

Struggling to hold back, my limbs shook. I never wanted this to end. Ever. But my toes curled, tingles zapped around my body like I was an arcade machine, and all I wanted was more. This. Forever.

I reached out, amazed I'd held back for so long, and cupped his head, gripping his soft hair. When I made contact, he groaned. Through my bleary eyes, I caught movement. Smirking, I moaned, unable to stop myself, my stomach tightening when I saw him humping the sheets.

"Jay." I grunted his name. The need in my voice ricocheted around the large room. In response, he doubled down, and I was gone. "Fuck." I jerked, moaned, maybe blacked out for a second as I spilled into his mouth.

I felt his moment of hesitation.

"It's okay, you don't—" My words cut off with a strangled cry when he sucked harder and swallowed. I shuddered, tried to look at him, but the edges of my vision were fuzzy.

Jayden's grunt caught my attention, and the look in his eyes held it there. On his knees, bare-chested and the towel long gone—which I'd totally missed happening—he took himself in hand, jerking himself off. The frantic movements were mesmerizing.

"Come on me." Eagerness chased my words.

He edged forward, the glimmer of a smirk on his

face. And then he was coming, spilling on my abs, the cream-white stark and so perfect against my darker skin. I reached down, swiped my finger through, and brought it to my mouth.

I paused, making sure I had Jayden's attention. Still stroking his cock with a slow rub, he arrowed in on my mouth. I sent him a smile before sucking my finger. His body jerked and groaned, and he stared wide-eyed as one more shot of cum spilled out of him.

Before I could savor the taste of him, he collapsed, stomach pressed to mine, lips descending. I captured his kiss and chased his tongue when he devoured my mouth. We kissed and sighed, our caresses languid. When Jayden finally eased away, he leaned up on both palms, staring down at me.

Our gazes were soft and searching, and I wondered if he felt the shifts in what was happening between us too.

"So, what secret are you keeping from me?" A satisfied grin appeared.

Amid the doubling of my heart rate, it was impossible not to smile back. How could I resist when Jayden was pink-cheeked, had sex-mussed hair, and his lips were puffy from stealing my soul?

"Since you've already got my soul," I said, and his brows furrowed in confusion, "maybe I need to tell you that you've had my heart for a while too." I cringed inside, feeling like a sap. But the emotion ruling the day was absolute fear... that it was too much, too soon. And what if he told me I was talking shit? Or maybe told me to fuck off?

I tried my hardest to not hold my breath, but it was impossible.

Staring down at me with those expressive dark-oak eyes of his, Jayden angled his head a fraction. He was taking in my words, my expression, letting everything make sense in his brain.

Knowing his tells was a hell of a thing.

His smile was sweet and gentle. Instead of speaking, he angled down and pressed his mouth against mine. When he eased back, his brows knotted. "Last year after my kiss...?"

I cringed. "Yeah. I kinda panicked. Started having all these feelings," I admitted, my skin heating in embarrassment. By the intensity of Jayden's gaze, it didn't seem like I was escaping this conversation.

"You started popping boners around me, huh?" Wagging brows followed his words.

I snorted, relieved this was the man my heart had chosen. "Something like that."

"And you didn't tell me."

While there wasn't a thread of accusation in his voice, there was curiosity. I wanted to rub a hand over my face, feeling weary, but Jayden had me trapped.

"The last thing I wanted was to plant seeds or make things even more uncomfortable between us." I sighed. "I mishandled it, and the more I reacted and distanced myself, the deeper the hole I dug. Then I just couldn't find my way out without making things even worse."

The twitch in his jaw was the giveaway. Hurt and pissed, he seemed to be working out the best way to react.

"I'm sorry. I fucked up," I admitted. "But we're here." My pulse spiked at the plea for understanding, easy to hear in my tone.

After several seconds, his cheeks puffed out, and he exhaled. "I could be so pissed at you."

"But you're not?" I asked, wrapping my arms around his waist.

"I was but, now?" He shrugged. "What's the point? Just no more secrets, at least between us, okay? Not if we're really doing this."

I held him firmer. "Oh, we're doing this."

The smile, broad and happy, pulled at his mouth. "I'm down with this plan."

He followed up by kissing me senseless. When my cell rang from the floor, we ignored it for two rings, but whoever was calling clearly wanted my attention by the third.

I grumbled as Jayden pulled away and picked up my phone, taking a look and passing it to me.

"It's Jonas." Wide eyes peered back at me when he handed me my cell.

Why would the team's manager be calling me? Depending on the topic, any communication was always done via the coach, PR, or HR.

"Answer it," Jayden said with an urgency already thrumming in my veins.

"Jonas," I answered.

"Sutton." Jonas's Southern-accented voice rumbled down the line. "You got Moore there with you?"

"Yes, sir."

"Good. I need you both to head over to the main office for a meeting at three this afternoon. I know you've only just flown in, but it's important. Can you make that happen?"

"That should be fine." I looked at Jayden, my eyes widening a little. "Uhm, is everything okay?" I refused to ask if we were in trouble. The question reminded me too much of being a rookie.

"Sure is. See you soon." He ended the call with no further explanation.

"What's going on?"

"He's asked for us to attend a meeting at three." A

quick glance at the time told me it was already just after one in the afternoon.

"What did he say when you asked if everything was okay?"

"Said it was fine. Nothing else."

"Urgh, what the hell's this about?" I saw the moment he thought the same thing that had just entered my overworking brain. "They couldn't be talking trades, right?" He paled, looking as horrified as I felt.

I hoped they weren't. The last thing I wanted was to leave the team. That both Sutton and I were creeping toward the end of our basketball careers was obvious. Our ages pretty much guaranteed that. But since we had just signed new contracts, I'd have been surprised if that was the case.

"Let's not jump to conclusions. He said there wasn't a problem—"

"One or both of us being traded wouldn't be a problem for him. We're just numbers on a jersey."

While Jayden wasn't wrong, I couldn't imagine the manager calling us in about that. Shit, unless there was a trade offer and with us sharing our relationship status, they wanted to make sure there weren't any legal issues.

My stomach sank. That could totally be it.

"What? What is it? You just thought of something."

I twisted my mouth a little, wishing I could control my expressions better around this man. Hell, I had pretty much done so all last season by concealing my feelings, so why couldn't I now?

"You better just fucking tell me. Shit, we've only just agreed—"

"I know," I said quickly, cutting him off. The man was right, as frustrating as that was. "I just didn't want to panic you."

I glanced down, realizing I was still a mess, and Jayden wasn't much better. "Let's shower, and I'll let you know what I'm thinking."

Narrowed eyes stared back at me. "You better."

His pout was fucking adorable. I kissed him and smiled against his lips before pulling away. "I promise."

WHEN WE ENTERED THE ROOM, A HEAVY THUMP punched against my chest. Six people were sitting around the conference table. As well as Jonas, Monty and Coach Brentworth were here—Monty smiling at us both. There were three other people, one woman, and two men. None I recognized.

"Coach Jenkins," Jayden said from my side, stepping forward and taking one of the men's hand in his. "What are you doing here?"

My gaze bounced between them. While I didn't recognize him, I knew Coach Jenkins was Jayden's old coach from college.

"Good to see you, Jayden." Warmth lit his voice. "I'm sure once you sit your ass down, you'll soon find out." He chuckled and sat.

Casting a glance over his shoulder at me, Jayden shrugged, his brows almost touching his hairline. He pulled out a chair and indicated that I sit, my heart pitter-pattering at the gesture. I took the seat next to him.

"Thanks for coming," Jonas started, smiling at us. While the smile seemed genuine, I wasn't quite prepared to relax just yet. "I'm sure you're both exhausted." He focused on Jayden. "You doing okay? Head and hand okay?"

"Yeah. I'll be good for training."

Jonas nodded. "Excellent. Make sure you book in to see Doc Marlow in the next forty-eight hours, okay?"

"Sure thing." Jayden's voice was friendly, confident. No one would be any the wiser that it had taken a hand job in the shower to calm him down and stop him from having a meltdown about the meeting.

"So, we'll try not to keep you long. Today was the only day to get us all together, knowing you both were flying in. Let me introduce you all." Jonas glanced first at Coach Jenkins. "Sid Jenkins here is the coach at Montview."

"No shit," Jayden interrupted, receiving a chuckle from Coach Jenkins.

"Yeah. I took over five years ago. Best decision I ever made."

Jayden being Jayden, grinned, saying, "Makes sense. You were hard-pressed getting the quality on the court you witnessed in my four years."

I rolled my eyes, my lips twitching.

"Uh-huh. Sure, let's stick with that story," Coach Jenkins said.

Through the exchange, my brain was ticking over. Montview hosted an elite summer college program for athletes. I knew they had guest coaches step in a few weeks every year, but the summer program was already in session as far as I was aware.

"This here is Emily Meadows. She's Montview's outreach director."

The middle-aged brown-haired woman smiled at us. "Nice to meet you both."

"And finally, this is Harry Powell. He's the athletic administrator for QSA over in Indiana."

I had no idea what QSA was. Jayden beat me to the punch, asking, "QSA?"

Harry's grin was wide and bright. "Queer Sporting Association." He made eye contact as he spoke, his gaze unwavering, possibly curious.

My brows shot up, and I cast a look at Jayden since I saw his head whip in my direction. Somehow I managed to control my laugh at his bug-eyed expression. This was all surreal.

For barely a blink of time, I'd been in love with my friend, a man. Hell, I hadn't even considered a label, beyond clearly not straight and happily loving on Jayden. Yet here we were, in an out-of-the-blue meeting with someone from a queer association.

And fuck if I didn't feel like a fraud.

But here we were.

Becoming aware neither Jayden nor I had responded, I offered a small smile. "Good to meet you."

"And those are the introductions of people perhaps you didn't know. So, let's get down to business, shall we?" Jonas indicated toward Harry and nodded in his direction.

That appeared to be Harry's cue. "This year we've been working with Montview, specifically providing low-key educating opportunities to raise awareness, and honestly, cut through the bullshit involved in being a queer athlete. Our aim is to promote healthy conversation at college level with those players who will likely be drafted. You know, try to create an even playing ground for queer players so they can be out, should they wish to be, and hopefully establish an environment where their teammates are supportive and that all players feel safe. There's a counselor already involved, someone who's been there for a few years. We're just lucky he specializes in LGBTQ+ health."

I swallowed hard at his words. What they were doing was amazing. I thought of Pearce, who'd told us on one of our few calls over the past couple of weeks that he'd known for sure he was gay since he was twelve. That programs like this existed so that younger, hell, all players, like him—like *me*—had that support was incredible.

"We don't have any out pro players in the program yet," Emily said. "We think it would be an amazing opportunity for college kids to meet seasoned players, and with your recent news— congratulations, by the way—we'd love for you to spend six weeks out at Montview as guest coaches."

"We know this is short notice. Heck, it's no notice, as we'd want you there in four days, but I think you guys could really make a difference," Coach Jenkins added.

I was rendered speechless, overwhelmed by the opportunity, and heck, the privilege. But beneath all that was a layer of discomfort. This seemed too soon. Shit, I hadn't even seen my parents since being in a relationship with Jayden... being out. And even thinking in terms of being "out" was a concept I was struggling with.

I loved Jayden, all of him. The good, the stressful and painful, his heart, and his mouth and cock most recently. I wanted a future with him.

Did that make me bi? Queer? Something else?

I just didn't know.

My chest started to constrict, my breathing quickening. I fidgeted, wanting to get out of here.

The whole time, six sets of eyes stared back at us.

A hand appeared on my leg, stopping it from bouncing and pulling my attention.

Jayden.

His pale hand squeezed my thigh, and I inhaled, hoping like hell I wasn't making a dick of myself.

"Just give me and Sutton here a few minutes. That all right?" His voice was calm, soothing on my nerves.

"Absolutely." It was Harry who spoke.

And then Jayden was tugging me up, hand on my

arm and then holding my hand. He led me out the room and asked the woman at reception for an empty space we could duck into, and she must have given him the information, as I followed blindly before I heard a door closing and Jayden pushing me onto a small couch in an empty office.

Lips pressed against mine, soft and tender. Jayden's tongue skimmed my lips, encouraging me to open. I did so immediately, welcoming the contact, the intrusion. Needing him to ground me and help my emotions and head catch up with everything, especially my reaction to it all.

Slowly, tension trickled out of me, but I wasn't ready to stop. Wrapping my arms around him, I held on tightly. The perfect distraction from my addled brain was him, and I was loath to let go.

Jayden sank against me, giving me what I needed. Tender touches. Sweet kisses. A steady reassurance he was with me.

All too soon he pulled away. This time I allowed it and met his concerned gaze.

"What's going on in that bulging brain of yours?" he asked, his words gentle. He traced his fingers on my temple and down to my cheek.

I looked back at him, not expecting to find amusement or disbelief, but I checked anyway. Nothing but curiosity and affection shone back at me.

When I eased back onto the sofa, Jayden moved off his knees where he'd been camped out between my thighs and sat next to me.

"I think I panicked." Uncomfortable heat spread across my skin, admitting as much to him. Rather than respond, he nodded, the look in his eyes encouraging me to continue. "I feel like a fraud. Then when I realized I felt that way, I started to freak. Then when I started to panic, I felt ridiculous for reacting that way. Still do." I rubbed my palm over my short hair, frustrated by the spiral of emotions.

When I risked a glance at him, his smile was thin, tight. "So…" He paused, twisting his mouth, swallowing hard, and then exhaling. "A fraud?" His brows knotted. It was obvious he was trying to figure me out, my reaction. I held back my derisive snort. *Good luck with that.* How could Jayden possibly understand, since I was just as clueless. "I don't understand."

"I don't know who I am anymore."

Hurt filled his expression. I saw the battle before me as clear as day. He wanted to understand, wanted to help, but the more confused I became, the more I could possibly hurt him.

I'd done enough of that already. No way did he deserve any more.

"You said you've had feelings for me for a while." His cheeks turned crimson. "Did I get that wrong?"

I shook my head. "No, you didn't. I have. I do." Annoyed I was doing an awful job of explaining myself, I ran a frustrated hand over my face. "That," I said, finally facing him again, pushing every trace of certainty I could muster into my words as possible, "I am sure of. I know how I feel about you. You're the only thing I'm certain about at the moment."

He exhaled shakily and reached out and took my hand. "And?"

"But who am I? How do I identify? What changed? Why now?" The questions continued to spiral in my brain. "I'm such a fucking idiot. I prided myself on being so fucking smart, knowing my goals, my plan, and now I'm beginning to question everything." I gripped Jayden's hand firmly, terrified he'd pull away.

"Hey." He squeezed my palm. "I'm sure of my feelings for you too." A gentle resolve caressed his words, and fuck if I didn't love him the more for it. "All those questions you have, I have too." I nodded like an idiot, feeling like a bigger dickhead that I was the one having a meltdown while Jayden was here carrying me. "Hell, Sutton. I don't know any real answers to any of your questions. All I know is everything I feel for you is right. I know it and trust in it."

His words were like a sucker punch to my gut. Why the fuck couldn't I trust in it like he did? What was with the overanalysis?

"Listen, we're different. Our brains work differently," he said, the slightest edge of amusement creeping into his tone. "I'm the dumb jock who just goes with the flow, remember?"

"You're *not* a dumb jock," I said vehemently, hating when he joked about shit like that.

A look of satisfaction lit his face at my words, and I couldn't resist the smile that pulled at my lips when he was genuinely happy. "But you use your brain differently to me, and you wanna know what I think?"

"Always."

Jayden chuckled. "That right? I'll remind you of that answer sometime. But I think we should go, do this coaching thing. It sounds pretty awesome. Plus, you know, maybe it'll help you too. Everyone knows that what we have is new, only coming out. Though…" He tilted his head. "…we haven't actually officially confirmed anything yet."

I shook my head. "Not officially."

He huffed out a chuckle. "Those are big assumptions people are making then, right?"

"It means we could take it back." The words were out of my mouth before thinking. I regretted them immediately, even before seeing the look on his face.

That wasn't hurt staring back at me. No. Jayden was fucking livid.

"I didn't mean it," I rushed to say. "I don't want to change anything between us."

He narrowed his eyes. "If I didn't like them so much, I'd totally punch you in the nuts right now."

I nodded quickly, trying to keep a straight face. "And I'd totally deserve it."

"Damn straight you do, asshole." He gave me the evil eye for another second before smoothing out his features. "So, what do you think? You're not a fraud. It doesn't matter that we've been together for a hot second. It's no one else's business when our relationship actually started."

"And our engagement?" I asked curiously.

He waved off my comment. "We're in no rush, despite what either of our parents think." He rolled his eyes at that. The more he spoke, the more I calmed, and I thought he was probably right.

Spending time coaching college kids would be fun anyway. Adding in the outreach program and educating kids, trying to break down the hatred and bullshit surrounding homophobia would be incredible to be a part of.

And just maybe, being in such an environment would actually help.

Lifting Jayden's hand, I pressed a kiss to his wrist, smiling when I heard the hitch in his breath. "Okay, let's do this."

CHAPTER 13
JAYDEN

I HADN'T EXPECTED TO BE SO EXCITED ABOUT HEADING to the academy. But over the past few days, as Sutton and I organized ourselves, each step hadn't been a drag.

Sutton had been feeling more upbeat the past twenty-four hours, but it was harder work than I thought either of us expected it to be.

He was nervous. I got it. What neither of us anticipated was these role reversals of support. Sure, we both supported each other, but Sutton, being the caretaker he was, was so used to taking control and taking care of everyone and never needing anyone to step in to actually care for him.

Uncertainty had bounced around his gaze and almost every decision he'd made. It meant he sought out my support and wanted me to lead the way. After our initial surprise, I jumped all over the task.

Looking after Sutton? Heck yes, I was so up for it. Perhaps I exhausted him in the process with my overabundance of enthusiasm, but by his soft smiles and the way we wrapped ourselves up in each other whenever we could, he was taking it in his stride.

Something else we'd discussed was involving Pearce. Neither of us wanted to leave him in the lurch. We'd gone from a quick chat during practice or after a game with the man last season to speaking to each other on the phone at least three times a week.

He was fun. A little eager, maybe a little too much like me from what I knew about him, but he was easy to get along with.

I glanced over at Pearce as we stepped into the staff quarters. "You doing all right over there, Malcolm?"

He shot me a grin, and if he was nervous, it didn't show. "Sure am." He looked at the piece of paper in his hand. "Number fourteen. This is me." Pearce indicated toward the door of the room he'd been assigned to over the next six weeks.

When I'd spoken to Coach Jenkins, asking him if Pearce could be involved, he jumped at the chance. Understandable since the guy had been a first draft pick and was only three years into being in the

League. He was a hot commodity. Honestly, I wasn't quite sure how the Eagles had managed to keep their hands on him. I didn't expect he'd stay for long, though. Not based on his skills on the court.

Being young meant that joining the academy for a guest spot was a pretty rare and big deal. Young hotshots at the top of their game, earning the sort of cash they were, didn't seem to want to give back so much to the athletic community.

Traditionally off-season was all about blowing off steam. I totally understood that and had lived it. And peeking into Pearce's single room, it was clear that this wasn't a five-star hotel.

There was a shared kitchen for the staff and lounge and eating area. Honestly, at this point, I was just relieved we'd been promised a double room, and all came with en suites.

"See you in an hour," I said once he'd dumped his bag on the bed.

He looked over at us and nodded. "Sounds good."

Sutton and I carried on until we found our room. We unlocked the door and stepped into the space.

It was bigger than I'd expected, and thank Christ, there was a full-size bed. I muttered as much.

"I suppose they have to accommodate the above-average man."

I kicked the door closed and turned toward him, grinning. "I am totally up for accommodating an above-average man." I stepped into his space and wrapped my arms around his waist, rubbing up him to hit my point home.

Quirking a brow, he held on to me. "That right?"

"Have you not been making notes on my exceptional skills when sucking you off?"

"Exceptional?"

"The best you've ever had."

"That right?"

I narrowed my eyes. "You blew your load in under three minutes yesterday, so damn straight I'm claiming that title."

"You want a badge?" he sassed, eyes lit up with amusement.

"Fuck no. I want a trophy. 'Number One Cock Sucker.'"

His laughter was loud and abrupt. "Really, that's what you want on your trophy?"

I scrunched my nose. "Maybe I didn't think this through. Okay, maybe somehow make it clear that it's only your cock I suck, and I'm fucking awesome at it."

Humor sparkled in his gaze. "How about you leave it with me, and I'll see what I can do?"

"Sweet," I said happily, following up with a

smack of a kiss to his lips. Pulling back, I took a good look at him.

After the initial agreement to come here, post-mini meltdown, Sutton had been clearly trying to take control of his emotions and his reaction to our relationship. No word of a lie, I'd been freaked the fuck out myself at his reaction, agreeing wholeheartedly that if I had to put money on who'd be losing it, hands down, I would have bet on myself.

In the days following, he'd been calmer, and we'd talked more. He'd also had a proper conversation with his parents since being back on American soil. While I wasn't sure of every word exchanged, he'd ended the call a little happier, his shoulders less tense.

Having the focus on Pearce as well was a good thing.

While I didn't want Sutton to sweep aside his feelings, having something or someone else to focus on helped him. Admittedly, Pearce being here was also for that reason as far as I was concerned. Not that I'd admit that to anyone.

"You glad you're here?" I asked.

With his gaze on mine, he remained quiet for a beat, clearly thinking through his response. My chest warmed up that he took such good care trying to make sure he gave me his truth. "Yeah. It feels right to be here."

"I think so too. Shall we check out the shower? Get the stink of the flight off us before we head to the meeting?"

Heat flooded his gaze, and I barely held back from squirming from the need that one look shot through me. "Seeing you naked is one of my favorite things."

"One?" I asked, not giving a shit at the gruff desire in my tone. Sutton seeing me desperate and how much I wanted him would never be an issue.

"One of many involving you."

I grinned and eased back, tugging off my T-shirt. "Let's see how many other of your favorites we can tick off in the next forty-five minutes." I waggled my brows, grabbed his shirt, and got lost in his heat and touch.

***

"No fucking way," I said, far too loudly for my words to be subtle. "Milo Henderson is here."

There was nothing quite like stumbling upon your unicorn basketball player. Add in that Milo Henderson was a fucking legend, *and* he was a guest coach, and I was close to hyperventilating.

"Oh fuck."

"Huh?" I angled toward Sutton, who was shaking his head and pressing his lips together.

"No pissing yourself, humping his leg, offering to be his ball boy—"

"You know, they all sound seriously sexual. How did I not think of the hundreds of innuendoes I could have been having so much fun with?" Genuine disappointment colored my words.

"—no telling dad jokes"—I attempted to intervene at that. I *so* did not tell dad jokes. My jokes were freakin' spectacular. Sutton's raised brows stopped me as he didn't pause in his list of rules— "no asking him to demonstrate a spin jump sky hook—"

"Hey, now that surely will be something he'll be showing these college kids…" I trailed off, thinking.

"No way. You are not asking the guy for private lessons."

I pouted. He was no fun and took all of my awesome ideas away.

"Oh shit, and no asking him to sign your boxers," he tagged on quickly.

Pearce stood at our side, cracking up at our exchange. I rolled my eyes at him and refocused on Sutton. "Fine. For that, I'm totally introducing you to him as my fiancé. He probably won't even know who you are. Ooh, maybe we should practice, and we can start calling you Gale Moore."

Pearce snorted, and Sutton gaped.

"What?" I asked, oh so innocently. "Keep opening your mouth like that and I'll assume you want me to pop something inside."

"Oh hell, I'm out of here," Pearce said with a groan, quickly moving away from us and into the communal lounge.

While I wasn't sure how Sutton would respond, I didn't expect him to get all up in my business. "You want to introduce me as your fiancé and give me your name? You can go right ahead. It's not a hardship. In fact, it would make me so fucking proud." I gulped hard, heat sweeping through me at the intensity of his words and the emotion in his eyes. "And your cock in my mouth? I'm going to blow your fucking brains out later. Then we'll see if you contain yourself and not tell anyone who will listen just how fucking good I am with ball play."

He punctuated his words by a swift press of his lips against mine, just enough to leave his mark and my lips buzzing. Then the asshole smirked and walked away, leaving me breathless and with a giant boner.

I groaned, took a surreptitious look around, and adjusted myself.

That was one way to stop me from carrying on in front of Henderson. "Touché, asshole," I mumbled, my grin quickly following.

Once I moved into the room, I was introduced to Milo Henderson, the former All-Star player and MVP for four years in a row. Somehow I managed not to hump his leg or stare for too long.

At college, one wall may have been dedicated to posters of this man. There was no guarantee my cool could remain.

The additional two guest coaches were also former League players. Paul Carton had retired three years back with an impressive score average after twelve years playing pro. There was no shame in admitting his stats rivaled my own.

The final coach was Eddie Phelps. I grinned when I saw him, going in for a handshake and a bro-hug. "Eddie, hell, it's good to see you."

He smiled down at me as he pulled back. He was six-eight from memory and had always been a big, friendly guy. "Jay-bomb, I wasn't sure whether to believe Sid or not. Maybe questioned his sanity too."

"You and me both," I answered. "Damn, man, it's been what, five years?"

"Yeah, before you up and abandoned ship to head to Minnesota." His gaze flicked to Sutton, a smirk pulling at his mouth. "I always wondered why that was. A request for Minnesota of all places. Guess now we all know."

There was no denying it. Sutton had been the reason I'd requested Greg fight for a deal. We'd previously played on another team together before we'd parted ways. When I'd heard he was heading to Minnesota, I was all over that like white on rice.

It hadn't been a secret, to Sutton at least, that I'd made the move—legit begged, pleaded, and made deals—to make it happen. Maybe that should have been the lightbulb moment right then, shining on the rainbow flag that Sutton meant a lot to me.

More than was perhaps considered the norm in a friendship.

I bounced my brows up and down. "Can you blame me? Just look at the man." I flicked a glance at Sutton, whose cheeks had turned pink. His eyes were focused elsewhere, clearly trying to avoid being part of the conversation.

"I'll take your word for it. All I know is he can play ball," Eddie said, appreciation in his tone.

"Damn straight he can."

Eddie glanced around, and I followed his movements, realizing everyone was ready to go for the informal meeting. "Looks like we're holding everyone up. I'll catch up with you later." He slapped me on the back and went and sat, and I headed directly to the comfy-looking sofa and the empty space next to Sutton.

I grinned at him when I sat. I didn't put my hand on his knee or anything like that, which I really wanted to do, at least attempting to stay professional, considering the company. Instead, I sidled up close to him, my arm and thigh flush with his.

Harry, who'd been sitting patiently waiting for us, started us off. "It's good to see you all here." He sent a bright smile around the group. "I've already updated the staff who've been here for the past couple of weeks, letting them know to expect you. Our LGBTQ program has been up and running since the start of the summer academy, so everyone's up to date with our mission statements. So this is a general meet, so you could at least know who the guest coaches are."

"That's right," Coach Jenkins added. "As well as you guys, and the addition of Harry this year, we also have two other full-time coaching staff. They're running drills with the students at the moment. We'll head out soon so you can meet them and the college players who are spending the summer with us. There's also our counselor who's been with us the past few years."

"He's great," Harry agreed. "He runs a weekly group session with the college kids and has a one-on-

one session with each player and staff member. We were lucky the man's already a specialist in LGBTQ+ and has worked with several queer-friendly projects."

Hearing that, I pushed into Sutton a little, certain this was what he needed. In my peripheral vision, I saw the slight up kick of his mouth. It was so tempting to lean in and kiss the smile of acknowledgment he gave me. I refocused on Harry, not sure I'd be able to resist if I got staring at my... man?! At that thought, I pinched my lips together. *That* sounded weird as fuck. So different from the last time I'd used it when he'd just been my friend.

"—available for other appointments. The counselor has an open-door policy." Harry finished, glancing around the space, appearing completely at ease. I was impressed. In the midst of six giants and Coach Jenkins, who could squash a player should they be fucking around, the man held his own, effortlessly so.

He was probably two or maybe even four inches shorter than six foot and had a rounded face that looked almost boyish, but I was sure he was about my age. His eyes were bright and kind, though, and it was kinda awesome how enthused he was.

"Since Eddie, Paul, and Milo are familiar faces here and know the drill, we're going to pair the three of you up with one of them." I perked up at this information from Coach. If he said I was with Milo, I would likely pee my pants. "Malcolm, you're with Paul. Sutton with Milo, and Moore, you're with Eddie."

I narrowed my eyes and turned my head slowly toward the man at my side, whose shoulder vibrated ever so slightly. Sutton turned to me and grinned. "Fucker," I mumbled, and he pressed his lips together, gaze alight with amusement.

"Eddie, Paul, and Milo all have at least two years' experience of working with the academy, so they'll show you the ropes. Questions?" He barely waited two seconds before saying, "Great. Let's go meet the other coaches and the players you're going to be working with. And a heads-up, they have no idea you're joining them." Humor buoyed his words, and I couldn't help but grin.

Hell, when I was nineteen, and if I'd had the opportunity to meet more pro players, let alone be coached by them, my mind would have been blown.

We all stood and followed Coach.

Montview had an incredible reputation, and the grounds were impressive. Between a couple of gyms, a lap pool, and what looked to be high-standard communal spaces, I understood why summer attendance was so competitive. It was expensive as shit, too, but there was also a 40 percent scholarship intake.

I loved that the opportunities on offer weren't limited to the wealthy. It made being here and having this opportunity even more fulfilling.

Angling to look at Sutton, who walked alongside Milo, deep in conversation, I smiled. Being here was the right move for him, for us. I hadn't lied a few days ago when I'd told him my head spun just as much as his. The difference was, I believed everything happened for a reason. I also trusted my heart—and my dick's reaction.

Both wanted the man. Both perked up whenever he was near, or I even thought about him.

Accepting that was as easy as shooting a hoop when I had all the time in the world.

"How's your hand healing?" Eddie asked from beside me.

"Good." I lifted the offending finger, still strapped. "I got another X-ray a couple of days ago, and the team's doc is pleased with how it's healing. If I wasn't going to be on the court here, he said I could take the strap off, but he wants me to keep it on for at least two weeks. Just as a reminder, if anything, while I'm here and working on drills and such." When the doc had told me, I'd been relieved as hell. A few basic physio tasks were also explained to me, which I could start working on next week.

"That's great. Did I read you've got a concussion too?"

I snorted. "You been reading the dodgy press?"

Eddie laughed. "Well, between your car crash and you and Sutton, it's been pretty hard to avoid it."

"True that. I've been avoiding it all like the plague, but yeah, each day it's getting better. Not sure how I'm going to go on the court, though. Sometimes a headache will hit out of nowhere, and occasionally it'll make me dizzy. The doc wasn't too worried. I just need not go all gung ho for a while, but I need to pick up my fitness. A few weeks in Australia and eating barbecue like it's going out of fashion is going to catch up on me."

"Ha. I hear you. Try being retired. Don't get me wrong, it's great not having to calorie count, but it's hard not to just let myself go."

I eyed him. "I don't think you have anything to worry about." The man was in shape. While he only had a few years on me, I wouldn't complain if I had his physique a few years after retirement.

His grin was broad. "Careful, not sure how much Sutton appreciates you eyeing me up."

I snorted. As if Sutton would think that. I rolled my eyes, gaze landing on my... boyfriend's. Nah, that still didn't sound right. I startled at the intensity of the stare being sent my way. Of course I grinned. I was an asshole like that.

At my side, Eddie laughed, shaking his head. Meanwhile, I shot Sutton a wink and blew him a kiss. It had the desired effect. He rolled his eyes at me and returned his focus to Milo. I didn't miss the slight twitch of his lips.

Sutton, jealous? That shouldn't give me so much pleasure, but I'd be lying out of my ass if I didn't admit that him being a little green-eyed didn't make my dick twitch.

"Gentlemen," Coach called to the players with a loud clap of his hands when we entered the court. It was full-sized with capacity for maybe four hundred spectators. "Take a seat, and let me introduce you to a few guys who've stopped by to help us all out."

CHAPTER 14
SUTTON

Out of the twenty college players, I recognized at least thirteen of them from the occasional college game I caught on TV. The seven I didn't know much about, I was interested to see their skill on the court.

Montview's admission was fiercely competitive. It had been when I'd been at college, with only one player on my college team being offered a place.

A buzz of excitement hummed to life at being involved in supporting these young players.

I loved the game, always had, and while I wanted to move on to a position where I could put my degree to good use, there was something incredible about being here on this court.

High energy vibrated around the room as Coach spoke, and all twenty guys' gazes drifted over the three new coaches. Taking in some wide eyes, a few whispers, and a couple of double takes, I could admit to myself that this was a heady feeling.

Sure, every time I was on the court, the rush was indescribable. Being here with players who were on the cusp of greatness, striving for their own kick-ass careers in the League, though, was something special.

After Coach did the intros, he split the group into teams, directing them to have ten-minute games. It allowed us to sit and watch the players perform.

While I knew our invite was based on my relationship status with Jayden, and hopefully being here would cut through any tension or uncertainty for queer, gay, or bi players, I wanted to get out on the court and prime their existing skills.

"Damn, Holland's got some talent," Jayden said at my side. Everyone in earshot nodded.

The kid was fast.

"Jimmy Lindt," one of the full-time coaches we hadn't met yet said, introducing himself and passing out some paperwork. "Here's some basic stats on the players for you to look over."

Immediately, I dug in, keeping half an eye on the court and the other skimming over the twenty names, their stats, and basic details. The Holland kid was just nineteen. But his age didn't hold him back against some of the guys who had a couple of years on him.

"The players here this year are a good bunch," Jimmy carried on, taking a seat in the middle of us. "There's been the usual sort of dick-measuring going on, but after two weeks, it's clear some are moving on and no longer feel the need."

I bobbed my head, still half listening as he continued to give us more of a breakdown. Eddie, Paul, and Milo pitched in, giving their two cents on their observations of the players.

You could discover a lot about a player in a couple of training sessions and games. A whole two weeks of intensive strategy, and that knowledge moved to building an understanding of the person, rather than just the player.

I cast a sneaky look to Jayden. Since he caught my smile and winked, my attempt to be stealthy failed. But that was okay. I sent him a warm smile, remembering the first time we'd played off on the court during camp as kids.

He'd been cocky and fun, sure of himself.

The first time I'd really noticed, though, was when he'd screwed up a pass. It had been an amateur move, and he was ribbed for it by other players. I'd been expecting him to kick off or maybe even be embarrassed. Instead, fourteen-year-old Jayden had surprised the hell out of me by smiling, rolling his eyes at himself, admitting his screwup before he went on to legit saying out loud where he screwed up and what he should have done to get it right.

Not long after that, he'd winked right at me and gone ahead and played ball.

The group played for a while longer before Coach pulled them up. We all rose and headed to the court. Once there, Coach split them up into three groups, and Milo—thank Christ—took the lead and led them to the far right of the court, me in tow, curious about Milo's style and plans while questioning what the hell I'd been thinking by agreeing to this.

I stood by, hoping I didn't show my growing nerves. Heck, half an hour ago, I'd been keen. Now, with seven college kids staring at me, a mixture of curiosity and uncertainty on their features, I hoped to hell I didn't screw this up.

The group hunkered down as Milo started picking apart their moves, intermittently offering praise, then following up with a reflection exercise asking for one thing they did well and one thing they needed to focus on.

I half expected eye rolls and sneers at such an exercise, but either Milo had already whipped out that reaction, or they were simply good kids. Well, young men, since I knew a couple were twenty-one.

Reflective practice was essential in this sport, though. It was the only way to improve your game and excel.

"Jacobs," Milo continued, "you need to be upping your focus in zone defense." Jacobs winced a little at that, which I understood. So often defenders were focused on one-on-one, but it didn't mean players shouldn't know how to defend a zone properly. "Sutton, what do you think?"

I nodded, checking, "Jacobs, right?" The dark-haired player nodded in response. "Zone defense is a great way to slow the game down. Use it to your advantage. Let it give you and your team the time needed to take control of the game and the play's tempo." I cast a quick glance at Milo, who stood back, arms crossed, smiling and nodding in agreement.

"Remember, no layups in zone defense. Plus, talk to each other. At this stage, you're not mind readers. Sure, when you've played for a while together, there'll be some of your teammates you gel with, can read from a simple look or read of their play, their body language," I explained.

"Like you and Moore, right, Coach Sutton?"

Immediately alert, I flipped my attention to the redheaded kid who'd seemed too gangly to be a player. But since I'd seen him on the court, that impression didn't hold. When my gaze snagged his, I'd expected cockiness to be staring back at me. Instead, curiosity filled his features, and there was no sass or derision in his tone.

"Yeah," I finally answered, keeping my tone neutral and focusing on Moore my teammate, rather than Jayden my... fake fiancé? "On the court, we don't need to share a word most of the time. We got to that point by hours of practice, of studying replays—"

"—of hooking up," a wiseass said alongside a ridiculous cough.

"Murphy." Milo stepped in immediately. "Pipe down unless you want you and your team to run laps until you collapse."

Murphy, a guy who was quick on his feet, simply grinned, hands held up in a defensive gesture. "No disrespect, Coach Sutton," he said, eyes bright with amusement. "Just pointing out that being... uhm... friendly off the court has to mean you can read each other on a whole other level, right?"

I glanced around the small group. All of their attention was on me.

The need to deflect niggled at me, but then I remembered one of the reasons why we were here. Why we'd been invited.

The only way to cut through the bullshit and

negativity surrounding queer players was to tackle this head-on.

When Milo spoke up again, I smiled over at him. "It's okay, Coach. I can field this and any other *reasonable* questions," I emphasized for good measure. Heck, I didn't want a complete free-for-all. Nor did I want my private life to be at the center of gossip.

Taking a discreet, calming breath, I channeled the version of myself that could handle this and any other shit that came my way. Hell, I was an African-American man with a good sprinkling of Polish in me brought up in a working-class neighborhood. The amount of bigotry and prejudice I'd challenged and tackled over the years had been too numerous to count.

Why the hell not add in a queer label to that list for good measure? Somehow I held back my snort and focused on the young guys before me.

"Murphy's right. Connecting with your team-mates can improve your game twofold. You have to build mutual trust and respect. That's not always easy, especially if you have a few mouthy players on the team who don't know when to shut up." I quirked a brow and followed up with a smile to soften the blow. Murphy and the rest of the group snorted out laughs. "Having a player in your team who's not gelling for some reason can hurt a team's mindset, their morale. Playing pro is so much more than you being a kick-ass player, and as clichéd as it sounds about there being no I in team…" I rolled my eyes and chuckled. "I know, I know, I said it was clichéd, but it doesn't make it any less true. If there's upset in the team, it can mess up all plays."

Taking in the group, I hoped I wasn't screwing this up. At least they were listening or at least pretending to. But shit was about to get seriously real. For me anyway. It was kind of empowering that not a single person in this group would understand the significance of the words I was about to say either.

"Dissention in the group can spark from such minor things, like not leaving the emotions of a pointless argument in the locker room. Heck, it can be nothing to do with the team. Maybe you've had an argument with your parents, your girlfriend, your boyfriend," I added for good measure, "and rather than sharing that and talking it out, you bottle it up, take it on the court, and end up screwing your team over.

"Then of course there are the bigger things. Perhaps bullshit you've read in the press. Maybe it's one or two of your teammates identify as LGBTQ+, are queer, like me, and it throws you off your game because of some preconceived opinion of what that looks like or means."

Each pair of eyes in the group was a hundred percent focused this time. I pushed ahead, refusing to waver. "I can tell you all right now, sexuality, faith, race, none of it matters on the court. Ever. On the court, you're players, a team. And off the court, I can only hope you're all educated, decent human beings."

My words were met with silence. Ignoring the golf-ball-sized lump in my throat, I focused on keeping my breathing steady and shoulders relaxed. I then looked at Milo. A soft smile formed on his mouth, directed my way. He nodded once, winked, and turned back to the group.

"Right," Milo said, garnering the players' attention and thankfully removing their intense stares from me. "You all have your one area of focus. Form pairs and one three and get your asses moving. You've got thirty minutes to prove you don't want to be staying till midnight tonight working plays."

When no one moved immediately, Milo looked to the ceiling and raised his hands in the air. "Sweet Jesus, Coach Sutton asked for educated, but all you gave me were these guys."

My mouth twitched, appreciating the giant

change in subject and the break in tension. My thundering heartbeat began to steady out a little.

With one look at the sitting team, complete with raised brows and a scowl, Milo's expression did the trick. All seven guys were off their asses and racing to the court.

"What do you think?" he then said, moving to my side as we watched the group sort themselves and work on drills.

"About?" I asked.

"Think they've got what it takes?"

"Maybe ask me again in a month."

Milo snorted. "Right. You should have seen them two weeks ago. And these guys are the cream of the crop. I swear, have you seen Parker, number fifteen, in a game?"

I nodded. I'd watched him a few times when I took in a televised game. "The kid was impressive."

"Yeah, that's what I thought, but who the hell knows what happened between those games and them getting their asses here. The first week was a shit show. My elderly grandmother could have wiped the floor with them."

I chuckled.

"I'm serious. Be grateful you missed out."

"In that case, I definitely am."

We stayed on the sidelines watching the practice, exchanging a few observations along the way.

"It's good you're here," Milo said after a few moments of quiet.

Confused, I angled a look at him.

"What you said to them was important. They all need to hear it. I hope you got that shit memorized."

A little embarrassed, I cleared my throat. "Well, it wasn't really rehearsed. It just seemed like the right time to start, you know?"

"I think it was better for it. That it wasn't a prepared speech. These kids are still in the thick of an environment filled with lectures at college. It's important they don't get that here. Sure, we're coaches here, professionals, so there's a clear division, but sharing our truths without the aid of a PowerPoint presentation means a hell of a lot more to them."

My tentative smile grew, relieved I'd followed my gut. "Thanks." I hesitated before saying, "This, everything is all so new…." When I trailed off, he side-eyed me and bobbed his head, letting me know he was listening. "I don't like screwing up at the best of times, but especially not this." Whether he knew I was talking about Jayden and the coaching position, I didn't know. It didn't really matter either; it applied to both.

Thinking about Jayden, my gaze sought him out. It didn't take long to find him, and when I did, I groaned.

The asshole was dribbling the ball and dashing around the place like he wasn't still dealing with a concussion. I wasn't concerned about his hand since he was limiting his moves to his uninjured right one, but bouncing around like that, he'd end up with a killer of a headache.

At my side, Milo chuckled. "From your reaction, I'm going to assume he shouldn't be doing that."

"The word 'shouldn't' seems to mean something very different to Jayden." I rolled my eyes. "He's not meant to be doing anything super physical for another week at least."

"He's like one of those Energizer bunnies."

"As annoying as one too," I shot out, lips curving into a grin, because as much as I wanted to shake Jayden and get him to rest, I loved watching the man on the court.

He moved fluidly, almost gracefully. But in total juxtaposition, he had a raw, effortless strength. Every time he pressed on the balls on his feet or feinted a shift or a pass, control radiated from him. The ball became an extension of his hands.

He was fucking beautiful.

"Not bad for a guy with a broken bone and a concussion," Milo said from my side.

I shook my head. "He's fucking magnificent." As soon as the words were out of my mouth, heat enflamed my cheeks. I cleared my throat, mortified. "Uhm, so, what about those Maple Leafs? You catch yesterday's game?" I cringed. I was so damn lame.

Milo clapped me on the shoulder, his chuckle hearty and loud, catching the attention of several pairs of eyes. "I can't say that I did, but if the game was *magnificent*, feel free to tell me all about it."

He continued to laugh through my groans, which soon turned into a smirk.

This coaching gig wasn't too bad at all, and after I told Jayden that Milo had become my new best pal, it'd top off the first day spectacularly.

CHAPTER 15
JAYDEN

For two hours I managed to ignore the increasing pounding in my head. As we crept closer to the third hour, I was toast. My vision became more blurry, and if I didn't get my head down in the next ten minutes, I expected to crash where I stood.

"Coach Moore."

I squinted against the harsh light as I looked up, trying to focus on the speaker of the voice.

"Jay-bomb." A hand on my elbow accompanied my name. "You don't look so great."

My vision swam, ears ringing, vying for my attention alongside the heavy thump behind my eyes. I heard mumbling, shuffling, and was mildly aware of concern in the tones around me.

I wanted to speak. Let Eddie know I'd be fine

after sleep and some painkillers, but the thought of hearing my own voice made me hold my tongue.

And then a warm arm wrapped around my waist. Comfort, heat, and a scent that registered through the painful fog clogging my brain.

"I've got you, Jay. Eddie's just going to help me get you to our room."

I tried to smile, tried to let Sutton know him looking out for me made my heart happy, managing to cut through the stabbing jolts determined to bring me to my knees.

But screw that.

We were only two days into our coaching gig. There wasn't a chance I'd buckle and let the shitfest in my brain break me. Sutton knew that. He'd know being in pain was one thing I could just about handle in public, but on my back or on my knees, no fucking way.

With no idea how long it took us to get to our room, I focused on putting one foot in front of the other. Sweat trickled down my spine, and I was vaguely aware of the quiet, tight voices on either side of me.

Then I was on the mattress, my sneakers being tugged off, Sutton taking care of me in that assured way of his.

"Take these, baby." Five tablets appeared in my

hand. I didn't need to see to know which ones they were.

I attempted a smile and a whispered "Thanks" before swallowing them down with the cool water he offered up. A niggle on the edges of my mind latched on to his sweetness. Before I could think more, I melted into the mattress and the soft touch of his fingers against my skin.

"Let me just talk to Eddie." He followed up with a kiss on my temple, and legit tucked me in as I settled under the sheets, grateful that my head was finally touching the soft pillow.

Soft voices drifted in and out of my consciousness. The sound of a door closing, another opening. A dip in the bed. Something cool against my neck, making me sigh.

A touch of a tender kiss against my head.

Shuffling sheets and a warm embrace. Safety and comfort.

Each sound and movement intermittently reached me. Each one soothed me, helping the pounding ease and the loudness of my breaths plateau to gentle wisps.

I had no idea how long I slept. A warm body pressed against me, and that was all I cared about. And maybe the fact I could string more than a few thoughts together without my brain cracking open felt pretty much like magic too.

I prized an eye open. Just one, to test the light.

When I managed without burrowing deep under the covers, I lifted the second lid, blinking a few times to get my bearings.

Sunlight flooded the room.

I thought back to what time my head had finally told me who was boss. It had maybe been three or four in the afternoon. Since it was summer and dusk didn't change the color of the sky until at least seven thirty, it could be dinnertime. Either that or I'd slept right through and it was morning.

A sliver of frustration crept to the surface, hoping the latter wasn't the case. The knowledge of not surviving a day on the court, and not even training or playing, but doing a tenth of the physical activity I usually did, sat heavily on my chest.

Logically I was aware concussions impacted everyone differently. But I was what, about four weeks or so in, and my brain and body had shut down after a morning giving instructions and after lunch organizing a few drills and doing a few basic demos? No way could that be happening.

Not to me.

I was Jayden fucking Moore, and sitting still for so long made me itchy.

I had to fight this, push through it.

A simple smack of my head against a car window was not going to screw me over.

A flush of heat swept over me so fast, I struggled to breathe. I threw the covers off and swung my legs out of bed, sitting up.

What if this continued? What if the bang had knocked something loose?

What if I couldn't play again?

I jumped out of bed, refused to acknowledge how I staggered a little, and all but charged to the bathroom. Having just enough sense to tug off my tee and shorts, I stepped into the shower, throwing on the tap as I entered.

Cool water beat down at me. I gasped, taking a shuddering breath. I closed my eyes, trying not to fall down the well of what-ifs, too terrified that by doing so, my panicked thoughts would come true.

The sound of the shower door opening reached me. I jerked open my eyes, gaze immediately landing on Sutton's face. His smile slipped, worry bleeding into his expression.

Without saying a word, he stripped, stepped into my space, and wrapped me up in his arms. I went willingly, indulging in his strength, his calm, and mumbling, "Tag, I'm it."

His low snort was an attempt at amusement, but

neither of us believed it. Sutton held me tightly, saying, "I'm happy to take one for the team and for you to pass the tag back."

Gratitude for this man flowed over me, pulling a smile from where it was buried below my self-pity. I dotted a kiss on his neck and angled away to see his face. After reading my expression, his knotted brows eased a little.

"I don't mind holding the mantle for a while. Just as long as we take it in turns with hurting."

Immediately, concern flooded his features. "Hurting as in…?"

I rolled my eyes at myself, forcing out a chuckle. "Nothing. Just my head. I'm getting tired of migraines and dizziness, is all." While we'd attempted to tease each other, with Sutton's feelings still unresolved, there was no way I was adding to his burden. He already worried about my concussion. If I laid another load on his shoulders about my fear of not healing right and it impacting my career…. No way was I sharing my bullshit fears.

I'd be fine. It had only been a few weeks, which meant that I needed to suck it up and just take each day as it came, pushing myself a little at a time.

I totally had this.

"I'm feeling much better today," I offered. Maybe

it was because I was telling the truth that he finally relaxed in my hold this time.

"That's great," he responded. I was grateful he didn't question me, asking if I was sure. When people did that, it irritated the heck out of me. Though I was guilty of pushing myself on more than one occasion. "I was worried. You missed dinner last night."

My brows shot high. I hadn't even bothered looking at the time before stumbling into the shower. Just then, my stomach grumbled, obviously hearing the mention of food and letting me know it needed filling.

"No wonder my stomach's caving in."

Strong fingers brushed against my stomach. Goose bumps rose, and my stomach clenched at Sutton's touch. "I can't feel any hollowness there."

I simply nodded, tugging my bottom lip into my mouth and not so subtly encouraging him to keep touching with a thrust of my hips. "Perhaps you need to take a better look." I quirked my brow at him in challenge, thinking back to the spectacular blow job we'd ended with our first night here.

Fuck, was that really only a couple of nights ago?

Sutton trailed his fingers up my stomach, toward my chest, totally in the wrong direction. When my stomach growled, loud enough that it almost shook the shower walls, he paused, wide-eyed and chuckling.

"You need food."

"I need my cock in your mouth."

He smirked, but rather than dropping to his knees, he kissed me gently and stepped away, opening the cubicle door.

"Seriously?" I groaned, attempting a sulky pout that simply had him laughing.

"Yep. Food. If you wait any longer, your migraine will come back." He passed me a towel and started drying off.

"You know you're an asshole when you're right," I grumbled, toweling myself down.

"Wow, so you're saying I spend 99.9 percent of my time being an asshole?" He raised both brows and gave me an amused, pointed look.

"As if."

"Uh-huh."

I flicked the towel at his perfect ass when he turned to leave. He jumped and grunted, flipped me off, and headed to get dressed.

My traitorous stomach doubled its efforts. *Fine*, I thought. When my stomach was cock blocking me, I reluctantly listened.

We got ready, had breakfast, reassured the team I

was okay and wouldn't push it so hard today, and then we finally got to work.

Despite how yesterday afternoon had turned out, I was having a blast.

There were some cocky assholes on the court, which was how I'd got a little too involved and enthused yesterday. But sometimes, a twenty-year-old hotshot who thought he was all that needed taking down a peg or two.

Thank Christ I'd managed that and hadn't had a spell on the court when showing Lincoln how the pros did it and that he definitely wasn't the king of the court. But I'd suffered the consequences because of it. I ignored the taunting voice in my head that mumbled something about keeping my own ego in check.

I spent the morning with Eddie and a group of the guys, giving directions, running drills and plays. After a short break, we gathered, and the guys played a few games. My cell vibrated just as we were about to start a new set of drills, and I tugged it out. Greg was calling.

Giving my apologies to Eddie, I stepped out of range and climbed a few steps before taking a seat and answering. "Hey, Greg."

"Jayden, how are things? You settling in?"

I smiled. "Absolutely. There's a really good bunch

of guys here. Facilities are great. Everything okay over there?"

"Yeah, just thought I'd give you an update on the Axle thing."

"You get a chance to speak to Marshall?" Ken Marshall was my lawyer, with a reputation for being a shark. He was worth every penny of his crazy fees.

"Sure did. Unfortunately, your contract is iron-clad. Axle is perfectly in their rights to cancel and—"

"You're shittin' me. How is that—"

"Jayden, just let me finish, yeah?"

I sighed and stretched out my legs. "Sorry, yeah, go on."

"So their contract is airtight, and it was just shit timing it was at renewal time. But, backing out of the verbal deal just as you came out is clearly bad form and raises all manner of questions. Marshall jumped all over that, and while there's no chance of them offering you a new contract—"

"I don't want one with them."

He sighed at my outburst. "—they have agreed to a five-year contract directly with the charity, agreeing to a 6 percent donation over the five years."

Something loosened in my chest. "For real?"

"Yes. Marshall has spoken to the charities lawyer and managed to get all of that locked up tight."

I huffed out a relieved breath. "That's fucking awesome. Thanks, Greg."

"No worries. Just remind me never to get on the wrong side of Marshall," he said with a chuckle. "The man is a fiend with contract law."

"I really appreciate it, Greg."

"I've also started to look around for a couple of endorsements for you."

"Please make sure they're not assholes."

He snorted. "I'll try. I'm assuming you want to still look for a charity tie-in?"

"Definitely." One of my uncles was treated for testicular cancer seven years back, and knowing Bounce Your Balls still had funding was brilliant. Maybe it was time to refocus my effort. "Let me think about charities, okay?"

"Absolutely. I do have a couple of ideas. Obviously, we can go the LGBTQ+ route. I know there are so many great but underfunded charities around. Or we can focus on something closer to home and your mom. If that's too close for you, I can keep searching."

Contentment eased through me, so grateful for this life I had, the opportunities it gave me. "Thanks. I'll let you know."

"Sounds good. Have you guys thought any more about your official statement yet?"

I groaned.

"It's not that bad."

"I know," I agreed with a sigh. Obviously no one was aware that Sutton and I weren't technically engaged. It was the one thing still hanging over us. "Let's just get through this summer, okay. When we're back in the real world, we'll talk then."

Greg was silent for a beat, and I could just imagine how antsy he was about the whole thing.

"Okay. Have a great time and stay out of trouble, yeah?"

I snorted. "Do you not know me at all?" I teased.

"Yeah, that's what I'm afraid of. Speak soon, Jayden."

"Bye." I ended the call, ecstatic that the whole Axle bullshit was over and wasn't a complete bust. Smiling, I headed back to the court to carry on with the drills. It wouldn't be long till we stopped for lunch and I'd be able to update Sutton.

AFTER LUNCH, WE HEADED TO OUR FIRST STAFF counseling session.

With no idea what to expect but aware that Sutton was unusually quiet, I stayed glued to his side. I talked overtime and nonsense, trying to distract him and ease some tension. When that didn't work, I didn't even hesitate to take his hand in mine.

He angled his head, our gazes connecting, the smallest of smiles playing on his lips. Squeezing his hand, I watched as he loosened his tight muscles. Happy I'd reached out to him, I smiled, so relieved we were here together, doing this.

As far as I was concerned, I didn't need to understand the how or why.

Sutton was mine. That was all I needed to know. That it wasn't the same for him, that he wasn't having such an easy time accepting the how or the why wasn't ideal, but I expected it, truth be told.

Sutton was almost zen in his approach to life and his understanding of himself. The guy prided himself on being open and honest and so real in every avenue he followed. And this all being so new and unexpected, well, that could screw with a guy.

"So, Saturday's our day off," I started as we got closer to the room where we were meeting. "You thought about what you want to do?"

"Not sure yet. As long as we're hanging out, I'm good. It doesn't matter where we do that."

A zap of emotion hit me. It did whenever he said such things. I grinned at him. "You know, I never took you for a romantic."

The look he attempted didn't quite work. His

usual deadpan expression was wrecked by the twinkle in his eyes and the twitching of his lips. "Hanging out and doing literally whatever is romantic?"

I shrugged. "Maybe it's not beer and Twizzlers, which by the way also works when you want to get down and be *really* romantic," I said, "but just wanting to spend time with me is."

"But that's what we've been doing for how many years? Five or six when we've actually played for the same team?"

"And the four years at college when I totally made sure I was at the closest school possible."

His gaze softened, and he paused, Eddie almost running into us.

"Sorry," Sutton said quickly, tugging me closer to the wall so we were out of the way.

"What is it?" I asked, bemused.

Sutton's attention swiveled around the hallway. With no idea who or what he was looking for, I glanced around too but didn't see anyone. Once my focus returned, my breath caught, and I groaned when he slanted his mouth against mine.

The kiss was fast and possessive, full of need and so many unspoken words. When he pulled away, his pupils were blown, and I was panting, my cock hard, and seriously wondering if one of these doors led to a dark room.

Just as I intended to suggest we find out, Eddie called, "When you guys have finished necking, we're waiting to get started."

I grinned, my smile smug. "I'm just so hard to resist," I hollered back, latching on to Sutton's arm and heading toward the room. The other coaches had been incredible from the moment we joined the ranks. And I was so grateful it had been that way and we'd been surrounded with positive experiences. Of course, that was completely ignoring some of the ridiculousness on social media.

As we stepped into the room, I threw Sutton a wink and sought out Eddie to give him some more shit. "I can't help it that I'm irresistible. These lips have been known to change lives."

"I can testify to that," a smooth voice interrupted.

My brows shot high, and I searched the room and did a double take, my gaze landing on a man I hadn't seen for over ten years. *No way.* "Mark Lonsdale." Shock had me pausing before his words registered fully and the reality that my old college friend was here, in this room, hit me.

And looking at his name tag, he was the academy's counselor.

CHAPTER 16
SUTTON

Mark fucking Lonsdale. Life had to be messing with me.

The guy looked nothing like I remembered, not that I'd known him all that well. But with the tight hug and back slaps he gave Jayden, his bright eyes and flushed cheeks, my stomach bottomed out, and my chest tightened.

"I can't believe you're here." Jayden's voice was light and excited. "Man, it's been what, ten years?"

"Eleven."

That response right there had me moving my feet. "Mark," I said with a chin lift, forcing myself to offer a hand.

Jayden flipped a look at me, a grin on his face as he stepped away so Mark could shake my hand.

"Good to see you again." While I couldn't find it in me to smile, I kept my tone pleasant. Unaffected.

Yeah, that was totally me, dealing with an unhealthy shade of green for the first time in my life and freakin' the crap out.

He gripped my hand and gave me a friendly shake while I worked hard at not being a dickhead and squeezing tightly. I pulled away, calling myself all manner of names in my head.

I was not a prick. I was not this guy.

"You too," Mark answered, the same smile he'd given Jayden directed my way. Something eased a little at seeing it, and I attempted a slight curve of my lips. "How about we all catch up later? For now, we should get started."

I slowly exhaled, keeping the action light, controlled.

It took me only a couple of seconds to deduce he was the counselor. That meant he had to be a good guy, right? Sure, I was grasping, but if he was an asshole who liked hitting on other people's boyfriends, these guys wouldn't have offered him a job. Because of course that was part of the interview process.

I silently groaned and angled toward an empty chair, disliking how irrational I was being. Spotting two open seats, I headed that way, turned, sat, and changed my mind completely about Mark fucking Lonsdale when I caught him wink at Jayden.

The session started, Jayden at my side. Meanwhile, I could barely concentrate.

This was not how it was supposed to go.

Being here, agreeing to this gig was filled with good intentions for sure, but there was also the pull of using the time to figure things out. Part of that was embracing counseling in a safe environment, one that was mandatory so I wouldn't feel in the spotlight or singled out.

Nothing about this felt safe, and I wondered whether Mark knowing us would be some sort of conflict of interest, meaning our sessions, at least our one-on-one session, wouldn't be able to go ahead. Certain that was the case, I relaxed a little, shoulders losing some of their tension. And when I felt a soft touch at my neck, I angled to see Jayden reaching out and briefly touching me. Ease swept over me.

My smile was real, receiving one back immediately.

"—why you were interested in being part of the program. A reminder that in this space, we respect opinions, and we also request privacy. You can share as little or as much as you want."

Shit. Having not been fully paying attention, I'd missed at least five minutes of whatever Mark had been saying. But it sounded like I had to participate in some way.

Nerves leaped into my throat, something so unusual that my reaction had me sitting up straighter in my seat. Speaking in crowds had never been an issue. Nor had informal group sessions I'd led when back in college as part of my course.

Hell, I spoke on national TV regularly, had done so in packed stadiums, never once breaking into a sweat.

My reputation for keeping my shit together and being the epitome of reasonable while keeping my cool wasn't something I aspired to. It simply was.

Until now.

And I didn't like spiraling one single bit.

"I'll go first, as I can already see some squirming in seats." A few chuckles bounced around the small group of staff. "Yes, I know it's perhaps a different environment from what many of you are used to, but I promise no hard questions and no pressure. At the end of the day, we're here to support players who have a solid future going pro. *You* are the people with years' worth of experience. You know the highs and lows. We know they're here for the athletic program, the court time, to have the opportunity to play with past and current greats," he said, stroking a few egos while also speaking the truth.

He was right, though. It was the main reason we were here.

"But as you know, part of their time here is about developing skills off the court, arming impressionable young players with the skills necessary to not get lost in the League, its pressures, the demands it expects from you, especially in their private and personal lives. This is my fourth year of helping with the program," Mark continued, "and I keep coming back because I see the difference the program makes, see how impactful your support is, especially when you can offer your wisdom and share your experiences of staying grounded. Being real and not losing sight of the world around you or your futures."

He glanced around as he spoke, his tone friendly, calm. Those same bright eyes he'd greeted Jayden with stared back at us all. The guy appeared genuine and passionate, so much so, it cut through some of my nervous brain fog.

"As you already know, this year we've been approved to build in LGBTQ+ awareness. Since joining the team, I've fought for this and have had several successful years running similar programs and sessions. As a gay man, I have a vested interest in it. The aim is to expand awareness and understanding of sexual orientation, gender identity, and gender expression. With more and more athletes feeling safe enough to come out in sports that have a history of toxicity, we want to celebrate those moments while helping to change reactions, build acceptance, and honestly, cut through the toxic bullshit surrounding queer players."

The heavy thudding in my chest ached, the noise so loud it filled my ears. *This* was why we were here. It was what we agreed to. Blood rushed to my cheeks. Heat zipped across my skin, making a path to my hands, which started to sweat like crazy.

I was a fraud.

I'd thought it before and admitted as much to Jayden. He'd managed to talk me down. But here, now, it felt wrong, so fucking wrong that my head spun and I could barely see straight.

Heedless of the torrent of heat and loathing storming my body, Mark continued speaking, and I tried my hardest to listen. "While some of the awareness opportunities will be built into sessions like these with yourselves and the students, the aim is for you to be your authentic selves while you're here, building trusting relationships with the players. There's no prescriptive text about how you do that, what to say and do. That's not what this is about. It's more that you step in if you hear or see anything derogatory. You open up and respond to discussions in a way you feel comfortable."

"This year, yes, we have familiar faces as well as new ones, but you were all invited specifically to assist in raising LGBTQ+ awareness, something I'm so happy and excited to have you all on board for. Very quickly, and then I promise I'll stop droning on and we'll do a quick share..." Mark gave a self-deprecating chuckle.

The gesture drew my attention enough for me to take a breath. *Authentic self.* My mind played over those words. That was the problem right there. I thought I had been precisely that, always. I just wasn't sure what that looked like anymore.

With clarity came a much-needed calm.

I knew the problem, could verbalize it and analyze it to death. That also meant I could plan and problem solve and get some answers. I needed to know myself. Be sure I was the same person I had been before my heart had shifted and dick had woken up to just how hot my friend was and how perfect he was for me.

I wiped my hands on my shorts, popped my neck, and full-on stared at the man at my side. Not giving a damn that we were in the middle of a group session. *Him,* I was sure of.

At my movement, his concerned gaze turned my way, traveling over my face, reading me. A genuine smile pulled at my lips, and I reached over, took his hand, and brought it to my mouth, kissing it before settling our joined palms on my lap.

Wide-eyed and smiling, Jayden maintained eye contact longer than was appropriate, but I didn't give a shit. When a throat clearing and chuckles broke my focus, I dragged my attention away and peered around the group.

All eyes were on us. Friendly, amused, accepting.

I gave a sheepish grin. "Sorry. I got distracted."

Mark's lips twitched. "Understandable." I narrowed my gaze at him, and he snorted out a laugh. "I mean, understandable. You're newly out, being able to touch each other in public for the first time. It's *understandable* that you're taking the opportunity to do that whenever you can."

I gave a light shrug and a nod. Not quite an apology for thinking he was hitting on Jayden, but rather an acceptance of his words.

"Perhaps one of you can start us off with my original question. Why did you agree to join the program this year?"

While I'd known it was coming, my brain was still caught on my own epiphany. Was that something I could share here… in this group?

Jayden saved me from being the one to start, saying, "Honestly, being asked was unexpected. But it felt good, you know, especially considering the focus on me and Sutton." He squeezed my hand and cast me a small smile. His voice remained steady. "I thought it would be a chance to get away from the media attention," he admitted, receiving several nods, "and being here, with players, especially those who will be drafted over the next few years, it's a chance to, I don't know, dispel myths or something?"

My heart leaped at his explanation, filling with love and pounding hard at how incredible and articulate he was. The man tended to play the jock card and had disparaged his own intelligence on more than one occasion. It was all nonsense. He was one of the smartest people I knew. Smarts didn't always come in packages of super-high IQs or the highest grades. But he read and understood people. Could figure out what someone needed.

He always described me being the carer, the man who had his back. While I absolutely did, he gave it all back twofold.

"I thought it would be a good opportunity for the two of us." He cast another glance my way, gaze darting over my face. I gave his hand a squeeze, silently letting him know he was doing great. Turning his attention back to the group, he said, "Being together in public is new for us. We've got a lot to figure out. Then there's the team and playing together next season… so yeah, things to work out." He followed with a shrug, indicating he'd finished.

"That's great, Jayden. Thanks for sharing that. You all have different experiences in the spotlight, and with this new focus on you, not only being in a same-sex relationship but also teammates, it will undoubtedly take some navigating." Mark's smile was friendly. "And starting here to do that is a positive idea." His attention moved to me. "How about you, Sutton?"

I cleared my throat, projecting a calm that wasn't quite a lie. "You mentioned earlier about being our authentic selves." Nerves danced in my chest, threatening to catch in my throat. I focused on Jayden's hand in mine, energy, and support. I swallowed down the forming lump. I could do this. "Being here allows me to explore who I am. Maybe doing so openly with these younger guys witnessing that will give them insight into just one version of what that looks like. That even a guy of thirty-three doesn't have all the answers off the court, and that discovering things about yourself that perhaps you'd never even considered doesn't have to be terrifying."

I avoided moving in the intensity of the quiet room.

"Each of our experiences and situations are unique," Mark responded, his gaze flicking to me before darting around the rest of the group, seeking out eye contact. "It's so invaluable, sharing that with each other, especially in an arena where perhaps you're expected to keep everything bottled in. And," he continued, his focus returning to me, "new experiences, reactions, our thoughts can be terrifying and confusing. And that's okay too. It's recognizing that our strength comes in so many shapes and sizes. That there's no set rule about how to react to our own discoveries and journeys." Mark smiled. "Thanks for sharing, Sutton. It's really brilliant you're here."

Mark then looked around the room while I focused on processing his words and what I'd shared. Despite the tightness in my chest, I felt happier, a little less foggy. I begrudgingly admitted that Mark still seemed like a stand-up guy.

It didn't mean I liked the fact that he'd kissed Jayden, though.

Feeling Jayden's attention on me, I angled to look at him. His soft eyes, filled with warmth, latched onto my gaze. I tilted my head in question. In response, he rolled his eyes, flushed, and smirked. Now *that* was a look I was becoming more familiar with.

With a slow glance down his body, I took in the slight bulge in his shorts. He shifted his leg, trying to conceal what he was packing. My gaze snapped to his, a shit-eating smirk appearing on my face.

This time he narrowed his eyes at me. The look sent a rush of pleasure into my system. Did I love that he was turned on? Heck yes. I loved everything about this man.

I offered a careless shrug and deliberately darted my tongue across my mouth, earning me a scowl this turn. Grinning, I turned away from him, intent on listening to the rest of the team. They'd listened to me, heard my story; it was only right I offered them the same courtesy.

It was also a chance to wind the man at my side up. No way would I miss out on an opportunity to do that.

CHAPTER 17
JAYDEN

We left the meeting with a promise to catch up with Mark for dinner and headed straight for the gym. My arm brushed across Sutton's with every step. Maybe I should have been taking more time and the opportunity to get to know some of the other guys better, but after that whole share fest, I was feeling needy.

While my neediness wasn't anything new in the grand scheme of my friendship with Sutton, I'd sensed his vulnerability, his words hitting me hard before curling up and making a home in my heart. With that, my need had flipped a little. The desire to be with him, let him know unequivocally that I had his back zapped possessiveness in me I'd never felt before.

We were quiet as we maneuvered through the

corridors, the sound of conversation from the guys ahead and behind us. It was unusual for me to stay silent, embracing the moment. While Sutton had long bouts of being soundless—not from pulling away but from observing those around him—I was a certifiable talkaholic.

It wasn't that I necessarily felt uncomfortable in silence, rather I had shit to say, and I liked to share the bullshit on my mind, especially with Sutton, who, let's be real, had the patience of a saint.

"You're going to follow the directions of the coaches when at the gym, right?"

Sutton's question pulled my attention to him. "Yeah. After yesterday, I'm not going to push it." When he bobbed his head, I smirked. "You see, I can be sensible as shit."

"Can shit be sensible, though?" Pearce asked from behind.

At his side, Eddie snorted. "You've known Sutton, what, a couple of years?"

"Yeah, that's how long I've been with the Eagles."

"You'll soon learn Jay-bomb mixes his imagery and lives for alliteration."

I flipped Eddie off. "How many points is that, Sutton?"

He responded immediately. "Twenty."

"What's that?" Eddie asked.

Pearce answered first, saying, "They do this whole Scrabble word count thing. Or they did." He paused a beat. "Not so much last season. It was weird."

My gut clenched at the mention of last season and my and Sutton's distance. While it already felt like a lifetime ago, the year had been so epically awful, it had left a lasting impression.

"Why not last year?" Eddie asked.

I side-eyed Sutton, more than happy to take over. Seeing the discomfort on his features, I stepped in. "Well, you know that kiss?"

"You and Sutton when Ryan Broadwater came out?"

"Yeah," I answered Eddie, aware he had his own bi coming out story not long after retiring from the League. "Well, that kinda changed everything." A genuine grin crossed my mouth, impressed with myself that I'd told the absolute truth. This was the first time we were really answering the question about last year and potentially our secret love affair and subsequent engagement. The latter wasn't something I dared deal with yet, but only because I'd have way too much fun thinking of elaborate plans for our upcoming fake wedding. And then there was the whole proposal. I had so many ideas bobbing around for that story.

Sutton would threaten to kick my ass or maybe get me to sign a gag order or something if he got wind of the fabricated stories in my brain.

"The team already had a wager going before I joined." Pearce chuckled. "Apparently it had been going even before that kiss blew up the media."

"Yeah?" Eddie asked, glee in his voice.

"I still can't believe I never got wind of that," I sulked. I would have totally got involved. My thoughts froze. Heck, I would have lost, which would have been totally mortifying.

"It was popular too. A few grand all up by the time the reports came out."

I shook my head and noticed Sutton's mouth twitching. We could have really screwed that up for Pearce, who'd won, if we'd admitted the truth when I was in the hospital. "You do know that was all gossip, and nothing official was announced. What would you all have done if it had been bullshit?"

I glanced over my shoulder, and Pearce shrugged, his cheeks pink. His reaction made me pause. I wondered how he'd felt with all the betting going on? Pearce hadn't come out publicly yet. He'd already shared with us that his family knew and that he'd had a couple of boyfriends over the years. But we were the only people in the industry who knew.

A stab of sympathy hit me at what that must be like for him.

What had happened between Sutton and me was rare, I expected. I hadn't had years of being afraid, being in the closet. Hell, being ashamed, as I understood that was a far too familiar feeling. Instead, while my attraction and the depth of my emotions had come out of left field, I'd embraced them, hadn't hidden from them. That was who I was.

And I was so lucky that was the case.

I made a mental note to talk to Sutton and make a greater effort with Pearce, find out if he had a plan. The young forward didn't know it, but it was his bravery that had led to Sutton sharing his truth with me, and me opening myself up to the unknown.

We both owed him a lot.

"It's all good," I said with a smile, wanting to close the conversation down. I glanced at the gym door ahead. "If I pass out, no drawing dicks on my face or anything, okay?"

Eddie and Pearce snorted. Sutton didn't. Instead, his concern beat down at me. The man knew I could deflect like it was an Olympic sport.

THE TREADMILL WAS GOING THE SPEED OF AN INJURED snail that had been doused with salt. But after thirty minutes on the thing, I couldn't hear the music pumping out of the sound system anymore. Not with the loud beating of my heart in my ears.

A migraine hadn't brought me to my knees, which was a win. I had a feeling one wasn't far behind.

"Ten more minutes," Jimmy instructed, eyeing me carefully. Since the man apparently had a whole laundry list of experience with working with athletes post-concussion, I was willing to trust him.

He'd put me through my paces. I'd been concerned at first after the mountain of questions and the brief physical he'd pulled in the on-site doc to do. But Jimmy didn't seem to be holding back.

It did wonders for my headspace, if not my abs and ass that weren't quite as toned as they were a month ago.

"Hey, Sutton," I called out, trying to steady my breathing so I didn't come off as an unfit tub of lard.

He grunted at me from the weights bench where Antonio, the other full-time coach, was spotting him.

"You think you can bounce a quarter off my ass yet? It says here I've walked 1.8 miles. My glutes are feeling it."

The metal bar clanged as it hit the frame before

the sound of laughter erupted around the gym. Half of the college students were with us as part of their gym routine and "get to know the coaches" task. I expected from the way I'd been running my mouth off, they'd be forming an opinion about me real fast. Just the way I liked it.

"Jay-bomb," Eddie said with a snort of laughter. "Didn't we ascertain, what… seven years ago, that you were third in line for the greatest glutes?"

Pearce shot out, "Do we really wanna know?"

"It's all lies," I called out to anyone listening. "The contest was rigged. And my twenty-six-year-old ass wasn't in the glute-envy condition it's in now. Just ask Sutton."

"Don't bring me into whatever you're talking about," he said with a grunt, arms straight up in the air, weights bar steady.

"You see, even your boyfriend can't defend your ass." Eddie wiped his face with a cloth, throwing it in the laundry bin before moving to the rowing machine.

"Fiancé," Pearce corrected.

Eddie snorted. "Damn, Jay-bomb, even the man who's taking one for the team and getting you out of circulation won't defend your mediocre glutes."

"Whoa," I shouted. "Mediocre. I'll show you fucking medi—"

"Jayden, your pants stay on."

The patient voice coming from Sutton was laced with a kinda hot firmness. While everyone laughed their saggy asses off, my head totally stuck to the sexy firmness I'd heard in Sutton's voice.

"Damn," Pearce said, "I always wondered how you were able to keep Jayden in line. Now I know." He waggled his brows at me. The room erupted in more laughter, and Sutton just shook his head, carrying on with his reps.

"Patience of an angel," Eddie confirmed.

"I don't think there's anything angelic about Sutton," I defended breathily, not convinced it was the fast-paced walking that made it sound that way.

"Old guys getting it on…," Lincoln called out, grabbing my attention, "I think I need to bleach my ears and eyes out." His shudder was over-the-top and totally something I would have done. Okay, perhaps would still do. I examined him closely, seeing if some of the arrogance I'd witnessed yesterday had developed into more.

The guy grinned, though, his tone surprisingly light and filled with humor.

Happily biting, I hollered, "Old guys? Eddie, you're the closest. Give the toddler a pacifier to shut him up. Add a nut punch for good measure." I grinned at Lincoln, sending him a friendly chin lift.

"Okay, gentlemen, time to cool down, then grab a shower," Jimmy interrupted, his features full of amusement.

"Perfect." I slowed the machine. "Communal showers. Glute contest is a go!"

I lost count of how many stinking, damp face towels were thrown at me. And even though one managed to hit me in the mouth at the unfortunate time I was about to tell them to piss off, it was worth the disgusting taste and stink up my nose.

I'd had a decent workout, hung out with some good guys, eye-fucked Sutton, who looked delicious with a trickle of sweat down his dark skin, and walked away migraine free.

Halle-freakin'-lujah.

"You good?" Sutton sidled up to me and wiped his face dry.

"Yeah."

His smile was immediate. "Straight to the room for a shower?"

"No glutes contest?"

He arched a brow at me, his face deadpan.

"I'll take that as a no."

"You interpreted correctly."

I chuckled, heading out of the gym. "You know, if you'd just admitted my ass was firm enough to bo—"

"The only 'firm' you need to be thinking about

when it comes to a sentence containing 'your ass' is my cock."

I stumbled, mouth gaping. I would have hit the floor if it hadn't been for Sutton's fast reflexes.

"Or you can keep your mouth open that wide for a while longer. I'm sure we can find a good use for it."

I stopped dead in my tracks, wide-eyed and gaping like a damn fish—or rather a man who was imagining sucking Sutton off. "You just… did you just…" I shook my head. "Who the fuck are you, and what have you done with my best friend?" I ended up saying, my mind spinning at the delicious filth coming from him.

Never, as in ever, even with the weeks of mutual masturbation, had he ever said anything like this before. Never about anyone he was dating, never to me, about me. My dick was hard before I could even contemplate putting one foot in front of the other again.

He leaned in, moving me closer to the wall and away from the final couple of guys leaving. After giving them a nod, he trapped me with his gaze.

"You know how fucking sexy you are working out, happy like that, in your fucking element?" With his nose to my neck, he inhaled and licked a short column up my throat.

Surprise and a weird giddiness battled for the top spot at his words. "Yeah?"

"As soon as we're in our room, I'll show you exactly how sexy you are."

I nodded numbly, my brain misfiring as all the blood rushed to my throbbing cock.

"Let's go." He took hold of my hand, and we raced to our room. Anyone looking at the security cameras right now would be wondering where the fire was. In my pants, I thought, grinning.

After a gazillion steps, we finally unlocked the door and fell inside, my mouth on Sutton's the instant we were in our space. Teeth, tongues, and desperation, our kiss was frantic, messy, and hot enough to be combustible.

"Shower." It took an effort to push the word out, but then we were moving, straight for the en suite, tearing at our clothes, stumbling to kick our sneakers off.

"Your bandage," he gasped out, mouth against mine.

"Don't care," I garbled. A wet bandage was the last thing I cared about.

Finally, blissfully naked, we toppled into the shower, a mess of limbs, somehow keeping each other upright so we didn't fall on our asses. I chuckled when Sutton whacked his shoulder in the enclosed space and cursed.

"This shower needs to be at least five times bigger." The words were mumbled against my shoulder, the now warm spray wetting our skin.

"I am a big guy," I sassed, thrusting my hips against him.

A snorted laugh was his response before he cupped my dick. "That you are."

The witty response didn't manage to fall from my lips, not when he squeezed like that and moved his hand in strong, sure strokes. Instead, I grunted. The sound was loud and downright filthy, full of need and impatience.

I wanted it all. To shoot my load but for this to last forever. For Sutton to kiss me, possess me, and never stop. To suck me so hard, it would feel like he was extracting every part of me that mattered.

"I want you." It was all I could manage, unable to grasp exactly what I needed from this man right now.

"You've got me."

Fuck if I didn't like the sound of that. The words pushed me to take action. "Fuck this. Need you on the bed so we can suck each other's brains out."

The smirk he shot me was sinful, full of dirty promises. "Hold that thought."

I groaned when he grabbed the shower gel, rubbed it over my body, paying careful attention to my cock and balls. Unable to resist, I thrust into his hand, willing my hips to listen to reason. "Stop," I grunted. "I want your mouth."

He chuckled as he eased off and quickly lathered himself up and washed away the suds.

"Fucking hell, could you be any slower?" I complained, earning me a pinch on the ass.

"You're sexy when you're all sweaty, but you don't want to be anywhere near my ball sac after my workout."

I laughed. "Then my tastebuds appreciate the sentiment and you being such a gentleman."

"I can assure you there are absolutely no gentlemanly thoughts firing through my brain."

I quirked my brow at him and turned off the shower, impatient with the wait. "Prove it."

And holy sweet-scented cock did he.

In no time at all, I was flat on my back with Sutton's dick in my mouth, on the verge of going cross-eyed with how he sucked and lapped at me.

On top of me, his weight on the right side of perfect, I groaned as I squeezed his ass cheek and pulled him a little deeper. He moaned around me, the sound causing a vibration and a tingle at the base of my spine.

This was all too fucking fast, too good.

I wanted it to last forever, stay this way, top to tail, and give each other such pleasure I could barely see straight. But then, all I could actually see was a close-up view of his balls. They were so tempting this close.

I released his dick with a pop. Once again he moaned around me, and I didn't hold back the shiver at the sensation. Somehow, I stayed on mission and drew one ball in my mouth, appreciating so much they were super smooth. I sucked gently before moving onto the second, aware his thighs shook, and he was rocking.

Putting him out of misery, I wrapped my lips back around his sensitive head, licking and sucking before taking him deeper. He mirrored the action, and my hips jerked of their own volition.

His mouth, the heat, hell, the taste of him made my brain misfire.

And then I saw stars as he swallowed me so deep, I felt his throat contract around me.

I reacted instinctively, sucking and bobbing for all it was worth. I breathed through my nose when I could, squinted tightly, trying to make him come before I lost it completely, but I shattered and forgot how to complete this most simple, delicious task.

Spurred on by his grunts, by the increased

shaking of his limbs, I dragged my finger through his crease, tapping gently on his pucker, not quite daring to breach with no lube. On the second rub, his body turned rigid, hip movements erratic. I focused on not choking, centered on making him relive this moment anytime he simply heard the number sixty-nine.

His release spilled directly into my throat, and I pulled back a little to sweep my tongue to get a better taste. It was the last rational thought I had—the desire to taste him—before my cock pulsed, my body shuddered, and then I pulled away, head sinking into the mattress.

Another shudder rippled through me when he eased his mouth away.

Opening my eyes, I zeroed in on his dick. Cum trickled, pooled into a pearl. Sticking out my tongue, I reached up and licked it. He grunted at the action.

I somehow managed to chuckle. "Better than getting pink eye." I released an oomph when his knees gave way, some of his weight landing on me. With my nose practically implanted in his ass, I grinned, the movement lazy. "I've never been more grateful that you washed your ass."

He huffed a laugh, the movement making me groan.

"You've killed me."

Sutton grunted against the mattress, half of his body resting on top of me.

I attempted a tap on his ass but failed miserably, my muscles like jelly. "Brain cells gone."

He grunted again, this one sounding a little close to a tired chuckle.

"'S okay." Still, I couldn't get my arm to move. It would have been nice to feel his butt cheek in my hand, but… nope, still no movement. "You can keep them," I finished, feeling super generous.

He shifted a little and collapsed onto his side on the mattress, freeing me from being pinned down.

"I've decided we should do that every day. Twice." I could barely pry my eyes open, and a yawn followed my words.

"I thought you were killed."

"Your spunk is an elixir. Swallow that creamy goodness down and *ping*, back to life."

Loud laughter broke free of him as Sutton maneuvered the right way up on the bed. "You're so full of shit—"

"Nuh-uh. Your jizz."

He groaned and rubbed his face. "If you can get up and walk to the bathroom, right now, on steady legs and without collapsing, I'll believe you."

With a narrow gaze, I angled to look at him. "You're so fucking mean. I can't even feel my legs."

His grin was beautiful and completely mine. I wanted to capture each smile and commit each one to memory. The thought made me smirk and roll my eyes at myself. My inner sappiness was strong.

"Shit, what time is it?"

"No idea." Sutton reached for the bedside table but failed on the first attempt. "Too far."

"Seriously, move your ass and check the time. We said we'd meet Mark for dinner." That, my old college buddy being here, was something I still hadn't had time to process. Seeing him had been a surprise. A good one. Strange in a way, but how he'd run that session and had Sutton opening up like that, it was a hell of a thing.

"*You* said, not *we*."

I arched a brow in his direction, wondering at the hint of grumble in his voice. "You want me to go to dinner alone?"

"No," he was quick to say. "But the phone's all the way over there."

I snorted, not used to witnessing an almost petulant Sutton. Reaching over him, I snagged his phone, relieved to see we weren't late. Dinner was served between six and seven thirty, and I'd agreed to meet Mark at seven.

The food here was good. There were fancier places in the nearby town, but that would mean venturing out in public and dealing with the drama that came with it. We'd be living back in our real world in a few weeks, so for now, I'd savor the safety of the academy. Heck, only three days in and the college kids were no longer looking at us with wide-eyed awe.

All of that had fizzled away after we'd put them through their paces, earning us grumbles and under-the-breath cusses. Plus, me suggesting we had a glutes competition went a long way to wiping clear the rose-tinted glasses.

It was no good. We had to get moving. "We need to shower."

"You're very talkative for a dead man."

"A brainless dead man," I agreed. "You see, my talents will forever surprise you."

Sutton angled and leaned on his elbow, peering down at me. "I'm good with you surprising me."

Goose bumps dotted along my skin at the heat in his gaze and the sweet sincerity in his voice. That was followed quickly by the memory of his heated words after our gym session.

"Speaking of surprises." I arched my brow and gave him a pointed stare. "You mentioned something about a cock in my ass." Just saying the word sent a rush of warmth to my cheeks. My ass cheeks clenched, wondering exactly what that would feel like.

Sutton's brows shot comically high, his eyes widening. "Is, uhm, that something you want to try? That we're ready for?" A roll of his eyes later, he shook his head. "Fuck, why is it that I feel like a fucking virgin all over again?"

I chuckled. "Because both our asses are virgin holes." I furrowed my brows. "Well, at least mine is—"

"Mine too," he was quick to say.

"What are you thinking?"

"That I'm both mortified and turned on by this conversation." He collapsed back onto the bed, covering his eyes with his arm.

"Me too," I admitted. With the man being honest with me, I'd absolutely be giving it him back. "We really do need to shower. We can talk about this later." I sat up, having a great idea. "Perhaps we could talk about it with Mark. He's gay, so is probably down with the whole anal sex thing. I'm sure—"

"No fucking way." Sutton sat up, the whites of his eyes super visible with how wide-eyed he was.

I frowned. "But he's a counselor. And does the whole LGBTQ stuff."

"And he's also had your tongue in his mouth."

Surprise blasted through me. The emotion was quickly followed by amusement and a huge grin. "Huh… is that where you're at with Mark? Interesting."

"It's so *not* interesting." He shook his head at me and stood.

I jumped up to follow him into the bathroom, too entertained by this turn of events to leave it be. "You know, some people say jealousy is an ugly emotion."

He turned on the shower and stepped inside. I was close at his heels when he said, "Not jealous."

I ignored him. He totally was jealous. "You wanna know what I think?"

"Do I have a choice?"

I grinned. "I think it's fucking hot." My dick had done a valiant job of perking right up. I pushed against his butt, so he could join me with the admiration my growing hard-on deserved. "So much so, every time it's clear you're jealous, I think you'll deserve a blowy. Maybe a hand job. Either way, you'll be blowing your load."

From over his shoulder, Sutton looked at me, his pupils blown.

"You like that, huh?"

He attempted to harden his gaze, look unaffected, but I reached around him, latching on to his erection. His breath caught. I had to give it to the man. Sutton schooled his features impressively. Not so much when I squeezed gently and gave a tug.

"I think there's probably something really unhealthy about being turned on and offering sexual rewards when your b— I'm jealous."

"You're talking too much. I'm clearly not getting my point across." I stroked more firmly, picking up speed, still pressing against his back and feeling his body vibrate.

He grunted, and I pressed my mouth against his neck. Angling a little, he gave me better access.

"I swear I could come with just getting you off." I thrust against him for good measure and gasped when my cock glided through his ass cheeks, angling down. "Holy fucking yes." Sensation flooded me. If getting off with the crease of his ass was this good, how fucking incredible would it be sinking into his tight channel? I grunted at the thought, going to town with my thrusts and keeping a fast rhythm on his cock.

"And don't think I didn't notice," I managed, rubbing up against him, "you didn't know what to call me."

Once again, he angled to look at me. With his bottom lip trapped between his teeth, he looked hot. Complete with flushed cheeks, he was well on the way to the image of him I loved seeing the most. Thoroughly debauched.

"Boyfriend… sounds weird," he said with a groan, pushing against me one second and then pushing forward into my grip.

I agreed completely. More than once I'd hesitated about terminology. And then he was spilling into my hand. I barely had time to react before he turned, smashed his mouth against mine, took my cock in hand, gave a few short, tight tugs, and I released.

The sound echoing around the bathroom was loud, a relieved grunt and groan as he once more had me seeing stars.

"I think I need to work on my jealousy," Sutton said as he pulled away. "Much more of that, and I don't think I'll survive it." The sweetest smile beamed back at me, making my heart do a loop-de-loop, my stomach adding an extra fizz for good measure.

"How about me telling you that you have nothing to be jealous about?" Despite my smile, I was deadly serious. With the way Sutton made me feel—whole, complete, understood—how could he possibly think I wanted anyone else? "Plus, there's the whole my dick's-only-hard-for-you thing we have going on." I bounced my brows up and down. "Is bi for you a real thing?"

Rolling his eyes, Sutton groaned, pressing his face against my neck.

"What, it's a legit question?" Mirth lit my words, but I was kinda serious too. "Another question we can ask Mark."

The bastard nipped my neck. I hissed and pulled away, noticing the smug grin on his face.

"You've got issues, man," I grumbled, dotting a kiss to his puffy lips and somehow managing to pull away before I devoured him.

"That right?"

"Yeah, apparently you can't decide if you're the Hulk or… what's that guy's name, from that movie? It's old as fuck now. Shit." I racked my brains as we washed off, then grinned when the name came to me. With a click of my fingers, I said, "Blade. You know, the vampire? It's also the name—"

"I know the name of the movie," he deadpanned.

"Yeah, that whole crackpot Wesley Snipes vibe going on. Teeth to yourself."

Turning off the shower, Sutton eyed me with something akin to wonder on his face. *Scratch that.* Rather than wonder, it was bemused tolerance, maybe.

"Just get your ass moving. Apparently we have a friend of yours to meet."

"Roger that, *lover.*"

Honest-to-God befuddlement crossed his features.

"No? Okay, no use of lover. I'll keep trying."

We dressed while I considered other alternatives. Thinking of something wild that would really get under Sutton's skin.

"How about suitor?" I suggested as we stepped into the canteen, which was nothing like the canteen from my college days. Here was all nice silverware, quality plates, and well-cooked, albeit healthy food. Since I didn't have to fend for myself, I took it as a win.

"Nope."

I peered around the room and saw Mark sitting with Milo and Pearce. My back straightened. I still hadn't had real quality time with Milo yet. Sure, there was Mark to catch up with, and there was Pearce, who we needed to check up on, but Milo Henderson was right there.

A hand clamped on my shoulder. "I know playing hard to get has never been in your vocabulary," Sutton said quietly next to my ear. "Now's the time to try it on for size."

Narrowing my eyes, I glanced at him. "I'm not that bad."

The asshole responded with an arched brow that distracted me for a second at how gorgeous he looked. I shook my head out of my Sutton fog. "Uh-huh."

"Please," I drawled, "if that was Tommy Leroy sitting there, you'd already be hyperventilating."

He didn't correct me, since I totally spoke the truth. If I had a baller crush on Milo, Sutton had a full-on swooning kinda crush on Leroy. The man definitely had some mad skills on the court in the day, but Milo would have totally been able to kick his ass.

With a twitch of his lips, Sutton sighed. "Have at it then. Just remember we're here for weeks yet."

Taking my time to head on over, not wanting to appear too eager, I eyed the spare seats, planning my move. The chair opposite Milo was empty, plus the one next to him. I hesitated before settling on the chair opposite. That way I could listen intently to everything the man had to say.

"You made it," Mark greeted.

"Sure did. Everyone doing okay tonight?" I asked to the table as a whole, my gaze drifting to Milo.

After a round of smiles and yeses, Mark said, "I was just explaining how we know each other."

I grinned. "Got it. Badge of honor awarded for that kiss."

Pearce spat out his drink, Milo's brows rose, Sutton shook his head, while Mark stared at me wide-eyed. "I meant college. We took a couple of classes together."

"Oh." I bobbed my head, not quite sure why he hadn't shared the kiss too.

"You guys made out in college?" Pearce asked after clearing his throat.

"Sure did," I said smugly. "The kiss that changed Mark's life." I shot him a wink, a little perplexed at Mark's gaping-fish expression "Shit, shouldn't I have said that? Fuck, are you not out here?" Panicked, I shot a look at Sutton, hoping for some sort of assist. "You did say you were gay in the group session, right? I didn't imagine that?"

He stared at me, and just when I thought he would let me open my mouth and carry on digging, he saved me with another small sigh and a wink.

"Maybe while we're here, part of the time needs to be conversations about privacy, oversharing, and ensuring respectful conversations are had, ones that could impact on someone's life before talking."

"Yes." I pointed at Sutton. "Totally what my significant other"—Pearce spat out another mouthful of water at that gem—"said." Focusing on Mark after seeing Sutton glare at me, I scrunched my face in apology. "If I know someone's secret, I absolutely do not share any of that. But other stuff, I just assume. Sorry." I made sure not to look in Pearce's direction.

Mark's smile did a lot to ease my shoulders. I swore I wasn't usually such an idiot. I didn't even glance at Milo, figuring my overenthusiasm and my mouth running away with me was me being hyper-aware of my idol. "Relax, Jayden. You heard right. I'm absolutely still out, and I think anyone who knows you trusts that you'd keep their confidence."

Relieved, I nodded. "Scout's honor." I shot Sutton a pointed look before he could throw his usual argument at me.

"Honestly, I've never told anyone about what happened in college. It's one of those sorts of rules, if you like, about not making assumptions or oversharing. Not when it comes to sexuality."

"These rules… please tell me they're written down in a handbook. I could totally do with one of those. Speaking of—"

"Jayden." Sutton cut me off, eyeing me with the sexy stern look he was a master of.

I grinned at him, only half planning to carry on and be ridiculous in my questioning and topic of conversation. He winked, knowing I enjoyed razzing people just like I enjoyed being the entertainer. It was also a great distraction from my potential faux pas earlier.

"So, anyone else starving?"

Nods around the table followed.

"Excellent. Let's get food, and then Milo can tell us all about how he plans to talk to Coach about letting him forget these kids, and he should have one-on-one sessions with the sexiest and most talented player in the League for the remainder of the course." I rubbed my hands together, ridiculously so.

Milo looked startled for maybe a fraction of a second before he nodded. "Absolutely. I'm up for that. Sutton"—he glanced at my bae—"I'd love to offer you extra sessions. Just let me know when."

The table erupted in laughter as they stood, Sutton patting Milo on the shoulder.

"Laugh it up, wise guys." I followed them toward the serving area. "Don't think I've forgotten about the glutes contest. No chance anyone else will be winning that one but me."

CHAPTER 18
SUTTON

THE FOLLOWING TWO WEEKS RACED BY. BETWEEN working with the trainees, getting in some gym time, and making sure Jayden wasn't overdoing it, it had been both full-on and just what I needed.

Being so busy and being surrounded by a decent group of guys was exactly what I needed to help clear my head. I was also spending more time with Pearce, who I hadn't really made an effort to get to know so much before now.

He was a good guy and was easy to talk to openly and honestly. Except for the white lie of me and Jayden being a thing since last year, and that he was my fiancé.

Admittedly that was a not-so-great secret to be holding on to, but I justified it to myself with increasing ease. Jayden and I most definitely were a couple, for a start. Our label remained unknown, but thank the basketball gods, he was running out of possible names for us to try out. Plus, my relationship really was no one else's business, nor was it hurting anyone.

While we'd started out with a small lie, intended for good reasons, in the grand scheme of things, it didn't really matter.

Not anymore.

That didn't mean we'd be sharing our origin story. What would be the point?

"What time will Jayden be finished?" Pearce caught the ball I passed him in the triple shot position. He jab stepped, shifted position as I made to defend, dribbled, then executed a jump shot.

The ball passed through the hoop effortlessly.

I snagged the ball and got back into position as we continued to run a couple of basic drills. "He should be done by five." He was having his official one-on-one meeting with Mark. There'd been some discussion about how appropriate that was, but since it was Jayden at the center of that discussion, of course he'd have his say and get what he wanted.

The man always did. The sexy jerk could convince a straight man he just might like it up the ass, after all.

Pearce followed the same training pattern, faking impressively.

"What about you?" I asked. "Still feeling good about your session a couple of days ago?"

A grin appeared and he bobbed his head. "It felt good. More official somehow, even though I know it was all in confidence." He shrugged. "Mark said he'll meet with me again and offered to be there when I call Monty and my agent. It feels good, though."

I caught the ball after it slid once more through the hoop. "I'm pleased for you, man. Must be a weight off your shoulders."

"It was. Not as much as the relief I felt at the news of your engagement blowing up the internet."

My gut tightened, but I forced a smile.

"I'm sure that's a shitty thing, you know, all of the comments, the backlash and bullshit, how people react. I'm dreading it."

I passed him the ball. "There are fewer assholes than I expected," I answered. "Honestly, Jay and I didn't spend time looking at the hate. It was easier to block it out." I didn't add that we hadn't really invested time looking through the positive comments too much either. The support had been incredible but had added to the layer of guilt that had pressed heavily on my chest.

It was easier now, though. Easier to swallow and

handle. Easier to accept the smiles we sometimes received when Jay and I were having a PDA moment or reading the occasional comment or message when we ventured onto social media.

"People are crazy vocal," I added. "Everyone has an opinion. I expected it but still struggle to believe it's happening. Like, why on earth would we be making a headline, just for being together?" I shook my head, despite knowing the reason why.

All too well I understood there was a fascination with professional athletes, including their private lives. It didn't mean I was comfortable with my personal business being speculated on. I'd suck it up, though. It was part of the package of going pro, being in the public eye. Fans and non-fans all wanted a piece of you and had vocal opinions to share as well.

"You'll be fine. You'll breeze through. You know the team is great, and while our fans may be curious, they're more interested in us winning."

Pearce bobbed his head. "You're right. Maybe—"

"Sutton."

The sound of Eddie's tight voice made us pause. Immediately, my thoughts went to Jayden, my heart tripping over itself. "What's wrong?"

Mouth tight and brows knotted, Eddie looked serious. Hell, expressions like that usually came with bad news. His gaze flicked to Pearce before traveling back to me. "You mind if we talk in private?"

My brows shot up, pulse quickening. Pearce shifted his feet and glanced at me, a silent question in his eyes. I nodded.

"I'll go to the locker room. I'll catch up with you later."

As soon as he was out of earshot, I asked, "What is it?" Worry threaded my tone.

Pulling out his phone, Eddie hesitated a beat. It took all my patience to not demand he hurry the hell up. But pulling out the phone meant Jayden was okay, right? His concussion seemed to be finally behaving itself. With fewer and fewer migraines, he was getting back in shape and really giving the young guys a run for their money.

"I just needed to show you this before you overheard anything. I have no idea how accurate it is, but I didn't want either of you caught out and taken by surprise, or at least with an audience."

He keyed a few buttons on his phone and then passed it. I frowned, trying to prepare myself. Not quite sure what to expect, I simply stared at the screen.

"You need to click on the top left image for it to play."

Recognizing it was TikTok, I did as he said. The

video clip opened. Loud music erupted from the phone, along with laughter and catcalls. The video was dark, and the occasional strobe lighting and flash of colors drew some people into the spotlight.

And then it registered what I was seeing.

Jayden was on the dance floor, kissing a woman. They weren't exactly discreet or even dancing. There was the occasional movement of his feet, small tilts of his body. It was all I could focus on, not wanting to watch Jayden making out with anyone. Well, anyone but me.

I exhaled, my brain ticking over. The video stopped, and it moved to the next. I clicked on the video to pause it and handed the cell over with a shrug. "I don't get it. So Jayden was with a woman. Everyone knows he used to date and hook up."

Eddie pinched his lips together. "There's a state-ment in the comments indicating this video was from four months ago."

I froze. Four months ago I was being an asshat and pretty much avoiding Jayden. But as far as everyone else was concerned, we were already fully invested in a committed relationship. I rolled my eyes, saying, "Well, clearly it's bullshit. That could have easily been from eighteen months ago or even four years ago."

This right here was the problem. The only way to

deal with this was to deny, speak to Jayden, and, if necessary, come out with the truth. The thought of the deception made my stomach knot. It didn't make it any easier that this was all my fault.

Sympathy filled Eddie's expression. "I thought that too, but in the video is Paul Steinburg." The defenseman who'd been traded to the Eagles six months ago. *Fuck.*

I shrugged, aiming for nonchalance. "I'm not worried." He searched my gaze, and I offered a reassuring smile. "I'll speak to Jay. Give him the heads-up."

Eddie nodded, not looking especially confident. "Sure thing."

I grabbed my towel and turned to leave before focusing back on Eddie. "Listen, man, if this starts doing the rounds here, can you do me a favor and try to squash any bullshit? We're here to play ball, not talk about my relationship."

"Of course."

"Can you also send me the link?"

"Yeah, sure."

With one last smile, I turned and headed straight to find Jayden. At least I knew where he was.

Relieved I didn't pass anyone en route, I huffed out a fortifying breath before knocking on the meeting room door. Hearing Mark's invite in, I pushed the door open and peered inside. Jayden swung a look in my direction, a smile immediately appearing. Not even a second later, it dropped, and he stood.

"What's wrong?"

I flicked my gaze at Mark. A frown pulled his brows low. I offered him a nod, saying, "You mind if I talk to Jay a minute? It's important."

As he stood, Mark bobbed his head. "How about I just give you the room?"

"That'd be great. Thanks."

Before Mark left, he glanced back at us. "I won't be far if you need me." His genuine smile was the last thing he offered before he left us alone. I winced, wondering if he'd be quite as helpful if he knew my and Jayden's relationship had started on a lie, one we'd never cleared up.

"You're freakin' me out, Gale."

Our gazes connected, and I pinched my lips together, feeling all levels of weird about this whole thing. I tugged out my phone, finding the link Eddie sent me. Once I opened it, I handed it over. "Best take a look at this."

Loud music erupted from my cell, along with conversation I couldn't quite make out, plus laughter and hollers. Watching intently, Jayden stared at the screen with a pinched expression. It was apparent when he spotted himself, his brows shooting high, color dotting his cheeks.

He flashed a look my way before returning his attention to the video. The repeat kicked in on auto. The same sounds spilled from my cell.

"Who put this on?" he finally said, gaze still on the device.

"Not sure. But there's a statement saying the video was from four months ago."

That got his attention. Wide-eyed, he stared at me. "Four months?" He shook his head. "You sure?"

"That's just what the comment says. Paul Steinburg's in the video too." I could see Jayden's brain ticking over, making the same links and no doubt drawing the same conclusions as me.

"Fuck." He backed up and sat, elbows on his knees, my cell in his hands. "Who showed you it?"

"Eddie."

"So what, everyone's seen this and thinks I cheated on you?" The pink in his cheeks bled to red. Panic flashed over his features.

Knowing exactly how he felt, my heart stuttered, and I reached out for him, stepping into his space. He stood immediately, his gaze unwavering. "I don't like how this implies that I cheated on you." His jaw tensed. "I'd never do that."

I did know that. Jayden was a lot of things, but in

all the years we'd known each other, a cheater was never one of them. "I know. I just don't know what to do about it."

"We put everyone straight. Tell them we weren't together then. So what the media ran with the fiancé story. We've never confirmed it."

"But we haven't denied it either. It'll just come across that we were lying, which we were. It doesn't matter the reason. Plus there's the academy. This year was the trial year for the LGBTQ+ focus group. How's that going to be impacted when everyone discovers we lied?"

"But we're together. We *are* in a relationship." The fierceness of Jayden's tone took me by surprise.

"I know." I reached out and swept my thumb over his cheekbone. My heart beat loudly, making it difficult to think my way through this. Trying to decide what was for the best.

All I could think about was how it would likely make a mockery of Montview's summer program. Plus our team was involved at the highest level with our manager's backing of the new program.

Then there was Pearce.

He'd trusted us with his secret because of the lie we'd let him believe.

"I just don't know how we make it clear you weren't cheating on me without destroying all of the good we've done. Plus, there's the Youth Pride program visiting tomorrow. We're meant to be role models, for fuck's sake."

Jayden winced. "Shit. I'd forgotten that."

I cracked my neck, trying to relieve some of the tension. The preliminary program put into action this year at Montview was incredible. Sure, it was the usual focus of offering elite training. Add in the additional outreach work they were incorporating with LGBTQ+ organizations, and we couldn't mess up.

Our deception could discredit what Harry and the team were working toward.

What they were doing here mattered. It would have mattered two years ago, but now, with my own letter somewhere in the long list in the Pride alphabet, it mattered so much more.

"Maybe we should just say—"

"No fucking way am I saying I cheated on you." Jayden's voice was firm, resolute.

A flare of guilt ignited in my chest.

"You'd prefer me to be a fucking pariah rather than us simply telling the truth?" Hurt bled through every word, making his voice shake. "Screw you, man."

I winced. "I know it's shitty, but if we don't find a way out of this, work out how we're going to handle it, it could screw up the LGBTQ+ inclusion. No way will there be a chance of growth… of other programs following the same model if we mess this up for them." A burst of determination pushed me to continue. "Then there's Pearce and everyone else here. They'll fucking hate us and—"

"Yet it's okay if they hate me because I'm the fucker who cheated on you?" He shook his head, his hurt morphing into something more. Disgust maybe? Anger? "We wouldn't want that, would we? Gale fucking Sutton, the genius star player who can do no fucking wrong." He backed away completely, shaking his head.

Exasperated, my hands shook. Frustrated at Jayden, this situation, and most of all at myself. But then there was the unmitigated spite to his words, ones that had me pursing my lips, holding back my desire to simply tell him to fuck off. "That's *not* what this is about."

"If you say so."

I threw my hands up in the air and shook my head. "Jay." The word came out harder than intended. I huffed out a breath, attempting to control my irritation. Taking the edge from my words, I said, "You know that's not what this is about. This isn't about me or you."

He scoffed. "If the roles were reversed, I wonder if you'd be saying that."

Jaw clenched, I ground my molars together, words spiraling around my brain, a flash of words he'd told me a few weeks ago rising to the surface. "If you hadn't bullshitted me in the first place, saying I was the last person you kissed, then this is something we could have prepared for. Tried to cut it off before anything like this happened." The more I thought about it, remembered his sweet lie about me being his last kiss, it made me wonder if that moment had meant as much to him as it did to me.

Fuck, I was an idiot.

"So much for not partying and getting laid." My hurt surged forth, transforming into anger. Not once had we ever argued. Not once had I ever raised my voice at him. Not like this. But fuck, he'd lied to me, and for what? Why keep it a damn secret? It wouldn't have mattered. It wouldn't have changed anything.

Jayden's mouth opened and closed a couple of times. As he shook his head, he said, "I didn't. Haven't."

My brows shot up, and whatever he could read on my face hardened his own expression.

"You know what? Fuck you, *Gale*. You fucking started this. What, you couldn't handle me kissing you a year back, so freaked the fuck out and decided to treat me like shit, and all because I got your dick hard?" He sneered and shook his head. "All the fucking time since the day we met you've talked about integrity and honesty. As soon as it doesn't suit you, you're so fucking quick to judge and turn the other cheek. This, all this… is on you."

As if the wind had been completely knocked out of his sails after sharing his cutting words, sadness shadowed his expression. His shoulders slumped, his eyes became watery, and he swallowed hard.

"How about you do whatever you want? Deal with this how you decide. This past year's already been a shit show because you chose to handle things by yourself rather than opening up to me. I don't see how this is any different, not if you're asking me to lie."

He strode toward the door while I stood rooted at the spot, gut churning and heart aching. Before he pulled the door open, he glanced at me. Sorrow and hurt contorted his features. Pain slammed into me at the look he shot my way.

"Whatever you decide, I'll do. You need me to take one for the team? I will." He shrugged, raking his watery gaze over me one last time before he turned his back on me and left.

The silence in the room was deafening. Thick with anger and sadness, the air seemed too thick to inhale.

What the fuck had I done?

CHAPTER 19
JAYDEN

A BITING RAGE NIPPED AT MY HEELS THE FURTHER I walked away. I embraced the chase of anger, much preferring it to the agony that ripped through me.

Fifteen minutes ago I'd been baring my soul to Mark, all but gushing about Sutton, how my feelings for the man had first grown, my initial confusion realizing what we had was so much more than I'd ever envisioned.

What a clusterfuck.

"Whoa."

I all but smashed into Pearce. If he hadn't grabbed on to my arm, we both would have been flattened.

"Where's the fire?" The smile on his face slipped a moment later when I didn't shoot back with a wiseass remark. "Man, you okay?"

"Sure." I nodded and avoided eye contact. The

last person I wanted to see was Pearce, not after the fight Sutton and I just had.

"You don't look okay." His gaze searched mine, but I couldn't be here right now.

"All good. I just have to be somewhere." I stepped around him. "I'll catch you later." Then I was out of there.

There wasn't a chance I could go back to my room. The one I shared with my— I caught the thought, cutting it off abruptly. What I needed was a bar.

I patted my pocket, relieved I'd shoved my wallet in there this morning, and made my way to the exit, pulling out my phone as I did so. The plan was to get the hell out of here. I needed space to think and cool off. Drink my aching sorrows away.

Managing to make it all the way to the front of the main building without spotting anyone, I inhaled the fresh air. A quick look at the map on my phone told me there were plenty of bars within walking distance. I chose one that was tucked away off the main drag of the small town and followed the route to get there. The whole walk I focused on everything but the ache in my chest, and somehow avoided clutching onto it, sure at any moment my heart was either going to break in two or stop beating altogether.

The sun was lowering, but it wouldn't be dark for a few more hours. Between the steady heat of the sun and the gentle breeze, I managed to slow down my stride, still doggedly ignoring that damn ache.

Twenty minutes later, I turned into the smaller side street, seeing up ahead the sign for Wessex Bar. And not a moment too soon. Ignoring Sutton's barb, his words and accusation were too hard, I tugged open the heavy door, glancing into the quiet bar.

It was a little too early for after-work drinkers, so the place was almost empty. The lighting was dimmer than I expected, taking me a moment to readjust from the bright outside. I zeroed in on the barstool right at the end of the bar, the farthest away from the door. It had my name written all over it.

Once I sat, the bartender, a middle-aged man with a headful of dark hair and just a whisper of gray on the edges, approached. I wondered if, before Sutton, I'd have noticed a man's appearance, considered if he was decent-looking or not. My gut lurched, and before my emotions could spiral, the guy greeted me with a chin lift. "What'll it be?"

Eyeing the bottles on the shelf, I winced. Hard liquor wasn't my friend. It never had been. Give me a decent beer any day. Anything stronger tended to taste like shit. But this was cause for desperate measures. "What's going to get me wasted but doesn't taste like crap or make me gag?" I asked honestly.

Considering my life was about to implode, and people would start to believe I was a cheating bastard, what was one more humiliation?

The bartender stared at me for a beat, nodded, and reached for a bottle. "I've got just the thing."

"Actually, get me a couple and use your imagination, please." I considered asking for six right off the bat, but knowing I tended to gag when attempting to knock back shots, I didn't want to risk it just yet.

A few moments later, two shot glasses were set before me. "You wanna know their names?"

I eyed both drinks, one a light pink that looked watery, another creamy with what looked like whipped cream on it. "I'll taste them first, you know, rather than letting the name sway me to my poison of choice."

The bartender's mouth twitched. "Have at it."

With a nod of thanks, I grabbed both glasses, knocking back the pink concoction first, already wincing and preparing for the burn. When I didn't gag and my eyes didn't water, I nodded in relief at the sweetness. "Not bad." Then it was onto the second. How the fuck was I going to get that down with all that cream?

I examined it, figuring out the best course of

attack, investing far too much energy in the brilliant distraction this moment provided.

"Best to wrap your lips around it and down the whole thing."

My gaze shifted to the bartender, and while he seemed amused at my focus, he didn't seem to be setting me up. Nor did I see a camera in his hand. With a shrug, I lifted the glass to my mouth, wrapped my lips around the rim of the glass, and knocked it back.

It was sweet and creamy, and I readily dipped my tongue in to catch the last remnants of the cream.

"Do we have a winner?" he asked.

I pulled out a smile, knowing after a few more of these I'd be happily wasted, without the humiliation of gagging, and I could drift into oblivion for a little while. "This one for sure." I indicated toward the creamy shot glass. "Hit me with their names, and I'll have two more of those."

"Sure thing." He returned to the ingredients, saying, "The first one was a wet pussy."

I snorted, because how could I not?

"Your favorite was a cum shot."

My laughter was loud and a little overzealous. "Are you shitting me?"

The bartender smiled. "Nope. It's all in the cream."

I snorted out a hard laugh. Figured between a pussy and creamy cum, I'd opt for the latter. Story of my life at the moment. "Can I grab a beer too?" I eyed what was on tap and indicated toward what looked to be a local beer.

I knocked back the couple of shots as soon as they were in front of me, then took hold of the beer with thanks. "You the owner?" I asked, seeking additional distraction. My stomach felt warm, my head a little fuzzy, but it did nothing to distract me from the bitterness and hurt turning over my stomach.

"Yeah. Had this place for six years now. Moved out here from Minnesota."

"No shit. What's your name?"

He grinned and held out his hand. "Name's Blake." With a firm grip, he shook. "And you're Jayden Moore."

My shoulders sagged a little. Of course he'd know who I was.

Not only were we a stone's throw away from Montview, but he hailed from the place I now called home.

"You support the Eagles?"

He folded his arms, stance relaxed, and an easy smile on his face. "Sure do. Used to have season tickets back in the day."

"You been able to pick up a game recently?"

He bobbed his head. "Last season I caught the game against Ohio."

I grinned, my shoulders easing a little. Given the chance, I could talk all night about basketball. Add in cum shooters and maybe I'd found the perfect distraction after all.

"Yeah? Good game to catch. Close game from memory."

"Sure was." Blake grinned. "One of your players especially had an impressive game, as I recall."

I knew exactly who he was talking about. "The rookie's got something, right? Game changer for the kid, that one."

"He dominated both ends of the court. Not bad for a kid so young."

I chuckled. "Shit, man. Twenty-four does seem young, right? Pearce gets pissed off, though, when I call him a kid." I sipped at my beer, no longer feeling like I needed to neck the thing.

"You're here coaching at Montview, right?"

It was no secret Sutton and I had joined the academy for the summer. "Yeah. It's been a different pace. Interesting to be on the other side of the line."

"They do some good work over there." His gaze dropped to my hand. "You all healed? Was sorry to hear about the accident."

Lifting my hand, I turned it this way and that,

wriggling my fingers for good measure. "Finger's doing well. I've finally been getting some decent ball time this week, when I can pry it away from these college kids."

"I've heard they do like the limelight."

"It will only get worse once they're drafted and go wild those first few years."

"First few years?" He raised his brows, amused.

I grinned. "Well, maybe eight or ten."

Blake laughed. "Nothing wrong with making the most of your peak." Another customer headed toward the bar. "You want another beer once I've served Marvin over here?"

"That'd be great, thanks."

He tapped the bar counter and served Marvin. Left alone, I tugged out my phone, unable to resist taking a peek. It was still on silent, since I'd been in the middle of a session with Mark.

There were no missed calls, no texts. Well, at least not from Sutton. Rather than feeling relieved, my gut twisted. I'd left the academy a little less than an hour ago, yet he hadn't reached out to me. I didn't know what to do with that.

Just the thought of him pinched my heart.

I hated we'd argued, just as I hated that he'd expected me to perpetuate the lie and run with it. Honestly, him all but suggesting I do so had knocked the wind out of me. The Sutton I knew and I— I sighed and shook my head, finishing off my beer. The tang of hops didn't stop the flow of my thoughts.

Of course I loved him, something I'd already known and an emotion I'd never shied away from. But *loved him* loved him? Heck. That was too big of a minefield considering his out-of-character reaction to this whole mess.

Plus there was the whole thing about me not remembering that fucking kiss.

I hadn't lied when back in Australia I'd told him he'd been the last person I'd kissed. As far as I knew, he had been. The film footage told a different story.

The club was one I recognized. Considering I could count on one hand how many nights out I'd had with some of the guys like that, I knew which night it was.

It was my birthday, which I always spent with Sutton. We always headed to my favorite Mexican restaurant if we were local, ending the night back at mine or his with a Hollywood action movie.

This year that had not happened.

There hadn't been a game on my birthday. Nor had there been a birthday text from my best friend.

My solution had been to call some of the guys, who'd made it their mission to get me wasted when they discovered it was my birthday. I didn't make it home that night, instead staying at Morgan's pad. The following day he'd told me none of the others would take me as I'd vomited in the cab. That was after getting us kicked out of the club for trying to strip.

I'd been grateful I didn't remember a thing.

"Here you go." A new beer was placed in front of me.

"Thanks." I picked it up and took a generous couple of gulps. The momentary distraction from talking with a fan was gone, my brain too full of Sutton. Fuck, I'd thought dating women could be hard work. Dealing with this mess with Sutton made me reconsider that.

"You doing all right over here?"

My gaze snapped to Blake's. "You in a relationship, Blake?"

Surprise registered on his expression. "Yeah."

I mulled that over, taking my glass in both hands and spinning it slowly around. "Been in one for long?"

"Three years now."

"It get any easier?"

A small smile settled on his mouth. "Relationships can be hard work. But when you meet the right person, going all in, warts, intricacies, and all are totally worth it. But I'm not sure 'easier' is the right word. Sometimes I'm still taken by surprise, kept on my toes, and have to think through my reaction."

"She's worth it then?"

He angled his head and examined me. "*He's* worth it, yeah."

"Shit, man, sorry."

"Nothing to be sorry for."

"No, but still, always the assumption, right? I was brought up with totally open and accepting parents, yet immediately I assume people are straight." My brows dipped low. "What the fuck's with that?" I shook my head and finished off my almost full-to-the-top beer. When I finished, Blake's brows were high.

"I'm serious. I'm still thinking shit like that, yet I'm bi or queer or whatever the fuck label I'm meant to be, and I still make assumptions." I shook my head, pissed off with myself. "I can't even get this right. I swear—"

"Hey, man." Blake latched on my forearm, stopping my tirade. "There's only a few of the locals here, but you were getting a little vocal." He pulled away after a light squeeze.

The fire inside me doused quickly, and my shoulders sagged. "Sorry. Thanks." I took a quick glance around, and no one seemed to be paying any attention.

"Listen, I don't know what's going on. Sure, I've seen some press, but I know to absolutely not believe even half of what's posted or printed. All I do know is if some of what I've read is right, it sounds like you've gone through a big change and realization recently. So give yourself a break. And as for labels…" He shrugged. "You're not on anyone's timeline but your own. Figure yourself out, what you want, what feels right. When you've got that sorted, focus on your relationship. If you see a future together, you'll work it out."

Absorbing his words, something tight loosened a little in my chest. "You know what they say about bartenders doubling up as counselors… well, I think you'd give the guy I know at Montview a run for his money."

A large smirk appeared immediately on Blake's face. "Is that right?"

"Sure is."

Blake chuckled and shook his head. "Best not tell Mark that."

Startled, my brows shot up. "You know Mark?"

His smirk turned into a knowing grin. "You could say that."

Just as I was about to ask a question, the bar door opening pulled my attention away and directly to the man of conversation. Smiling softly, Mark entered, and from that look alone, it was clear he knew something about what was happening.

I sighed and turned to Blake. "Isn't there some sort of confidentiality or something that exists between barkeep and patron?" I groused, not really pissed off.

"I think that's something between you and a priest or you and your counselor. And he just happened to text me a few moments ago, and I might have mentioned I had a runaway who looked in need of some company." He shrugged, gaze moving to Mark. A very different smile lit his face, and I immediately knew who Mark was to him.

"Huh, you're Mark's dreamy boyfriend the guy's mentioned a time or ten." I shook my head and smiled. "Mark, seriously, man. Blake's going to be gunning for your job."

"Is that right?" Mark slipped onto the barstool next to me, offering his boyfriend a grin and me a concerned stare.

"Dreamy?" Blake cut in and bounced his brows up and down.

"Hush, it's all lies." Leaning up and over the bar, Mark accepted a kiss from Blake. I took a cursory glance around, and the few patrons here didn't pause from drinking or even bat an eye.

"Beer?"

Mark glanced at my beer and nodded. "That'd be great, thanks."

"Coming right up." Blake left us to go and pour Mark's drink while I focused on my glass.

"You just had beer?"

I cast a look at my old friend. "Nope. Something about cum and pussy."

He snorted. "Which was your favorite?"

Angling to look at him, I narrowed my gaze. "You a mind reader?" When his brows shot high in question, I shook my head. "Just, that's a question I asked myself earlier, and I decided on the cum."

Concern crinkled his forehead. "Why do I have a feeling we're not actually talking about shots?"

"Just seemed, I don't know, like telling or something."

"I think it just means that the cream and the Baileys is creamier and sweeter, and I've seen how much creamer you take in your coffee, so it's not a surprise. There a reason you're reading more into this?" A beer appeared on the bar in front of Mark, but rather than sticking around, Blake moved away to the far side of the bar, giving us space.

"You tell me?"

Rather than answer straight away, he took a small pull of his beer. When he placed it back on top of the polished surface, he said, "I'm a counselor by profession, but I'm also your friend." He tilted his head, examining me. "You know, as soon as I read about you and Sutton in the media, it was my idea to get you involved?"

I nodded. "I kinda figured."

"You know why?"

"Because I'm the newest gay in town?"

Mark chuckled. "Funnily enough, no. I suppose I was curious, knowing you as I do, well at least as I did. How open you were to kiss me at college gave me a heads-up that perhaps you weren't quite as straight as you thought. I've followed your career enough and have always known you and Sutton were tight. I suppose it made me wonder why Jayden Moore, confident, a little bit cocky, and a man who's always been a hundred percent himself and honest, why he would keep such a big thing as an engagement to his best friend a secret."

My stomach hollowed out, and I wasn't sure if I was paling or my face was burning up. All I was sure of was that I lied for shit, and the thought of continuing to do so made me nauseous. Not willing or able to respond, I focused on my beer glass. Condensation dripped a long line, moseying on down, taking its time. It latched onto another drip, growing and building up speed.

It was exactly how I felt, like everything was rushing ahead and I had no idea how to stop it.

How could the best thing to happen in my life—namely falling for Sutton—have led me to this point?

"I saw the video."

I slammed my eyes closed at his words. A weight pressed down on my chest, uncomfortable and restricting. "I imagine millions have seen it by now." I wasn't even being facetious. It was how social media worked. News outlets would be picking up the story and running with it sooner rather than later, and I expected some reporters would show up in town by the end of the day, since it was no secret Sutton and I had joined the training academy this summer. Hell, our team had supported it, heralded it, doing a whole PR focus on it.

"Maybe. I'm just wondering why you're here and why Sutton's on campus looking like someone kicked his puppy."

A humorless snort escaped when I said, "Doesn't take a genius to work that one out. Didn't you know that video was from a few months back, which meant I was cheating on him?" I'd intended for my words to be dripped with sarcasm, but instead, they were low, quiet, and filled with my hurt.

"Something tells me you weren't cheating on

him." His soft words caught my attention and drew my gaze back to his.

"How can you be sure?" Fuck, my eyes stung, chest felt tight.

"Because I know years have passed by since we last saw each other, Jayden, but you cheating on anyone is not in your DNA. What's more, it's clear you love Sutton. You were on your way to admitting it earlier when we spoke."

"Why do you think that?" I asked, heart in my throat. "If he's my fiancé, wouldn't that be kind of a given?"

His unwavering gaze searched mine. "I think when you fall in love, you'd happily shout it from the rooftops and not keep it a secret for a year."

I huffed out a breath and wiped a hand over my face. Despite all the nonsense battling it out inside my heart, a chuckle spilled out of me. "How the hell do you do that?" I shook my head. "Am I that predictable?"

A gentle look was aimed my way. "Only to those who know you. And I also know what love looks like." He cast a quick glance toward Blake, his smile softening even more. "It's also clear whenever you and Sutton see each other or even talk about each other."

I nodded and took a fortifying gulp of beer. "I

know how Sutton feels about me." While he hadn't come right out and said those three words, he'd pretty much bared his soul to me when he'd talked about why he'd kept his distance last season. "I've always loved him. It was just as a friend."

"Until now."

"Yeah, until now."

"So you wanna tell me what's going on and why you're here, Sutton's there, and why by morning everyone's going to think you've been up to no good behind Sutton's back?"

When I hesitated, Mark reached out and squeezed my arm. "We can do this as a whole session or simply as me as a friend. Either way, I will not say a word if you don't want me to, but it's clear you're unhappy, and you need to talk."

I bobbed my head and eyed an empty corner booth; nobody was in the ones close by. "Okay. Best go and get comfy and grab a fresh beer too. You're going to need it when you hear about the mess I've got myself in."

CHAPTER 20
SUTTON

Damage control was never pretty, and since my visit to Australia, it seemed to be one thing after another. Since coming out, Jayden and I had pretty much ducked for cover, doing the bare minimum to squash the rumors. On top of that, any official statement had been about respecting our privacy, us confirming our support for the LGBTQ+ community, and our excitement about joining the summer program at Montview.

So while damage control had been sporadic and half-assed, we'd made sure we didn't confirm or deny anything. Nor did we lie in any statement we made.

Sure, it pissed off our agents and didn't make the PR team's lives exactly easy, but gut deep I'd figured something like this would happen.

It was the only lifeline we had.

"I'm catching the next flight out. I've booked a suite at the Sentinel. Meet me there."

"Why not just come here?" I asked Max.

"In the next couple of hours, the academy is going to be swarmed. Between your explosive coming out, Jayden's injury, the two of you being honestly shady about the whole thing." I winced as he took a breath, not even being able to deny it. "You know they're going to be lapping this up. Only a few weeks ago there was a leak that you're getting married, and now, just a few weeks later, there's trouble in paradise, and Jayden's caught—"

"He wasn't cheating on me."

A heavy sigh ricocheted around the line. "Okay, if you say he didn't, he didn't, but we need to get you out of there before it becomes a circus. My job is to support you. Let me do this, okay?"

Max sounded tired. A sliver of guilt—another one to join the many—hit my chest. Both in Australia and when I'd returned Stateside, I hadn't let him do his job. The fuck had I been thinking?

"Okay," I agreed in defeat.

There was no holding back his exhale of relief. "Great. Just get yourself there and behind the locked doors of the suite. I'll be there as soon as I can, okay?"

"Okay."

There was a beat of hesitation before Max asked, "You doing all right?"

"Not really."

"Just hang in there, okay?"

The call disconnected, and I looked across at Jayden's empty side of the bed. A pang of regret made it difficult to get my head straight. Even more reason to lean on Max. He hadn't steered me wrong yet.

The bucketload of regrets weren't going anywhere. It meant I had to get out of here after giving my apologies to Coach, then try to work out what to do.

Two things I knew. Jayden being the bad guy was not acceptable. In my panic, I'd been an asshole to him. He deserved better from me. And also there was no way I'd allow the program, either the training or the new LGBTQ+ initiative, to be affected. The thought was deplorable.

Knowing those were the main goals of my next move, I grabbed my small carry-on and packed a few things. I made sure some of my remaining clothes were visible as I did so. The thought of Jayden returning and thinking I'd skipped out on him was not okay.

I tugged out my phone, ordered a cab, and then

hesitated to call Jayden. Too chickenshit to call him without a plan, I shot off a text.

Me: I'm sorry.

I'd clear up the rest when I worked a way out of this.

Bag in hand, I sought out Coach. He frowned when he saw me with my bag.

"What can I do?"

Heat hit my cheeks. It was no surprise the rumor mill was working overtime. But as yet, the handful of people I'd seen had only asked if I was okay. Each time I'd bobbed my head, relieved that they didn't start cussing out Jayden.

"Nothing, thanks. I'm heading out to meet with my agent. I'm sorry this has happened while we're here. The last thing I want to do is put a negative spotlight on the academy and everything you're doing here."

He waved his hand, brushing aside my comment. "Don't sweat it, kid. We all know exactly what it's like to live the life of a pro player. Hell, if anything, it's an up close and personal look for these dipshit hotshots we're working with. They're dreaming of fame, of living the high-roller life while playing ball. Sure they hear the stories, but getting to know both you and Moore, seeing this happening now in real-time... it's shit for you to be a lesson for them, but you know, shit happens, and you just have to step up and deal, right?"

Gratitude helped my temperature drop a couple of degrees. "Thanks, Coach."

"Just get on out of here. I'll remind everyone not to talk to the press and not buy into social media bullshit. Go do what you've gotta do, then get your ass back here as soon as you can." He patted me on the shoulder and returned to his desk.

With a smile, I made to leave the room, turning before I pulled the door closed behind me. "Thanks for understanding why I need to leave."

He nodded, calling out, "Good riddance," following up with a wink.

Head down, I headed outside to wait for my cab. I could fix this. Somehow, someway.

All my thoughts continued to spiral on the journey, the only possible end to each thread being inevitable. No more secrets and complete truths.

Not that I was talking about the media or even the public at large. While I was a well-paid athlete living my best life and so unbelievably lucky, my life was still my own. Plus I'd worked my ass off to be here. With that, I deserved privacy. All I owed my fans was that I played my hardest on the court and was a decent human being.

Nothing Jayden and I had done negated that.

No. All my truths belonged to Jayden. A few to some others too along the way, but still, Jayden was what mattered.

I managed to get into the hotel suite without too much fuss. While waiting, I turned on the TV, putting on a movie just to make some noise. Not long after the end credits were rolling, the suite door opened, and in walked Max.

His smile was friendly, genuine, and I stood, greeting him with a handshake. "You get here okay?"

I bobbed my head. "Yeah. No problems."

"Excellent." He dropped his bag on the floor and headed straight to the kitchen area. "Coffee?"

"No, thanks. Caffeine will push me over the edge."

At my words, he cast another glance my way, this one more assessing as he took me in. He huffed out a breath, his cheeks puffing out as he refocused on the pod machine. A few clicks and a hiss of steam later, he headed toward the sitting area and took a seat opposite me on one of the couches.

"The more I know, the better position I can be in to help you." He winced when he took a sip of the piping hot coffee. "Lay it out for me. I'll give you my ten cents, and then we can work this out, okay?"

I'd had nothing but time to think when the movie had played, and I'd waited for Max to arrive. I hadn't checked social media, only glancing at my cell to see if Jayden had returned my message. He hadn't.

With a bob of my head, I told him everything. The realization a year back about my feelings for Jayden. My panic, the word "fiancé" leaking from the hospital, our escape to the outback, Jayden, in that sweet, adorable way of his, telling me he thought us being together wasn't as crazy as it sounded. And then the here and now. Our commitment to the LGBTQ+ community, my desire not to make a mockery of everything Montview was hoping to achieve. And, of course, the video of Jayden not actually cheating on me since we hadn't been a couple at the time.

I didn't get into Jayden telling me I'd been his last kiss and the contradiction of the video. Nor did I mention Pearce.

By the end of it, I grabbed a beer from the bar, emotionally spent and a headache looming. Looking over at Max as I sat back down, I held his gaze.

"Let's take a step back a moment," he said, ankle crossed on his thigh and his foot bobbing up and down. "You and Jayden are in a committed relationship, correct?"

I nodded, feeling like I was back in high school. Max wasn't that much older than me, but with his black-rimmed glasses, crisp shirt and well-pressed pants despite his flight, and his confident demeanor, I felt very much the pubescent kid in this scenario.

Heck, since I'd fallen for Jayden, I'd felt this way in general. Perhaps it came with that giddy feeling of being in love.

"At no point have you confirmed or denied being engaged or even when the engagement started." He'd moved on to making statements. "Jayden hasn't been dishonest or strayed from your relationship." I held back my wince at that, thinking about Jayden not telling the truth. It was still something that didn't make sense. Needing to give him the benefit of the doubt, I remained quiet so Max could continue with his processing.

After a beat, he looked me dead in the eye, stating, "I don't get it."

Taken aback, I frowned. "Don't get what exactly?"

"Why you're freaking out about this. That's assuming Jayden is freaking out too." He left it hanging, knowing full well I hadn't mentioned where Jayden was. I may have left out the part about my reaction to the video.

With a grimace, I said, "I may have reacted badly to the video and panicked. Jayden went off somewhere."

Max's brows shot high. "And you don't know where? Has he called his agent? Anyone?"

I shrugged, feeling lousier by the minute. That I'd spiraled over the last year, then had a crisis figuring out my sexuality, then acted like this, pissed me the fuck off.

I stood up and shook my head. "I need to fix this and find him."

"While I agree, you traipsing around the place isn't going to work."

"Neither is me hiding here." For crying out loud, who had I become?

"Hold on. Let's get back to me saying I don't get it. Why not just admit you didn't get together until you were in Australia? That Jayden did nothing wrong? Nothing you've said or done will compromise… hell, anything as far as I'm concerned. If this is your pride—"

"It's not," I snapped.

In response, Max quirked a brow at me. He'd been my agent since going pro. He knew me well. While we didn't socialize, our professional relationship meant we had a firm handle and read on each other.

When he didn't say anything, I shook my head. "It's not," I repeated, even as I forced myself to open up to the possibility that it was exactly that.

"Listen." Max sat forward. "You've always been the unmovable rock. The voice of reason. The man who processes everything, weighs up the odds, and does the right thing. The man who everyone, especially Jayden, depends on. Whatever you're going through, been through, struggling with, heck, embracing and loving, that's all just the next step. It doesn't mean you've lost any of those qualities. But I know that brain of yours."

I grunted and leaned back, exhaling loudly. "People keep having to talk me down and help me get my emotions to make peace with my head." I shrugged. "It's weird, man. That's usually my job."

Max nodded. "So maybe it's your turn to let others support you for once."

"Everything you're saying, I understand. I agree with. But it's alien as fuck, letting go."

"That's just the control freak inside you talking. It's not a weakness."

I managed a smile. "I know. You know I could spout off about toxic masculinity for days." But he was right. It wasn't about feeling weak. None of it was about that. Letting someone who wasn't me take the reins, though, was the difficulty. It didn't help knowing I'd screwed up, time and time again.

"I know I'm not perfect."

Max scoffed, and I flipped him off.

"But I regret letting the story run about me and

Jayden when it wasn't true." There was still Pearce I would need to apologize to.

"Then maybe you wouldn't have ended up with the revelations you've had." The asshole chuckled when I blanched. "Relax, I'm sure it was meant to be, and whatever other romantic crap you want to assign to you figuring things out. Just find a way to forgive yourself for not always being perfect."

"And maybe that pride thing you mentioned holds a ring of truth to it," I admitted.

He laughed. "Okay, so what's the plan? Who are we talking to? And how much groveling is necessary to make sure Jayden doesn't dump your sorry ass?"

CHAPTER 21
JAYDEN

On surprisingly steady legs, I headed back to campus. I'd brushed off Mark's suggestion I call a cab or he'd escort me. I needed the time to think.

Having spilled everything to Mark, I wasn't surprised when he'd absorbed every word and listened intently, not once interrupting me. While he'd also shared pearls of wisdom afterward, all I needed was Sutton. Without him, I felt strangely numb.

Between our argument and my guilt at the poisonous things I'd said, I just want to shove my tongue in his mouth, suck him off, and set the record straight. Exactly in that order.

I expected he'd want to talk some more. But talk was overrated. Why hash things out when an orgasm was a hundred times more effective? Make that a joint orgasm, and we'd be blissed out and back to putting our world to rights.

I chuckled inwardly as I stepped into the courtyard, heading toward our room. Pulling out my phone to check the time, I winced, seeing missed calls from my agent. Adulting was the worst, as was fame at times. I closed out his text, not wanting to read it, and noticed a handful more calls and texts I'd missed since switching my cell to silent a few hours back.

My breath hitched when I saw Sutton had texted me.

Sutton: I'm sorry.

Relief swept through me. The likelihood of us sucking each other's brains out seemed more imminent since Sutton had reached out to me. I was actually impressed he'd held back and hadn't written a fifteen-paragraph breakdown of what he was sorry about. Those two words meant more.

I was all about keeping life simple. I smirked. Anyone looking back at my life would probably argue that concept, but they knew nothing. Maybe I got myself into situations and experienced life a little differently than most.

But my approach was to live life simply by taking chances and opportunities and living in the moment rather than analyzing everything to death. Sure, there'd been a few pitfalls along the way. Did I care? Not one bit.

I was here, had a career and life I loved, and a man who I felt deserved a capital L when I considered my feelings for him. That asshole Mark was too wise for his own good.

Scanning the door with my key card, I waited until the locks disengaged and entered the building. A sense of certainty and rightness beat against my chest, right alongside every certain step I took closer to our shared room.

"Jayden, you got a minute?"

I stopped in my tracks at the sound of Pearce's voice. While Sutton was my mission and I was desperate to get to him, I liked Pearce a lot. I could imagine what he'd heard by now, so this was as good a time as any. "Absolutely."

Turning to him, I eyed him carefully, trying to get a read on the guy. From the dip of his brows and his curious stare, whatever he thought he seemed uncertain about.

"It's all over social media." A wince followed, making him look younger than his twenty-four years. "You okay?"

Surprise had my eyes widening. "Yeah, or I will be as soon as I find Sutton."

A more pronounced wince followed, right along-side a grimace.

"What is it?" I asked.

"It's Sutton. He left a while back."

The heavy thump of my heart made his words muffled. "What?" I shook my head, not under-standing.

"I heard him tell Coach he was leaving. He had a bag with him, then jumped in a cab."

Blood rushed to my ears, confusion clouding my vision. "I don't understand."

The hand on my forearm startled me. I hadn't even realized Pearce had moved. "Shit, man. I'm sorry. I know there's stuff going down. I also know not to believe half the stuff I see and hear."

"I need to go," I managed to say, needing to get away, go to our room. Pearce had to be wrong. There was no way Sutton had up and left.

Racing to our room, I fumbled with the lock to let myself in and switched on the light. A quick scan of the room showed me Sutton's towel was still on the chair, and a glance in the wardrobe revealed his larger case and some of his clothes.

I exhaled in relief, just as I noticed his smaller bag was gone. Heading to the bathroom, I focused on not thinking the worst. Almost all his stuff was here. I paused when I looked at the sink. Sutton's toiletry bag was missing.

"Fuck." I yanked out my phone, moved to the bed, and sat down.

Maybe he just needed a night away? The thought twisted my gut. Though could I blame him, and exactly what did he owe me? Since dating, we'd never been apart, never had space. Somewhere in the recesses of my mind, I was sure more intelligent men than me would say that was unhealthy and probably have statistics about how relationships didn't last or anything.

So what that we worked on the court like a well-oiled machine? I knew our friendship confused most people. And why wouldn't it? Sutton was so together and smart, despite how much he'd tried to convince me otherwise over the past few weeks. Me? I spoke before I figured things out and acted without thinking all the time.

It also seemed I got so drunk that I couldn't even remember making out with some woman.

Why would Sutton want to stick around for that?

Maybe it was for the best this happened now, before we got deeper, before I screwed up his life any more than I already had.

With another look at the last message Sutton sent me, I swallowed hard.

I'm sorry.

It was funny how I'd interpreted those words so differently less than thirty minutes ago. The words could only mean that he'd left and that he'd made a mistake.

I switched off my phone and threw it on the bed.

What I was sorry for was always screwing shit up. I gave a humorless snort and lay back on the mattress, inhaling the scent of Sutton's bodywash and his natural scent.

THE BANGING ON THE DOOR JOLTED ME FROM MY SLEEP. Wincing, I took in my surroundings.

At some point in the night, I'd stripped down to my boxer briefs and crawled under the sheets. I'd even managed to close the blinds.

What I hadn't managed to do was get wasted. Nor did I figure things out with Sutton. It wasn't necessary to glance over his side of the bed. I knew he hadn't returned.

Once again the door thumped with a knock. I groaned. "Hold up." Dragging myself out of bed and tugging my jeans up from where I'd discarded them, I yawned. I unlocked and opened the door, surprised to see Eddie standing in the doorway.

"You missed breakfast."

I groaned and threw him the stink eye. "Seriously?"

"Get your ass showered and meet me in twenty minutes. I'll scrounge you up some food. It looks like you need something."

"I have no plans to leave this room today. Unless it's to get beer or pizza." I had no issue with feeling sorry for myself. The last thing I wanted to do was see, well, anyone. The gossip mill would have been working overtime. Dealing with that would take energy I didn't have.

Eddie pursed his lips as he adjusted his stance, stubbornness setting in. It may have been a few years since I'd seen the man, but we'd played on the same court for a couple of years, and I knew that look all too well.

With a sigh, I brushed my hand over my face. "Why are you here, Eddie?" When he folded his arms and quirked a brow at me, I dropped my head. "You just going to stand there and not leave me alone?"

After a beat or two of silence, he leaned against the doorframe. "Just please shower and don't forget today's visitors."

Guilt jolted me. How could I have forgotten today's activities? Fuck, it was something I'd been looking forward to. Not only because I was going to be on the court, whipping the young guys into shape, but more because the Pride Youth group was visiting for the day.

"Shit, yeah, of course. Give me twenty."

I took a quick shower, trying to get my head into what was involved in the day ahead. After dressing, I gazed around the room, looking at the unrumpled sheets of Sutton's side of the bed. My heart pinched. Would he be back for the game? How would that even work?

I picked up my cell with a sigh, not bothering to turn it on. Yesterday, after one long hard look at his message, I'd switched the contraption off. The thought of listening out in case he tried to call or text but not receiving anything had been too much. Self-preservation had kicked in, and I'd shut it down.

Maybe we'd find a way to figure this out, but feeling bruised this morning, I couldn't even begin to start wrapping my head around how to do that.

Rushing to the canteen, I was relieved when I didn't hear voices. Since it was well after breakfast, the college players would already be on the court, running drills and doing some last-minute preparation for the group's arrival. Once inside the canteen, I looked around and saw Marian in the kitchen. She spotted me immediately and grinned.

"Eddie asked me to put this aside for you." She reached inside the warmer and pulled out a heap of pancakes. Placing it on the tray, she set a dish of cut fruit next to it, along with a small jug of syrup.

"You made pancakes? Are they Coach approved?"

With a conspiring wink, she hushed, "Shh, if you won't tell, I definitely won't."

I leaned across and planted a kiss on her rosy cheek. "You're the best, Marian. Thank you."

"You're a good boy. Go and eat up."

I chuckled. "It's been a while since anyone called me a boy."

Her expression turned tender, kickstarting the emotions I wanted to ignore today. "My own boy has ten years on you, Jayden, which most definitely makes you a boy."

With a small smile, I took the plate, set it down, then went to the fancy coffee machine. One steaming mug of coffee later, extra creamy, just like I liked my cum shots apparently, I dug into the fluffy pancakes. I sighed, embracing the moment of contentment, not having realized how hungry I was or how much I needed the comfort food.

Noise at the door had me glancing up. My heart stuttered, and I swallowed my mouthful of pancake, grimacing as it clogged my throat, having not chewed enough. I coughed immediately and took a gulp of coffee.

"Chewing is an impressive skill to have. Clearly you take after your mother."

Confused, I stood and walked over to my dad. With my pulse thumping, we embraced. "What are you doing here?" I pulled away, searching his expression.

"It's been almost three months since I saw you. I can't just stop by to check in and watch your debut?"

I narrowed my gaze. Dad didn't do saccharine. "Uh-huh. For real, you being here is making my brain hurt. And debut, really? What's going on? Where's Mom?"

"I'll have a coffee from that machine over there." He led me back to the table and sat down, waiting expectantly, wearing a small smile.

There was no point arguing with the man, especially when standing between him and caffeine. Coffee made, I returned to my half-eaten breakfast, placing his coffee in front of him.

"Montview's something impressive, right?" He gazed around the room.

"You didn't come all this way to talk about what a great place this is."

His gaze locked with mine as he took a slow sip of his drink. I rolled my eyes at him and bit the inside of my cheek. It was no secret who I took after the most. The man teased, could win a stare down, pulled pranks, and spoke what was on his mind with practiced ease. It made him being here even more alarming.

And the bastard was waiting me out.

"Why are you here, Dad?"

"You look like your favorite Milo Henderson jersey has been doused with gasoline and set on fire."

Wide-eyed, my mouth dropped open. "It better fucking not have been." I had eight Henderson jerseys and most definitely had a favorite. When Dad chuckled, I fired him a dirty look.

"Your mom made me come. Said I should support you in case you swooned or something on the court."

I snorted. That was so not the reason. "You pissing her off?"

He snorted. "Always. Any excuse to get me out of the house."

I grinned. "Now that I believe. Who's staying with her?" While my mom was super capable of taking care of herself and the whole family, she had some additional medical complications that could spark up without notice, making it difficult to get herself in and out of her chair.

"Your cousin Lake's with her."

I nodded, relieved it was Lake and not Aunt Joan.

"You doing okay, kid?"

At the softness of his words, I froze and closed my eyes. "Dad, can we not?" When I opened them, I glanced away from him.

"We're worried about you. Between your accident and you telling us about your relationship, to all the rumors flying around the place, especially since yesterday, of course we're worried, and of course I came. I know there's a game today. Yeah, I know it's friendly and fun, but still, it may be a big deal to you."

Fuck. Emotion clogged my throat. Too terrified to see the compassion in Dad's gaze, I couldn't look at him. Listening to his tone was hard enough, making it difficult to not break down.

"Sutton called us last night."

That got my attention. I swung my focus to my dad. "He did? Why?"

"Said something about loving you and being worried about you."

The hammering of my heart had me shaking my head. "What? He did?"

"Perhaps if you had your phone on, none of this would be as much of a surprise."

Double fuck. I scrambled for my phone, my heart in my throat and a spark of hope in my chest. The thing took forever to turn on. "What else did he say?"

When Dad didn't answer, I flicked my attention to him. Amusement filled his gaze. While it was a lot better than sympathy, all it did was make me want to throw my slow-ass phone across the room.

"Perhaps you need to talk to him."

I clenched my jaw. "You see him around here anywhere?" Bitterness crept into my tone. "He was the one who pissed off somewhere yesterday, took some of his shit with him. Who does that?"

Dad angled his head and took me in. "I imagine someone who was hurt and confused."

"Well, I was fucking hurt and confused too."

"And what did you do?"

I slammed my mouth closed. I up and left. "But I only went to a bar." I sounded petulant.

"Isn't being an adult in a grown-up relationship the best thing in the world?" Dad sassed. Before I could flip him off, his tone softened when he said, "I know your life is different than most, what with the whole stardom thing." Somehow I managed to not roll my eyes, but I understood what he was getting at. "The rules are different for you. Fair or not. You're under scrutiny, and you simply being here"—he twirled his finger—"means you're stepping up and making a statement while trying to be a responsible adult."

I sighed, and Dad chuckled. "Thirty-three years old, Dad."

"Exactly. *Trying* to be an adult. That means dealing with the hard shit. I know you, my boy, and you don't run from the hard shit."

Of course he was right. "I'm here and not running."

He eyed me, and I returned his steady gaze, determination settling in my veins.

"Good." He took a swig of his coffee, set it down, and stood. "Get your ass up and come with me. You've got a game to get to."

CHAPTER 22
SUTTON

Each time I called Jayden, it went to voicemail. Since six this morning, I'd been trying, hoping he'd wake and get the thing switched on. By seven, I'd donned my cap and sunglasses to escape the suite only to be stopped by Max, who pointed out the media outlets camped outside Montview and that we needed to stick to our arrangement.

While I didn't know how he gathered his intel, I had no reason not to believe him.

Picking up my ringing cell, my heart tripped over itself, hoping it was Jayden. While it wasn't him, I wasn't too disappointed as Jayden's mom's name flashed on the scream. "Hey, Mrs. Moore," I greeted.

"How many times have I told you to call me Daisy or even Mom?"

My heart constricted, hoping that would be

possible one day soon. "Sure thing, Daisy. Maybe we can build up to Mom. Is everything okay?"

"Sure is. Just wanted to let you know Mike landed not long ago."

I smiled. "That's great. I wish you could have come too."

Her voice remained light. "Pish, don't you worry about me. You know I'm not a fan of traveling, and this contraption doesn't make it easy. Plus, you're doing me a favor."

"I am?"

"A couple of days without Mike, and it's like I'm the one having the vacation."

I chuckled. Considering Jayden took after his dad in so many ways, I believed every word.

"And how are you feeling? You doing okay, honey?"

I smiled and sank down onto a chair. "Yeah, or I will be. Just wish I hadn't left the academy yesterday, is all. Camping out there would mean I wouldn't feel trapped."

"I know, honey. Just don't worry too much about everything, okay? Things will settle down soon enough. I'm just so pleased you called us yesterday and caught us up to speed. You know we love you boys, don't you?"

I swallowed hard, surprised at the impact of her words. Yesterday when I'd called, I'd told them pretty much everything, or at least the bare bones of it all. How I loved their son. That we weren't engaged. And anything they read or saw was before we were together, so they shouldn't be concerned about Jayden.

The conversation had extended and gone deeper, hence why Mike had jumped on a plane. I'd been beyond touched, and regardless of what happened over the next few hours, I knew Jayden would love the surprise of seeing his dad.

"I do, Daisy. Love you too."

"Good, well, keep your cool and don't screw this up." A light laugh filtered down the line, and I grinned.

"No chance of that. I'll speak to you soon."

After we said our goodbyes, I managed to eat breakfast in between some fast-paced texting with Pearce, Eddie, and Coach. All three I'd spoken to last night, and we'd texted a lot over the past couple of hours.

"You ready?"

Max startled me from scrolling through my messages. "Is it time?"

His brows shot high. "Just a couple of hours ago, you were sneaking out. Now you're worried?"

I shrugged and stood, feeling so nervous I was going to puke.

What I planned was so not me, but it had Jayden written all over it. It was that knowledge that had me wiping my sweaty palms on my jeans and taking one step in front of the other to get to the elevator.

Max, a stoic presence at my side, clapped me on the back. "You've got this, man."

Somewhat numbly, I nodded, and with each step I took, I questioned my sanity.

This was crazy. Fucking ludicrous. My hand shook when I pressed the call button. Rather than Max pointing out the obvious, he remained quiet and passed me a cold bottle of water.

"The hotel's organized a car. It's waiting for us in the underground garage."

I nodded, watching the numbers count down, the movement feeling ominous. Shit, was it like a count-down to my doom, my humiliation?

I huffed out a breath and cracked my neck. This wasn't just about me. Sometimes it was necessary to put yourself out on a limb and hope like fuck it wouldn't break so you plummeted to the ground. At the end of the day, I'd handled yesterday badly. Again.

Today was about living my truth, this new

version of myself, and finding the comfort and love in that.

More resolved than just thirty minutes ago, by the time we were secure in the car and heading to the academy, I found a reason to smile.

Jayden.

He was going to go nuts over this. He loved this shit, and since I loved him, I'd do pretty much anything for the man.

LIKE CLOCKWORK, EDDIE, WHO WAS PROUDLY WEARING his pink, purple, and blue pin, and Milo had distracted the press with an impromptu conversation, talking to them about the Pride Youth group due to arrive in the next few minutes. It was the distraction we'd hoped for so they couldn't swarm me, while having the added bonus of focusing on the Pride Youth group, what their mission was, and how this year's program at Montview was supporting it as a whole.

Once inside the main grounds, Max and I headed to the court.

Today, with the group's visit, a short game was going on between the staff and the college kids. After that, the college players were spending time with the group, running some fun drills, answering questions, and spending time with them. After that, a movie was planned, obviously a basketball movie, complete with popcorn and other candy, before the group left.

It was something I'd been excited to be a part of. Still was.

"You know what you're doing?" Max asked before I entered the court.

No. "Yeah, I've got this." God, I was going to make such a prick out of myself.

Max's laughter wasn't reassuring, but he was clearly entertained by my pending humiliation. With a quick slap on the shoulder, he left me to it, heading into the small court to sit and watch.

There were no other guests attending today. The only people watching the game were Pride Youth. We'd agreed to their recording and doing basic social media about the game as promo, but the focus was on us and the game only, rather than the more personal stuff with the kids later on. All I knew about the group was that about forty kids were attending, all between twelve and seventeen, and all identifying as LGBTQ+.

I thought the whole thing was awesome, and with what I planned, I hoped they got a kick out of it.

"Didn't think you were going to show." Pearce

shook my hand and hugged me, a wide grin on his face.

"No chance of me missing this."

With his grin still in place, the guy practically vibrated before me.

"You doing okay? Too much caffeine this morning?"

"I told the staff and the college players this morning. Came out to them."

"Fuck, man." I engulfed him in a tight hug, tears springing in my eyes. "I'm so proud of you, man. For real."

I pulled away, not even giving a damn that my emotion was clear for him to see. His laugh was giddy, his own gaze watery. He sniffed and shook his head, clearing his throat. "Right, well, yeah. So that bit's done. I'll do the easy stuff later."

"Easy stuff?"

"Yeah, you know, the fans, America, the Eagles."

I laughed. "Well, I hope you know our team well enough to be confident that they'll have your back, completely."

"Shit, do you think they had a wager on me?"

I snorted. "If so, I didn't hear anything about it."

"Huh, I don't know whether to be offended or impressed as hell if there were no bets going." He bobbed his brows a couple of times, the energy pouring off him addictive. "You ready?"

I nodded. "Definitely." I latched on to his enthusiasm and gripped tightly. He was riding such a high, and he deserved every single second of it.

"Let's get going to the coach's office then. There's everything we need."

I FELT SEVENTEEN AGAIN. A GIANT BALL OF NERVOUS excitement bounced around in my gut, much like it had when I'd asked Libby Henshaw to be my date for the prom. Back then, the ball had been the size of a tennis ball. Now, it was definitely the size of a basketball, this moment feeling more significant than the day I got drafted.

I tightened my rainbow laces, something we were all wearing to celebrate today's events and our guests. I then shook out my hands.

Pearce had left me a while back. I just hoped he was doing a decent job of calming Jayden down. It was a risk not seeing him beforehand and waiting until we were in public to speak again. But this was my public declaration to him, and there wasn't a doubt in my mind he'd lap it up.

Okay, maybe there was the slightest possibility that he'd slam the ball in my face first. But I was quietly confident he liked my face too much to do damage. And honestly, if for one moment I was seriously worried or uncertain about his ready acceptance of our relationship, I wouldn't have organized it to begin with.

Certainty bloomed to life, and I smiled as I listened to the cheering kids who'd entered the court about thirty minutes ago. Coach Jenkins was emcee-ing. His voice over the microphone speakers reached me as I stood outside the doors, well away from the main locker room.

I gripped the cheap trophy that Max had managed to rustle up with the power of determination and cash and grinned at the *#1 Lollipop King* engraved on it.

Coach worked his way through today's players, their names, the small crowd going wild. My heart thumped loudly at hearing Jayden's name, and then there was just one left.

"Gale Sutton, star Eagles player."

And that was my cue.

A final check that my Eagles hoodie was zipped up fully, I opened the door and jogged out onto the court. It took me just a couple of seconds for my gaze to land on Jayden's. His eyes were wide, his focus intent, stare unwavering as I got closer to the rest of the guys on the court.

Before I forgot, I waved at our visitors, offering a big smile. Spotting Mike, I fired him a chin lift before refocusing on Coach.

"And these guys here will be entertaining you in a few moments. The only bets you should be making are on the coaching staff. You can be sure we're going to be wiping the floor with these guys."

At his words, the group cheered and our college players jeered. I laughed and zeroed in on Jayden. His focus hadn't strayed.

"Before we get to teaching these kids how it should be done—" A round of coughs, most muttering lower-level jibes that wouldn't get the players into trouble, interrupted Coach. "In recognition of you all, our distinguished guests, one of the newest members of our coaching staff is going to say a few words."

I swallowed hard, cracked my neck, and took the mic from Coach with a smile. "Thanks, Coach Jenkins." I glanced out to the group of kids, all wearing some sort of basketball paraphernalia, all sitting, eyes wide and seeming to pay attention. I doggedly avoided Jayden for a beat, sure his heavy gaze was on me.

"I know it's unusual for me to be talking

pregame, but before today truly kicks off, it seems only fitting that I say a few words—and I promise it'll be just a few, as I know you're looking forward to us taking these guys on—" I paused for some laughter. "But yeah, it feels right that someone just like you guys, someone who, like you, identifies as LGBTQ+, share a few truths." A few grinning faces stared back at me, making my heart lurch in my chest, reaffirming I was doing the right thing. For me, for Jayden, and for them.

"First off, I think you're all incredible. Not only the couple of you who are wearing Eagles jerseys but all of you for being part of such a wonderful group. It was only this last year that I felt I had to hide, that I kept a secret so big that I thought my world would implode." I risked a glance at Jayden. Pearce was at his side, his hand on my boyfriend's shoulder, a steady support that I appreciated. Jayden's eyes remained on me, though, and when I made eye contact, his mouth twitched before he offered me a tender smile.

"So about a year ago, you may have witnessed what I like to think of as a pretty spectacular kiss." When the spectators and the guys behind me cheered, I laughed loudly, ignoring the heat rushing to my cheeks. "I know, I know, that's how I reacted too, but the thing was, I didn't let the guy over there know that all it took was that one kiss for me to realize something had been missing in my life all of these years." I shrugged and huffed out a breath. "I'd only just had my rainbow epiphany and figured that maybe the long and wonderful list of letters was one I identified with. But with just a toe out, I jumped right back into the closet."

A few sympathetic nods were directed back at me. Fuck, I needed to move this on. Share my truth but get to the good stuff so I could win back my man and get everyone happy and on a high.

"But just a couple of months back, you may have heard that Jayden Moore was injured in Australia."

"While riding a kangaroo," he hollered out, amusement in every word. Happiness swirled around me, so relieved he couldn't help himself but get in on the storytelling in some way.

I chuckled. "I was going to say wrestling with a crocodile, but that's fine. But yeah," I refocused on the young faces before me, "when I flew out to be with him, we finally figured it out. I admitted how I felt, and was almost bowled over when Jayden told me he wanted to give our relationship a try. But we're not engaged—"

"Yet!"

My attention snapped to Mike in the audience, who stood and gave a thumbs-up. It was then I noticed his T-shirt. *Free Dad Hugs* was emblazoned in the colors of the rainbow. "Thanks, Mr. Moore."

"Anytime, son." He sat to a new round of cheers.

"So, we're not engaged… actually, we've been struggling to put a label on exactly what we are." Unzipping my hoodie, I pulled it off, revealing my T-shirt, again courtesy of the magic of Max and money. I faced the spectators first before turning fully to Jayden so he could read.

Will you go steady with me and be my…

One by one, the players tugged off their hoodies or jerseys to reveal their differently printed tees. T-shirts revealed, they stood at my side, so Jayden could read the printed words—as could our spectators from the same words printed at the backs.

A wave of hollers and stamping feet blew up the small court, crazy loud for only fifty or so people, and Jayden stood there laughing loudly, shaking his head.

Lover. Boyfriend. Sugarplum. Other half. Beau. Intended. Love. The list continued, filled with other dodgy alternatives Max and I had googled yesterday evening.

I stepped toward Jayden, lowering the mic.

"You almost made me shit myself. I thought you were going to propose."

I matched his grin. "You heard your dad. Not yet."

"And what's that?" He indicated the trophy that had been dangling from my fingers all this time.

"I promised you a trophy for a skill set of yours."

His eyes lit up. "Hell yeah, does it say blo—"

"No." I cut him off quickly and shook my head. "I had to be more subtle than that." I passed it to him, and he chuckled. "So what do you say? Can we choose a word, put a label to it, and make it official?"

He stepped into my space. "How about I just say you're mine?"

Feeling giddy at his declaration, I tugged him toward me and pressed my mouth to his. The kiss was brief and tender and did nothing to show him just how sorry I was or just how grateful I was that he'd agreed to be mine. Pulling away, more than aware we had an audience, one that included a video camera, I stared into his eyes. "I love you."

"I know." He dotted a kiss to my mouth. "I love you. And you can show me how much later. Once we've kicked these guys' asses."

I didn't miss the heat in his eyes and was more than okay with whatever he wanted to do. The pain in my ass loved me. I grinned. "Let's go show them how to play some ball."

CHAPTER 23
JAYDEN

The day had been incredible.

From the moment Sutton stepped onto the court, my heart had lodged in my throat. It had struggled to move, especially when I realized what he was doing. Sutton never pulled stunts like this. Ever. And that he did, meant all the more to me.

While the college players may have kicked our asses, I very loudly made it clear that it was only because twenty fresh-faced players had an advantage on the nine of us. We'd had fun, though, and long after the youth group had gone, and after we'd made sure Dad had got to his hotel safely, it was finally just Sutton and me.

"How's your head?" Concern pitched his voice low as we unlocked our room.

"Okay. Probably a good thing I took the painkiller

before the movie. It's shifted the headache that was forming." It was a huge relief. While it was far from a full-on game, on the court I'd played hard. And not once had my head hurt, nor had I gone dizzy.

The looming headache a little while after was more likely a combination of the exertion, on top of a fitful night's sleep, and the stress of what had happened with Sutton and me catching up.

I kicked off my shoes, Sutton doing the same. "Letting you know now that my codependency is going to be in full swing, and after last night sleeping alone, I have no desire for that to happen again."

He nodded. "I have no issues with that."

I grinned and paused to watch him tug off his T-shirt. The expanse of skin on display made my mouth water. Spending time kissing and tasting his skin had become one of my favorite ways to relax while having the added bonus of making us both horny.

Sutton tugged his cell out and focused on the screen. "I missed a text from Max."

"Everything okay?" We'd already caught each other up about what had happened since yesterday afternoon, right alongside heated kisses when we sneaked away and grabbed some time to ourselves before dinner with my dad. There'd been heartfelt apologies.

"Yeah. He's just about to board his flight. Said there's some footage of earlier that's going viral. Apparently the hashtag #jayton is exploding or something."

I snorted. "How'd you feel about Jayton and not Sutden or Galden." I scrunched my nose at both alternatives. "Well, apart from them sounding awful?"

"You before me... you on top... it has certain merits."

I'd been tugging my own tee off when he spoke. I tore it off quickly, eyes wide and my cock twitching. "As in merits about me fucking you?"

Sutton tilted his head back and looked at the ceiling. I was sure there was an eye roll in there too. "And they say romance is dead."

I grinned, stalked toward where he sat on the bed, and clambered onto his lap. He latched on to my ass and held me tightly. "You need me to romance you first? Will that make me getting inside you happen faster?" I tilted forward and rubbed against him.

A soft grunt escaped him before he said, "If romance means your mouth on me beforehand, then that's a hell yes."

Staring into his eyes, I looked for any uncertainty. Seeing none, I leaned forward and pressed a light kiss on his mouth. "Did you work out the prep stuff?"

Light pink spread across his cheeks. "I think so, or at least a quick version of it. Will that be okay?"

I nodded immediately. "Yeah, definitely." I was rock-hard already. "And we'll take it slow, yeah?"

"Okay. Give my fifteen, okay?"

Only the knowledge that we'd soon be having penetrative sex for the first time got me to move. Sitting on his lap, his erection firm and pressing against my butt, was a comfortable place to be.

Sutton stood and rummaged around in his bag for the anal douche we'd bought before leaving Minnesota. Both of us had experimented with it, just like we'd already experimented with the basics of fingers and searching for the prostate, which holy fucking orgasm… why hadn't we been doing this since we were old enough to suck each other off?

I figured good things came to those who waited. It was what I reminded myself while Sutton prepped himself.

Rather than using the time to simply play with my dick, I got the lube, grabbed a couple of condoms, and threw some of our clothes into the wardrobe to straighten the room up. I even turned off the light and switched on the bedside lamps. I also put some music on.

Sutton had gotten wonderfully vocal the few times I'd brushed against his prostate—so much more than when he came from me sucking or jacking him off—so I figured at least a little sound may cover some of the noise.

The room in a little better order and looking surprisingly cozy for a basic room, I stripped, thankful I'd already had a shower after the game, so I didn't stink.

I then lay on the bed to wait for him, my stomach fizzing with nerves, but the best kind. I wanted this, him so fucking badly that just the thought of being buried inside him made my cock pulse. I should have jacked off after the game. Though I don't think the rest of the guys would have appreciated the fact. I chuckled at the thought.

The bathroom door opened, and gloriously naked, Sutton stepped out of the room, closing the door behind him. My dick twitched in anticipation as I took him in. By the time I made eye contact with him, he had a brow quirked high at me, and I grinned. "You're so fucking sexy." And he seriously was. My mind still boggled that it had taken me so long to notice him this way.

Making his way toward me, he angled his head a little, gaze raking my body, pretty much the same way I'd done to him. His focus turned to the supplies on the bedside, and the slightest of pinks was just visible in his cheeks. A second later, his Adam's apple bobbed.

By the time he reached the mattress, I was on my knees and dragging him down. Patience wasn't a virtue I needed. Not when I craved his mouth on mine more than I needed anything else.

Once he was on top, I wrapped my legs around him, our mouths fused, tongues tasting, and soft groans spilling between the hottest of kisses. "On your back," I garbled. "I wanna suck you off."

Sutton eased back, his pupils blown and a grin forming on his mouth. "You going to earn that trophy?"

I laughed as we shifted so I could get him under me. "It was a pretty spectacular trophy. It seems only right." I kissed him again before swiping the lube and kissing a trail down his body.

His groans were breathy and needy, each grunt making me throb and so eager to be inside him. But we needed to do this right.

Finally eye to eye with his groin, I watched, mesmerized for a beat at the beading precum and the way his length twitched under my scrutiny.

"It's not going to speak to you."

I snorted a laugh between his legs. "That right?" I

licked a long trail against the underside, right along the thick vein I knew resided there.

He grunted, hips restless. "Just suck me off already."

I grinned and pulled back, loving teasing him like this, getting off on Sutton coming undone with barely even a touch.

"You want my mouth on you?"

"You know I do."

As he spoke, I opened the lube and squirted some on a couple of my fingers. Engulfing his cock with my mouth, I bobbed down once, sucked, and then came up for air, earning me another disgruntled groan.

"You want my fingers in you?"

Immediately, he angled to look down at me. Heat sparked in his eyes. "Yes."

A shudder of desire raced through me, and once again, I latched on to his dick and sucked just as I traced a finger around him before dipping inside his channel.

He clenched around my digit, so tight and hot I wasn't sure if my dick would survive it. But fuck, it would be worth trying.

Going to town, I alternated between sucking and licking, all while fingering him. After another loud groan that rivaled the music, I slid in two fingers. He grunted and moved against my digits, riding the damn things with such abandon I had to pull my mouth away to groan, the sensation too much.

"Holy shit," I gasped, fingers plundering his ass as he continued to slam down on them. "Fuck, I could come just from watching you."

Sutton swore a string of expletives until he managed a "Don't you fucking dare. I need you inside, now."

I didn't need to be told twice.

I pulled away, scrambled for a condom, covered up, and lathered myself with more lube, adding extra directly to his ass for good measure.

"Let me just get three in there first. I need you to be ready." The words pained me, and my dick cussed me, so desperate to be buried deep inside Sutton.

"No, just hurry up."

I gritted my teeth, controlling my urge to do just that. "In a sec," I grunted, entering Sutton again, this time with three fingers.

His legs shook, and an honest to God whimper fell from him.

"You okay?"

"Yeah, I just want you."

"I want you too, baby." I leaned forward and kissed him while my fingers worked him over. The kiss was sloppy and wet, almost desperate.

"Okay," he gasped, cutting off the kiss. "Just do it."

I grinned. "You say the hottest things."

His stare was fierce. "I swear to God if you don't—"

Nudging against his hole, I cut him off this time with my cock. I pushed in slightly, alternating between watching where we joined and taking in his expression.

Eyes closed, head back, and mouth open, Sutton looked the most vulnerable I'd ever seen him. My heart lurched in my chest, my love for this man pulsating and doubling as I took him in.

I pushed in more, saying, "I love you." He needed to know what we were doing, him… was everything.

His gaze locked onto mine, and he relaxed under me. I slipped in an extra inch. "I love you."

Another inch deeper, and he grunted, his stare unwavering.

"I'm okay," he said, answering my unasked question.

I nodded and went deeper still. Sweat beaded on my forehead. My limbs shook, finally giving myself over to the sensation of being buried inside him, wrapped up in Sutton's heat. And then I bottomed out. My head fell forward, and I paused, taking a breath before looking back at Sutton.

A deep frown burrowed between his brows, but then he nodded. "I need you to move."

That I could do. I took my time, finding a steady rhythm, and glanced at his flagging cock. "Touch yourself." I wanted to see him hard. Wanted him to get off so damn badly, not sure how long I would last with how tightly he gripped me.

With a groan, I fixed my attention to his hand, breath catching when his cock thickened. I refocused on his face. His eyes were half mast, and his bottom lip was caught between his teeth. Then I couldn't resist anymore. I need to see how we fit and how he took all of me. And fuck, it was so perfect and sexy. Just watching how I disappeared inside him had me grunting, my balls tightening.

Not lasting was becoming a real issue.

Reaching down, I moved his legs, holding them higher, getting a better grip so I could hit my mark. Sutton gasped, grunted, cried out "Fuck" so loudly that I doubled my efforts.

"Yes, fuck, right there," he gasped.

I nodded, too far gone to articulate everything I was feeling, just what his body and reaction were doing to me. With a renewed effort, I snapped my hips, pegging his prostate time and time again. His moan was louder, breathier, needier than ever at each contact. His hand worked double time, working so fast it almost seemed like a blur.

I focused on his face, needing him to anchor me to him. Without eye contact, I'd float away, explode, and, hell… I had no idea how I'd come back to earth.

His gasps were broken, stuttering. His eyes wide, frantic. The bite on his lip punishing. And I wanted it all. Every single sound was mine. Every gesture I wanted to latch on to.

I angled into him deeper, faster.

His moan was guttural, loud, and perfect. With a body jerk and a constriction of his abs, he came. Creamy ribbons painted his hand, his stomach, the image so hot that I bucked wildly. A heavy grunt escaped me as my toes curled, my vision whitened, and I finally spilled my release.

Gasping for breath, I angled over him, freeing his legs and pressing my mouth against his. After a brush of our lips, I rested my head on his shoulder, breathing heavily, my body still shuddering from the strength of my orgasm.

"You okay?"

Sutton wrapped his arms around me and nodded. "Yeah. You?"

"More than."

He chuckled, and I grunted, the movement with

his laughter making him clamp around my sensitive dick.

"Let me just..." I eased out of him, a soft gasp escaping Sutton when I did so. Free of him, I instead lay entirely on him, wanting the contact, stickiness and all. I wasn't ready for the closeness or the buzz of our connection to end just yet.

Once again, he wrapped his arms around me, this time tighter as there was no chance of breaking my dick off. I inhaled against his neck and relaxed.

"Not sure I'm going to be able to move for a while."

My smile was lazy, and I attempted a nod. "Fine by me."

He chuckled, his body rocking mine. "You might want to get that condom sorted."

I groaned. "We need to do the whole serious relationship shit. Get tested and scrap the latex."

"Agreed," he said immediately, and it was enough to have me moving, just so I could smile at him and kiss him again. "Tomorrow too soon?" he asked after I pulled away, knowing I really should move and get cleaned up.

"You just want to do a deep dive into my ass bare."

He grinned. "I'm not going to deny it."

My dick twitched valiantly, liking that idea a lot.

But there wasn't a chance there'd be more action than a twitch for a little while. I sighed at the thought. "You know, if we'd got around to doing this when we were ten years younger, I'd be ready to go for round two by now."

"That right?"

"With how good you felt around my dick, that would be a hell yes." I paused and angled up to see his expression more fully. "Was it really okay? Did it hurt like fuck?"

"Did you not see just how hard I came?"

I shrugged. "Well, yeah, but a dick up your ass, it's gotta be painful, right?" Nerves danced up my spine at the thought of it. It was something I wanted to try so damn badly, but it didn't mean I wasn't freaking out about it.

"It was sore, took some getting used to, but I knew it was you, and it was making you feel good, and then when you pegged my prostate, all that flew out the window, and it was then fucking awesome."

Relieved at his words, I smiled. The last thing I wanted to do was hurt him or be hurt either. Where was the pleasure in that? "So you'd do it again?"

"Definitely. Maybe not in the next twenty-four hours, though." He winced a little and wriggled.

"I know that should make me feel kinda guilty, but fuck, knowing you're going to be feeling me, remembering me buried inside you…" I trailed off with a groan, liking that idea a little too much.

Despite rolling his eyes, Sutton smirked. "Knowing I'm going to be feeling you for days gets you hot and bothered, huh? Good to know." He followed up with a slap to my ass. "Now shift it. Shower."

I reluctantly eased off him, looking down at the man who'd agreed to be mine. "I'm a lucky bastard."

His grin stretched wide as he stood, looking thoroughly debauched and completely pleased with himself. "How about we agree that we both are?"

I wouldn't be arguing with that.

CHAPTER 24
SUTTON

The dust had officially settled.

With just three days till the end of our six-week stint at Montview, it seemed like a million things had happened, and a whole lifetime of changes had taken place.

"Do you envy them?" I peered at Jayden, who lay by my side.

"Hell no." He chuckled. "I'm more than happy to be where I'm at, having navigated through all of the chaos of first going pro."

"You're making it sound like the last two or so months haven't been crazy."

He put his phone down, giving me his full attention. "Regrets are for pussies."

I rolled my eyes at him. "That's not quite what I meant."

"I know, but still, I wouldn't want to go back all the way to the beginning. We're where we're meant to be."

I grinned at him, and this time it was Jayden who rolled his eyes. "You remember that time you said you didn't talk about your feelings?"

"Fuck off." He punctuated his words with a kiss. "Shower. We need to get our asses into gear."

Tomorrow was the end-of-school game. We had another group of kids arriving just before game time. Plus, families had been invited. While it was a friendly game between the twenty guys split into two teams, I knew each and every one of them would play their hardest.

"How are your guys looking?" I asked as we got together enough to step into the shower cubicle.

"Like machines." He bounced his brows. "They're going to totally kick your team's ass."

"Not gonna happen. Between me, Pearce, and Milo as the dream coaches, there's zero chance your guys are gonna bring it." I grabbed the shower gel and took delight in rubbing it on his chest while he scowled at me.

Jayden wasn't handling the bonding Milo and I had done over the past six weeks well.

"Hey, don't forget he's invited us for a stay at his cabin when we get the time."

He seemed less pissed off when I mentioned that. "True." Tipping his face under the spray, he washed himself down. I admired the rivulets of waters as they darted a path down his skin. Jayden was too tempting for his own damn good.

I leaned against him, silently telling him as much. His grin was immediate.

"See something you like?"

I grunted and pressed my mouth against his before saying, "See something I love more like it," then went in for another kiss.

Smiling against my mouth, Jayden tugged me closer. "We so don't have time for this."

"Since when do you give a shit about such things?"

He angled away, a sparkle of mischief in his eyes. "True that."

Our mouths connected, and a bang on our room's door, barely muffled by the shower, pierced the bathroom. We both groaned and freed ourselves.

The hammering sounded again.

With a sigh, I stepped out of the shower, grabbed a towel, and opened the bathroom door, hollering out "What?" in the general direction of the banging.

"Coach wants to see you. Stat." It was Pearce.

"Tell him we're busy."

"Ha. No chance. Get your asses moving. Both of

you." He pounded the door once more for good measure.

"You hear that?" I angled around to Jayden, who'd turned off the shower and was already toweling dry.

"Pretty hard not to with the way he was shouting." He smirked a little, I expected thinking about Pearce.

The man still reminded us a little of Jayden, but he'd seemed calmer and more collected since coming out and going public a few weeks back. Sure, he could still be overenthusiastic and was a heap of fun. But he was less… wired, maybe.

"Wonder why Jenkins wants to see us."

I shrugged and dried off. "No idea, but it's a bit early for it. We haven't had coffee yet."

"Never fear. I'll make sure you get your caffeine fix this morning."

I smiled and leaned toward him for a kiss as he walked by to grab his clothes. A quick kiss was all he offered before he was tugging on his boxer briefs and shorts, pulling a T-shirt on afterward. Today's read *Sugarplum*.

Of course Jayden had gone around the guys and nabbed every single tee Max and I had organized. He took great delight in switching them out daily.

"Is that your favorite? It's done the rounds."

"It's the addition of the fairy Pearce added." We both glanced at the hand-drawn illustration of the "sugarplum fairy," which was actually an impressive piece of artwork considering he'd been armed with a Sharpie. It was a dude wearing a basketball jersey, complete with a tutu and fairy wings. "I even hand washed it."

My eyes softened at his sweetness. "Why don't you take a photo and get it made up properly so it's not going to run or fade or something?"

"Hell yes. Quick, do it now."

I chuckled at his enthusiasm, loving that he got excited and carried away about the weirdest things. After taking a quick photograph, or maybe two as he looked extra handsome with his bright smile, I dressed, we brushed our teeth, and made our way to see Jenkins, assuming he was in his office.

When we arrived, the door was open, and voices filtered through the doorway. I frowned at the voice, struggling to marry the accent with the location. My brows shot up when my gaze landed on Nate and Ryan.

"The fuck you guys doing here?" Jayden beat me to it, stepping more fully into the room and wrapping Ryan in a hug.

I grinned at Nate, and he moved toward me,

hugging me hard. "Holy shit. You guys are here," I said, stating the obvious. I then hugged Ryan.

When we finally broke free, still startled at seeing them here, I grinned. It was good to see them. Sure, it had only been a little over six weeks, but with all that had happened, on top of how busy we'd been, it felt like a lot longer.

"Heard there was a game tomorrow. Thought we'd come and check it out," Nate offered, appearing super pleased with himself that they'd surprised us.

"You'd have much preferred the last game a few weeks back," Jayden said without missing a beat.

"True. Watching you guys getting your arses handed to you by college kids would have been something. I had to settle on watching the high-lights." Ryan quirked his brow.

"Whatever. We all know we were going easy on the guys. Didn't want to destroy them before they had a chance to start their careers."

We all snorted at Jayden.

"Nice tee," Nate said, eyeing up the basketballer sugarplum fairy.

"Right!" Jayden grinned. "I'm going to talk to Pearce about getting a whole line on the go."

"That right?" I turned to Jayden, who gave a casual shrug.

"These things would sell. What's not to love?" A

legit twinkle appeared in his eyes, and I knew his brain was also rolling around the idea with a lot more seriousness. "We could do a whole range."

"We?" I asked. "And how are you contributing to this?"

"I'm the inspiration behind it, obviously. Hell, Pearce could design other fairy players. Do a whole line. Work directly with one of the LGBTQ charities. We cou—"

"Whoa there." I edged over to him as his hands flew about the more animated he got as his ideas poured out of him in the frantic way they tended to do. Standing at his side, I wrapped my arm around him. "Let's focus on these guys being here, then harass Pearce sometime next week, yeah?"

The stink eye he shot my way wasn't amused. "As if I'll remember anything by then. These ideas are here now. Once I've thought them, said them once, they flutter away, never to be seen again." I knew he thought he spoke the truth, but he needed to give himself more credit.

"How about we put a pin in it, and we'll talk it through together before chatting to Pearce?"

Jayden turned to me, taking me in, a smile forming. "Yeah?"

My heart leaped, enjoying the tenderness and openness in his gaze. "Definitely."

He leaned in and pressed his lips against mine. Immediately, obnoxious coughs exploded in the room, followed by Coach saying, "They don't stop." Amusement tinted his words, and I smirked against Jayden's mouth as I pulled away and returned my attention to the others in the room.

"So you guys really here just to see the game?"

Nate answered, "Mainly, yeah, Ryan also has a meeting in a few days in LA, so we came early to catch up with you guys first."

Curious about what meeting Ryan could have, I glanced over at him. Not that I'd ask.

"Who are you meeting in LA?" Jayden, however, had no such restraint.

Ryan bobbed his brows a couple of times. "How about I tell you about it later at dinner?"

"Sounds good," I said quickly before Jayden had a chance to complain. "You coming to hang out on the court? Gonna meet the guys?"

"Absolutely." Ryan nodded.

"You guys go ahead. I've got some calls to make," Jenkins said, waving us off.

We all left Coach's office, heading straight for breakfast and coffee.

I didn't take long to plate up our breakfast and get four decent cups of coffee before us all.

"Are you guys jet-lagged?" Jayden asked, his

attention drifting from the mountain of creamer he poured into his coffee.

"Not too bad. Ryan got us the good tickets, and we actually flew into LA yesterday morning."

Pearce took a seat next to me, grinning over at Ryan and Nate. "They were surprised, huh?"

"You knew?" Jayden asked.

"Yeah, since last week when Ryan reached out to me." He seemed thoroughly pleased with himself that he'd been in on the surprise visit.

"We've actually brought you a gift, Jayden." Ryan picked up a backpack, which he'd dropped on the floor when we'd sat. It was overfull, the zip barely containing what was inside.

"Sweet." Jayden reached out, stopping when Ryan stood.

"Actually, why don't you just come with me for five?"

I quirked my brow at that, already dreading what Ryan could possibly be gifting Jayden. "This sounds like it's a bad idea."

Nate chuckled. "It'll be fine."

I narrowed my gaze on my Aussie friend. Out of everyone at the table, he was the one person I trusted to be the most sensible.

"Please tell me you've got me sex toys." Jayden stood quickly, eagerness in his voice.

I spluttered out a laugh, not even touching that. Well, certainly not in public anyway.

With a sigh, Ryan shook his head. "Why would you think I got you a bag of sex toys?"

Wide-eyed, Jayden shrugged. "Because you're an awesome friend and want to make me happy."

My mouth twisted to keep from laughing, while Nate chuckled. Pearce snorted loudly. Ryan simply moved from the table, mumbling, "Fuck knows why it is I miss you guys so much. You drive me insane."

Watching them go, I asked, "Seriously, Nate, should I be worried?" His laughter tugged my attention away from Jayden's retreating form.

"Nah, mate. He's going to be in his element." He smirked and eyed me. "You guys had a good time doing this gig?"

"Definitely." My answer was immediate. Sure, we'd had a wobble a few weeks back, but that was about the secrets we'd kept catching up with us and not about the summer training. "We've even been invited back next summer, so we can't have pissed off Coach Jenkins too much."

"You guys accepted? You plan to come back?"

I nodded. "We've said yes. It's been fun."

From my side, Pearce added, "I've committed too. It's been good getting back to basics while pushing it.

Plus hanging out with some of the former players... yeah, it's been good."

The pink covering Pearce's cheeks as he spoke took me by surprise. He made eye contact with me before darting his gaze away. Rather than quizzing him, I looked at Nate. "Everything okay back home? That niece of yours okay?"

He grinned. "Ivy's great. Into everything and driving Ryan insane. He's loving spending so much time with her, though."

"Don't you have a store to run?" I asked, registering that he was here and planned to be in the US for at least a week.

He chuckled. "Yeah. From having so much time away last year, the guys have it completely covered. Me being there feels a little redundant at times." He didn't seem too put out by it, though. "It's made heading here last-minute nice and easy, especially with—"

A commotion at the entrance caught our attention. Laughter filtered around the room, starting off quiet before it spread quickly. My gut told me that Jayden was involved.

Turning and seeking out what was going on, I spotted Jayden immediately, rubbed my hand over my face, and laughed. Jayden entered the room with a huge-ass grin, complete with a kangaroo that he was riding.

"Where the hell did you find that?" I flashed a look at a laughing Nate.

"Isn't it epic? Found the costume online and managed to do a rush order so we could bring it with us."

With my attention back on Jayden, I watched as he all but strutted in, fake legs on either side of the partially stuffed kangaroo he was riding.

"Sutton," he hollered, bright-eyed and so in his element. "Get your phone out. I need to share this awesomeness with the world."

"I'm already videoing," Pearce said beside me with a chortle. He glanced over at me, smirking. "Just think, not only are you best friends with the guy, you also *chose* him as your boyfriend." He followed up with a wink.

True that. I stood and greeted the now bouncing Jayden, who jumped into my personal space. His eyes were sparkling with amusement, and genuine happiness flooded his features. The sight squeezed at my heart in all the best ways.

"You look ridiculous," I said with a grin. "And I love you the more for it."

Rather than giving me words, Jayden leaned in and brushed his lips against mine. The touch was brief and barely a kiss, but it told me all I needed to know.

Jayden was phenomenally happy, and I'd make sure he remained that way indefinitely. Kangaroo riding fantasies and all.

EPILOGUE

JAYDEN

"WE'RE GOING TO BE LATE."

I rolled my eyes, knowing full well Sutton couldn't see me. If he did, he'd only aim that piercing gaze of his at me. He thought it was intimidating, but it was sexy as hell. I was doing him a favor, considering I had no issues with being even later because I was busy jumping his bones.

"You're the one who insisted on changing your shirt. Twice." Not that I'd minded. Every strip show he gave, I was up for.

Sutton grunted and threw a damp towel at me.

"Hey." I quirked a brow, then all but swallowed my tongue when I raked my gaze over him. "Fuck, maybe we should stay in?"

"That'd be a no, and I think it means you'll be fired."

I mulled that over a second. Was it really that important as Ryan's best man that I get to the bachelor party on time?

"Whatever you're thinking, no. Just think of the hot and sweaty club and dancing all up me." It wasn't fair that his smirk was so delicious, but his words did have merit.

"I suppose, but just so you know, in case you're feeling frisky, I prepped ahead of time and wouldn't say no to some nasty restroom sex."

Perhaps I shouldn't have said that while he was gulping from the bottle of water, which he sprayed mainly on the floor of the hotel room rather than on his shirt that fit him like it was made for me to peel off.

"Nasty, really?"

I shrugged and threw him the towel. "If you could see how you look through my eyes, you'd be impressed as hell I can even manage to leave this room without stripping off for you."

His eyes heated. I grinned immediately, hand moving to my belt.

"No," he said firmly. His gaze didn't lie, though. It trailed down my body, landing on my crotch. Like the asshole I was, I put my thumbs in my pockets and framed my dick, one of Sutton's favorite parts of my body. "You're going to be the death of me."

I ambled over to him, my smile still in place. "Never." I pressed my mouth to his and tugged on his bottom lip for good measure before releasing. "No chance you're abandoning me that easily. Now, get your greedy eyes off the goods. We're going to be late." I walked past him, earning a heavy sigh. "I know you're just trying to steal my thunder and step in and be Ryan's best man last minute."

"Uh-huh. Yeah, that's totally it. Nothing to do with Nate pleading with me to make sure you don't screw up." The door closed behind him, and we headed for the elevator.

In answer, I flipped him off, then waited impatiently for the elevator, wondering how hot and revved up I could get him in the twenty seconds we were in the car. The doors opened, and my plan was immediately foiled. Pearce stood in the elevator.

"Hey, good timing."

Sutton edged me in, chuckling. I expected he'd known exactly what was on my mind. "Hey, you managed to get some rest?" he asked Pearce.

"Yeah. Slept for about three hours. That should see me through. It means I'll be dead to the world tonight." He'd flown in from the States this morning, in time for Ryan and Nate's bachelor party and their wedding in two days. We'd arrived two days earlier, but I'd planned tonight after countless messages with a guy called Elijah, the owner of the bar where tonight's festivities were being held.

It was a place I had meant to visit my last trip, a couple of years back. The car crash had derailed that plan. A quick glance at Sutton made me smile thinking about it.

"No plans on hooking up?" I asked.

Pearce was a good-looking guy, as well as a good friend. We'd all spent a lot of time with each other since the first summer at Montview. In all that time, I'd known he'd hooked up a few times but had no one serious in his life. Sure, he was only twenty-six, but Sutton and I had discussed a couple of times how lonely he seemed.

"Well, I won't say no if the right guy comes along and catches my eye." Pearce grinned, but I wasn't sure I was buying his enthusiasm, and from the side-eye Sutton gave him and then me, he wasn't either.

"The car should already be downstairs to take us to Bar QK. We caught up with Eddie earlier and a few of the guys who flew in yesterday." I hadn't even known until a couple of years back when Ryan and Nate flew out that Ryan knew Eddie, but apparently, they did. And since their reunion when out at Montview, Ryan had managed to get Eddie, hell, all of us on board with his own basketball camp he'd put together.

Last year had been the first year after meticulous planning. With the Australian summer being our winter, it made our visit tricky, since we were in season, but we'd flown out for one long weekend. That hadn't been a problem for Eddie, though, considering his retirement. Though I did know it could be a juggle with caring for his daughter.

For the wedding, Ryan and Nate made sure it worked out so as many of their friends Stateside could attend, planning the event for the off-season. That hadn't mattered so much to us anymore. Not since our retirement at the end of the season.

Realizing Pearce hadn't responded, I flicked a glance at him as we exited the elevator and stepped into the lobby. "You okay?"

His eyes widened, and he looked my way. "Yeah, sure." He smiled, but it was far from genuine.

"Eddie." Sutton lifted a hand, and I looked in the direction of his stare.

"Hey." He sent us a chin lift, his focus moving to my side. "Pearce, good flight?"

Pearce's cheeks pinkened. "Uhm, yeah, sure. You know, it's a flight. I got here. It was long."

My brows knotted as I took him in. Red-cheeked and tongue-tied, he looked like he wanted the ground to open up.

A noise escaped my mouth as reality set in.

Fucking hell, Pearce had a hard-on for Eddie. I opened my mouth, only for Sutton to snag me around the shoulders and tug me close to him.

"Come on. The car's waiting."

"But—"

"Nuh-uh."

"Did you—"

"Nope. Leave it."

"But they—"

"I swear to all that is good and holy, Jayden, if you don't hush it, I'm going to have to find a way to gag you."

Immediately I snapped my mouth shut and grinned. "You're thinking of dirty restroom sex, aren't you?" I bounced my brows.

He tilted his mouth close to my neck, his breath fanning against my skin. "If I say yes, will you promise to leave Pearce alone?"

"Didn't we say no more secrets?" I gave a lopsided grin and may have angled a little to accept the press of his lips against my neck like the hussy I was.

"I said no more secrets between us." He pulled away, and I only grumbled a little at the loss.

"Fine. I suppose you've got yourself a deal." I cast a quick glance behind me. Pearce followed with Eddie by his side, talking.

Sutton's sigh dragged my attention back to him. "You're incorrigible."

"How many points is that?"

He smiled. "Seventeen."

"One of these days, I'm going to marry up; you know that, right?"

His gaze flared and roamed my face. "As long as you know one of these days I'm going to be marrying my best friend, then that's fine by me."

Between the flipping of my heart, the flutters in my stomach, and the gigantic smile on my face, I had no plans to deny him or the likelihood of that statement.

"Come on. If you're lucky, I'll ride you like a kangaroo."

Sutton snorted, scrunching his nose. "It doesn't matter how many times you say it, it's not sexy."

I laughed loudly and opened the door for him, darting a kiss on his cheek as he angled down. "I'll spend my life seeing if I can change your mind."

Absorbing his soft smile and the feel of his hand in mine as we sat in the back of the car, I sighed, completely content. The accident, the injuries, they'd been absolutely worth it. Infinitely so. I wouldn't have changed a moment, not when I still pinched myself every day that my best friend agreed to be mine.

I HOPE YOU LOVED JAYDEN AND SUTTON'S SWEET romance. Be sure to check out RULES, SCHMULES!—Dean and Kieran's story in a brand-new spin-off series—the cute couple you met in NO TAKE BACKS. Looking for more low-angst loveliness? Be sure to check out STUMBLE (#1).

ALSO BY BECCA SEYMOUR

Zone Defense

No Take Backs | No More Secrets | No Wrong Moves

Fast Break

Rules, Schmules!

True-Blue

Let Me Show You | I've Got You | Becoming Us | Thinking It Over | Always For You | It's Not You | Our First & Last

Outback Boys

Stumble | Bounce | Wobble

Stand-Alone Contemporary

Not Used To Cute | High Alert | Realigned | Amalgamated

Urban Fantasy Romance

Thicker Than Water

ACKNOWLEDGMENTS

I fell in love with Jayden and Sutton as soon as I created their voices in No Take Backs. It meant writing their story was such a pleasure and so fun. But that didn't mean I wasn't filled with doubt. A special thanks to my sister who read this book as I wrote and it was a crazy mess. She reassured me it wasn't a pile of poop. :)

I can't thank you, my readers, enough for your support and encouragement to keep going and to continue creating stories. This writing gig is as wonderful as it is challenging. It's your faith in me that keeps me going.

As always, my team of editors, Liv, Donna, and James, deserve so much thanks and credit. You really are incredible.

Claire from BookSmith Designs reads my mind every single time. I'm so blessed to have your support.

A special thanks to Barb and Arden who work tirelessly behind the scenes supporting me.

A HUGE thanks to my group, RoMMance with Becca and Louisa, for your fun interactions and daily support, and obviously my bestie Louisa for keeping me grounded.

ABOUT THE AUTHOR

I live and breathe all things book related. Usually with at least three books being read and two WiPs being written at the same time, life is merrily hectic. I tend to do nothing by halves, so I happily seek the craziness and busyness life offers.

Living on my small property in Queensland with my human family as well as my animal family of cows, chooks, and dogs, I really do appreciate the beauty of the world around me and am a believer that love truly is love.

To check for updates head to my website:
https://beccaseymour.com
https://landing.mailerlite.com/webforms/
landing/r9f0i4
Plus, join my Facebook group, which I share with the awesome Louisa Masters here:
https://www.facebook.com/
groups/rommancewithbeccalouisa/
On TikTok, follow me here: https://www.tiktok.
com/@beccaseymourwrites

facebook.com/beccaseymourauthor
twitter.com/beccaseymour_
instagram.com/authorbeccaseymour
bookbub.com/authors/becca-seymour